SHE THRUST THE VIOLETS INTO REBECCA'S HAND

[Page 4]

REBECCA'S PROMISE

BY
FRANCES R. STERRETT

AUTHOR OF
MARY ROSE OF MIFFLIN, ETC.

ILLUSTRATED BY
E. C. CASWELL

GROSSET & DUNLAP
PUBLISHERS   NEW YORK

Made in the United States of America

PRINTED IN THE UNITED STATES OF AMERICA

TO

LILIAN JOSEPHA STERRETT

who believes in memory insurance
for you and for me.

ILLUSTRATIONS

REBECCA'S PROMISE

CHAPTER I

I NEVER should have brought you here," murmured Cousin Susan Wentworth, as she looked across the table at young Cousin Rebecca Mary Wyman, who sat on the other side of the white cloth like a small gray mouse with bright expectant eyes, a pretty pink flush on her cheeks and her head with its crown of soft yellow brown hair held high. "I should have saved my money for new kitchen curtains. The curtains in my kitchen are a disgrace to any housekeeper. But life wouldn't be worth much if we didn't occasionally do something we shouldn't, would it?" And she smiled at pink-cheeked Rebecca Mary. "The memory of this pretty room with the gay crowds of people, the music, the good things to eat will last longer than any curtains. And I can cut down the old bedroom curtains for the kitchen. Rebecca Mary, did you ever think that is what life really is, cutting down our desires to fit our necessities?"

1

Rebecca Mary sniffed. She had known that for twenty-two years. She did not have to be thirty-nine like Cousin Susan to learn that necessities always crowd out desires. And anyway she did not wish to talk of necessities, they were stupid and uninteresting, when for once in her life she was a part of what no one in the wide world could ever consider a necessity.

She let Cousin Susan study the card the attentive waiter handed to her, and while Cousin Susan tried to keep her mind from prices and on names, Rebecca Mary's bright eyes roved over the big brilliant room. She had never expected to enter it. She had scarcely believed her two pink ears when they told her that Cousin Susan had said, quite casually, "Rebecca Mary, suppose we go to the Waloo for tea?" Rebecca Mary had given a startled gasp, but here she was at the Waloo trying to forget that her old blue serge suit was wide where it should be narrow and narrow where it should be wide, and that her hat had only been given a good brushing to make it ready for another season.

Afternoon tea was served at the Waloo in the Viking room, a beautiful place with its scenes from the old Norse sagas on the walls above a wainscoting of dark wood and with lights like old ship lanterns

2

hanging from the beamed ceiling. The chairs and tables were suggestive of long ago days, also, but the linen, the silver, the dainty china, the music and the guests were very much of to-day.

Rebecca Mary watched the young people almost enviously as Cousin Susan hesitated over *foie gras* sandwiches, which were expensive and therefore suitable for an occasion which was to cost her kitchen its new curtains, and lettuce sandwiches which were cheap and which she made herself every time the Mifflin Fortnightly Club met with her. Rebecca Mary could easily imagine what joy it would be to come to the Viking room in smart new clothes and with a young man like—like that tall young fellow who was with the girl in the wistaria taffeta. It made the pink in Rebecca Mary's cheeks turn to rose just to think of what joy that would be.

There were any number of girls in the Viking room with whom Rebecca Mary would have changed places in the twinkling of an eye. It hurt almost as much as an ulcerated tooth to watch those radiant young people. And when you have an ulcerated tooth you don't, unless you are strong-minded or philosophical or stoical, laugh and chatter gayly; you know you don't. Rebecca Mary wasn't strong-minded nor philosophical nor stoical, she was just a girl who

3

had never had anything and, oh, how she did want something, and she wanted it right away. That was why her eyebrows frowned yellow-brownly, and the corners of her mouth drooped a bit.

"Oh, Cousin Susan!" she groaned, "why did we ever come here? Why didn't you take me to Childs'?"

"Eh?" murmured Cousin Susan, still hovering between expense and curiosity.

But before she could say another word a little girl ran up to them, an elflike little thing, who held a huge bunch of violets in her hand. She had been following a man from the room when she had seen Rebecca Mary and dashed around the tables, just missing a disastrous collision with a fat waiter, to arrive breathless beside her.

"Oh, Miss Wyman!" she whispered, her small face aglow with importance. "I'm so glad I saw you. This is my birthday, and my daddy brought me here for tea just as if I were all grown up. He bought me these violets, too, and I've had them all afternoon so I'd like to give them to you now because," her face grew crimson, and her voice rang out above the hum of voices, "I love you!" She thrust the violets into Rebecca Mary's hand and ran away without giving Rebecca Mary a chance to say one word.

4

Rebecca Mary just saw a portion of her father's back as he disappeared through the door, and she looked down at the violets with an odd flash in her gray eyes. No one ever had given her violets before. She had always picked them herself on the sunny slope of the bluff at Mifflin.

"What a dear child," smiled Cousin Susan. "Who is she?"

"One of my pupils, Joan Befort. Yes, she is a dear." Rebecca Mary buried her hot cheeks in the cool fragrance of the violets for a moment.

When she lifted her head she met the amused glance of an elderly woman at the next table. She must be a grandmother woman, Rebecca Mary thought swiftly, although she did not look like any grandmother Rebecca Mary knew with her smart and expensive hat and blue gown, on the front of which was pinned a bunch of violets and an orchid encircled with foliage. The smile which lurked around the lips of this most ungrandmotherly looking grandmother made Rebecca Mary remember little Joan Befort's fervent declaration of affection, and she smiled, too. How funny it must have sounded in the crowded tea room. "I love you!" Rebecca Mary giggled, she couldn't help it, even if she was most dreadfully embarrassed.

5

At the table beside the ungrandmotherly looking grandmother was a young man the very sight of whom sent Rebecca Mary into a quiver of delight. She had seen his picture in the Gazette too many times not to recognize him. He was young Peter Simmons, who had left college in his sophomore year to drive an ambulance in France during the second year of the great war. He had been awarded a *croix de guerre* for "unusual bravery under fire," and later had gone into the French flying service until he could fight under his own flag. He had been with the American Army of Occupation in Germany and had only recently returned to Waloo. No wonder Rebecca Mary thrilled all down her back bone as she realized that she was looking at a hero. She stared and stared for she might never see one again, and the hero raised his eyes and saw awed admiration written in huge letters all over her flushed face.

Evidently young Peter Simmons did not care for awed admiration, perhaps he had had too much of it, perhaps it made him unpleasantly self-conscious, for he scowled blackly and murmured an impatient something to the grandmother which made her look at Rebecca Mary again. Rebecca Mary turned a deep crimson and was horribly uncomfortable. She knew very well what they were saying, that such a shabby girl had no business among the fine birds in the Viking room, and she scowled, too. She could give scowl for scowl as well as any one. Peter's black frown made you laugh, but there was something rather pathetic about Rebecca Mary's bent yellow-brown brows, perhaps it was because her lower lip quivered as she hastily averted her shamed eyes.

On the other side of young Peter was a girl no older than Rebecca Mary, and 'she was so prettily and smartly clothed that she made Rebecca Mary feel like Cousin Susan's kitchen curtains, old and ragged. But every one in the room made her feel like that, she thought miserably, and she tossed her head higher to show how little she cared as her glance roamed on to the man on the other side of the grandmother. Of course the grandmother must be old Mrs. Peter Simmons, and old Mrs. Peter Simmons was one of the most important women in Waloo, so important that a poor little school teacher like Rebecca Mary could never hope to know her. Rebecca Mary rather liked the face of the man on the other side of Mrs. Peter Simmons. He was older than young Peter, and the most doting friend could not have called him handsome, but he had something much better than perfect features. He was the type of man who would do things, she decided, and then

7

she saw Mrs. Simmons turn to speak to him and with a little shrinking feeling of horror Rebecca Mary knew that they were talking of her, for the man who could do things raised his head and looked directly at her. For a moment their eyes met. Rebecca Mary was furious to feel her cheeks burn and her heart thump. She scowled before she turned her head quickly. She wouldn't look at that table again. I should say not!

There were other tables and other family parties, and, oh, dear! other couples. Old Samuel Johnson knew exactly what he was talking about when he said that "envy is almost the only vice which is practicable at all times and in every place." Rebecca Mary did find it so very very easy to be envious. About the only person she did not envy that afternoon was a short, stout, middle-aged man with a red face, who sat at a table by himself and consumed vast quantities of hot buttered toast.

Rebecca Mary had never imagined there were so many gay, light-hearted people in the world as there were in the Viking room that May afternoon and more would have entered if it had not been for the silken barrier which was held in front of the door by two very haughty waiters. Rebecca Mary felt blue and depressed to the very toes of her common-sense little shoes. She felt so hopelessly out of the gay and brilliant picture. She almost wished that Cousin Susan had not asked her to the Waloo for tea.

"Which shall we have, Rebecca Mary?" Cousin Susan found herself quite incapable of making such a momentous decision without assistance. "Lettuce or *foie gras*."

Rebecca Mary did not hesitate a second. She knew. "*Foie gras*," she said promptly. "I've never tasted them, and I've made hundreds of lettuce sandwiches, just thousands of them. What is the use of going to new places if you don't try new things?" There was just a trace of impatience in her low voice as if she thought that Cousin Susan should have known that without being told.

"H-m," murmured Cousin Susan. "The *foie gras*, then. They certainly sound mysterious and adventurous." And having given her order, Cousin Susan looked about her. "Isn't this an attractive place? I've read in the Gazette about the afternoon teas in the Viking room and how popular they were. I suppose all these people are very rich and important. None of them will pay for tea with kitchen curtains." And Cousin Susan's eyes twinkled.

Rebecca Mary's eyes twinkled, too, although really there was nothing very amusing to her in paying for

9

tea with ten yards of any kind of material. It was rather sordid to her and poor and generally horrid, like her very existence.

Cousin Susan looked at her frowning little face and fingered the silver in front of her with hands which although well cared for showed that they were more for use than ornament. Cousin Susan's hands exactly illustrated Cousin Susan's heart, which was so big and generous and helpful that the hands were often overworked. As she looked at Rebecca Mary Cousin Susan took a sudden determination and followed an impulse, which was nothing new for her, and which sometimes brought her great satisfaction and sometimes nothing but dissatisfaction.

"Don't frown like that, Rebecca Mary," she commanded like a general speaking to a very small private. "It is a lot easier to put a wrinkle in your forehead than it is to get one out as you'll learn some day. And while we are on the subject of your looks I'm going to take an old cousin's privilege and tell you what I think of you. It's a shame to do it here," she acknowledged ruefully, "but if I take the six-twenty train I shan't have another chance. You know," she went on in a firm low voice, "I don't like the way you live, and your mother wouldn't like it

10

if she knew. Why, you don't get a thing out of your life, Rebecca Mary, not a thing!"

"I don't see what I can do," murmured Rebecca Mary with a twist of her shoulders and a rebellious flash in her gray eyes. "You needn't think I like my life, Cousin Susan. It isn't one I should ever choose. I should say not! But I try to make the best of it."

"But you don't make the best of it. That is just the point. You make such a horrid worst of it. Yes, you do!" as Rebecca Mary indignantly declared that she didn't. "Listen. I've watched you and I never imagined a girl could detach herself from life, real life, as you have done. You haven't any friends, you don't go anywhere but to school, you don't do anything but teach the third grade in the Lincoln school."

At that Rebecca Mary did interrupt and there was a bright red spot on each of her cheeks, like a poppy in a bed of lilies. "It costs money to have a share in real life," she said in a suppressed voice which made you think how very thin the crust of earth around a volcano must be. "And I haven't any money. You know how awfully little we have and how much it costs to live now. I have to send something home every month and there are always taxes and insurance. And I have to provide for my old age! You

11

have no idea what a nightmare that is," tragically.
"I wake up in the night thinking what will happen
when I'm too old to teach. It's—it's ghastly!" It
was so ghastly that she shivered, and the poppies left
her face so that it was just a field of white lilies.

"You are thinking entirely too much of your old
age. You are robbing your youth for it. It is perfectly ridiculous for you to make such a nightmare
of the future. I know it isn't entirely your fault.
Your mother is rabid on the subject. She has
brought you and Grace up to think of old age as a
blood-thirsty old beast who has to be fed with youth.
Yes, I know all about your Aunt Agnes and your
second Cousin Lucy. But, my dear, they could have
saved and saved and their money might have been
lost just when they needed it. You can't be sure of
keeping money no matter how you save it. That's
why I spend mine." She looked at the dainty expensive sandwiches the waiter placed before her and
laughed. "It's gospel truth, my dear," she went on
soberly, "that the only thing you can be sure of
taking into the future is what you can remember, the
memory of the good times you have had, the people
you have met, the places you have seen, the books you
have read, the music you have heard. Don't you
know that youth should enjoy things for old age

12

to remember? And take it from me, Rebecca Mary,
that the old find their greatest pleasure in recalling
their youth. Will you have cream or lemon in your
tea? Lemon always seems more like a party to me."

Rebecca Mary took the lemon while a puzzled
frown appeared between her two eyebrows. "It isn't
that I don't like my work, Cousin Susan," she said
slowly, "for I do. I love children, and I love to
teach. If I had a million I should want to teach
somewhere, in a settlement or a mission, you know.
But I'll admit that the future does scare me blue.
Suppose I should be ill, suppose——"

"Suppose fiddlesticks!" Cousin Susan broke in
impatiently.

"It's all very well for you to talk. You have some
one to take care of you, a husband, and——"

"My dear, you can't guarantee a husband any
more than you can a savings account. Women are
left penniless widows every day. Don't misunder-
stand me, Rebecca Mary. I believe in a certain
amount of saving, but I don't believe in sacrificing
everything in the present to a future you may never
have. How do you know you will live to grow old?
How do you know that a grateful pupil won't leave
you an income?—that has happened if you can believe the newspapers. How do you know that you

13

won't make your own fortune in some marvelous way? That's the loveliest part of life, Rebecca Mary. You don't know what is waiting for you around the corner so you might as well expect riches as poverty; better in my opinion. I'd always rather look forward to a fried chicken than a soup bone hashed."

Rebecca Mary had to giggle when Cousin Susan suggested that a grateful pupil might leave her an income. That was even more improbable than that she would make a fortune for herself.

"Cousin Susan," she giggled scornfully. "You are a perfect silly!"

"That may be," admitted Cousin Susan, "but I'm telling you good solid sense. A proper amount of pleasure is as necessary to the real development of human beings as bread or boots. Every one admits that now. And you're not getting a proper amount, my dear. You aren't getting any! Why, you aren't living, you only breathe, and life is more than breathing. You are naturally impulsive. Can't you let yourself enjoy life instead of fear it? Yes, you are afraid of it. I've watched you. And from what you say I imagine that your room-mate was just another like you. I'm glad she has gone home. And

your clothes are a scandal. How many years have
you worn that suit?"

Rebecca Mary's face turned a bright crimson to
match the red-hot indignation inside of her. How
dared Cousin Susan talk to her like that? She was
doing the best she could. She shouldn't tell Cousin
Susan how old her blue serge was. It was none of
Cousin Susan's business.

"You wouldn't feel so shut out of the world if you
looked like other people and went where other people
go. I don't suppose you speak an unprofes-
sional word all day," went on Cousin Susan with
growing indignation at what she considered the waste
of a perfectly good girl. "It's a crime, Rebecca Mary
Wyman! A crime! And you needn't boast about
your old age provision when you haven't the brains
to make a sensible one. I'm as poor as a church
mouse myself. Your Cousin Howard will never make
more than a decent living, and we have two children
to feed and clothe and educate. I hadn't any more
business to come here for tea than I would have to
go to the Zoo and buy a baboon for a parlor ornament. But if I don't do something occasionally to
make a day stand out, something that it is a pleasure
to remember, I never should be able to keep on patch-
ing Elsie's petticoats, and darning Kittie's stockings.

15

I know,—I know!—Rebecca Mary, that when you are young you live in the future, and when you are old you live in the past. Some one has said that memories are the only real fountain of youth. And that's true. A girl is young such a short time that she has to cram the days full if she wants to be sure of a happy old age. I can't imagine anything more awful than to have no good times to remember. And all pleasures aren't like the tea here. Such a lot of them can be had for nothing. You can get such fun just out of companionship, and the world is full of people with whom we were meant to be friends. Why, life now means helping other people to have a good time instead of moping off by yourself. You should know that, Rebecca Mary. I know I sound like a sermon, but it is all so true. You must not turn your back to people and hide in a corner. You must face the world and take what you can and give what you can. I wish you would promise me something?" she asked eagerly.

Rebecca Mary didn't look as if she would promise any one anything, but she asked politely: "What would you like me to promise, Cousin Susan?"

"Just to say 'Yes, thank you' instead of 'No, I can't possibly,' when you are asked to do something or go somewhere," begged Cousin Susan, refusing to

16

be discouraged by the scornful toss of Rebecca Mary's head. "Please, Rebecca Mary! You talk so much about insurance and that sort of thing that I'm going to ask you to take out some,"—she hesitated and then laughed,—"memory insurance. We can't all hope to be money rich when we are old, but we can all plan to be memory rich. Please promise?"

Rebecca Mary put her violets on the table and stared at her. "Your tea is getting cold, Cousin Susan," she said stiffly. She shouldn't promise anything so foolish. Cousin Susan was the most irresponsible old silly, but Rebecca Mary couldn't be irresponsible. There was too much dependent upon her. She drank her own tea and ate her sandwiches and even had a bit of French pastry when Cousin Susan said she was going to try some even if it did mean going without the new magazine she had planned to buy to read on the way home.

"I can make the evening paper last longer," she said as she hesitated between a strawberry tart and a cream-filled cornet. "I've read about French pastry for years, but we don't have it in Mifflin, and I never had a chance to taste it before. Isn't it good?"

Rebecca Mary said it was good, but inwardly she

17

sniffed again and tried to think that it was ridiculous for a woman of Cousin Susan's age to become hysterical over a piece of pie. She could not understand Cousin Susan's enjoyment of little things. She never would have dared to spend her kitchen curtains and new magazine for tea and French pastry. It would have been too foolishly extravagant. But she had enjoyed her tea. And it was exhilarating to be a part, even a shabby part, of a world she had never penetrated before and never would again, she thought mournfully. That was the trouble with pleasant experiences, they came all too seldom and were over far too soon. But Cousin Susan had said when you had had a pleasant experience once you had it for ever. Perhaps there was something in that thought. Rebecca Mary evidently thought there was for her eyes were like stars as, with the violets pinned to her shabby coat, she followed Cousin Susan from the room.

She found herself in a crush at the door. Beside her was young Peter Simmons. Rebecca Mary thrilled as he brushed against her arm.

"Beg your pardon," he murmured absently, but he never looked at her.

It made Rebecca Mary so furious to be so coolly ignored that she did not see that Joan Befort and her father pushed by her and that close on their heels were Mrs. Simmons and the man who looked as if he would do things. The chattering laughing throng pressed closer. A hand even touched Rebecca Mary's fingers. She drew them away with a shrug of her shoulders. She did hate to be jostled.

"My dear, I must fly!" exclaimed Cousin Susan when they had emerged a trifle breathless from the crowd. "But first give me that promise? Please, Rebecca Mary! What is that in your hand?" she broke off to ask suddenly, for something green hung from Rebecca Mary's worn brown glove.

"Why—why——" stammered Rebecca Mary as she opened her hand and found, of all things, a four-leaf clover. She stared from it to Cousin Susan.

"Where did you get that?" Like Rebecca Mary, Cousin Susan scanned the faces hurrying by. Not one of them looked as if it belonged to a person who would thrust a four-leaf clover into the fingers of a girl in a shabby blue serge. Four-leaf clovers had been no part of the table decorations. They never are. They belong in meadows and are only found by patient seekers. Even Rebecca Mary had to admit that it was odd and that it gave her a strange shivery sort of a feeling.

"My, but I'm glad I didn't buy curtains!" Cousin

19

Susan was enchanted with the mystery. "You simply will have to give me that promise now, Rebecca Mary. You are sure to have adventures if you do. There's the sign." She pointed to the crumpled clover leaf. "There's magic in it!" she whispered. Really, Cousin Susan was a silly.

"I wonder!" Rebecca Mary looked at the talisman. Where could it have come from? Perhaps there was magic in it. There must have been, for suddenly Rebecca Mary laughed softly. She straightened her shoulders and looked into Cousin Susan's kind blue eyes. "Yes, Cousin Susan," she said swiftly, as if the spell of the clover leaf might be broken if she didn't speak in a hurry, "I promise to say 'Yes, thank you' instead of 'No, I can't possibly.'"

And then before Cousin Susan could say how glad she was, right there on the crowded avenue, Rebecca Mary put her arm around Cousin Susan and hugged her.

"I haven't been a bit nice this afternoon," she confessed frankly and with considerable regret. "I've been horrid, but it was because I did feel so out of place. But I do love you and—and I shall try and be more decent to people. And if you really want me to take one of your old memory insurance policies," she giggled as she thought of Cousin Susan as an insurance agent, "why, of course I shall. Perhaps—" she looked down at the mysterious clover leaf, and her eyes crinkled—"perhaps this might make a first payment."

CHAPTER II

REBECCA MARY walked home on air. If she didn't hippity-hop outside, she did inside. She held her head high, and her gray eyes were almost black with excitement. A delightful mystery tingled through her. Usually when Rebecca Mary walked home from down town she had to wonder whether she might have bought her gloves cheaper if she had gone to the Big Store or if the shoes at Ballok's were better for the money. But as she walked swiftly home from the Waloo that May afternoon she never once remembered what might have been saved. She had pleasanter things than saving to think of.

I doubt very much if Rebecca Mary would have kept her promise to Cousin Susan if it had not been for that mysterious four-leaf clover. Not that Rebecca Mary was the sort of girl to regard a promise as a new laid egg, easily broken, for she wasn't. When Rebecca Mary made a promise it was generally as solid and unbreakable as a block of concrete. But she did think that Cousin Susan was such a sentimental old silly, and anyway her old age could never be Cousin Susan's old age and consequently it didn't really matter a copper cent to Cousin Susan how poor and dependent Rebecca Mary was when she was fifty. Rebecca Mary shuddered at the mere thought of being fifty. Looking back, she saw a long stretch of yesterdays, an awful gray and uninteresting distance, and if she didn't wish to have it fifty years long, fifty times three hundred and sixty-five stupid gray days, why, really it was time to do something, as Cousin Susan had said, to introduce another color. The four-leaf clover presented quite a touch of another color, and the bright green was as puzzling as it was brightening for it never hinted in any curve or crumple where it came from.

But some one must have deliberately thrust it into her hand. It never could have reached her fingers by any kind of an accident. And who was the thruster? How Rebecca Mary would like to have that question answered in the way she imagined it might be answered! She wanted to be told in short convincing words that young Peter Simmons had given her the talisman, but Common Sense jumped to her shoulder and whispered in her ear that that was not only ridiculous, it was impossible. Impossible may be, as Mirabeau insisted, a stupid word, and yet it is a word which quite frequently stands like a stone wall in front of people. Rebecca Mary did not need Common Sense to tell her that young aviator heroes do not carry four-leaf clovers carelessly in their pockets. But then who does in a town like Waloo where patches of four-leaf clovers are as scarce as paving stones are plenty? It was curious and irritating and altogether amazingly delightful. Rebecca Mary scarcely thought of the third grade of the Lincoln school that evening, and she most certainly did not dream of the third grade of the Lincoln school that night.

You can easily imagine how disappointed Rebecca Mary was when she received the first invitation to which she was to say "Yes, thank you," instead of the "I can't possibly" which had always slipped so automatically over her lips. By all the rules of romance she had every right to expect that it would be to some gathering which would bring her at least in sight of young Peter Simmons, and so when Olga Klavachek begged her to come and see their new baby she did have to make an effort to keep the old negative phrase from popping out of her mouth, for what on earth would she get for her old age meditation, what memory insurance, Cousin Susan had called it, at Klavachek's?

24

But she had promised Cousin Susan so she let Olga take her hand and went to see the new baby. Mrs. Klavachek was as round-faced and as plump as Olga, and although she spoke no English, and Rebecca Mary spoke no Slavic, they managed to understand each other very well. A baby is a baby and even a baby tied in a big feather pillow cannot be mistaken for a new hat or a new arm chair. The Klavachek baby was as round as a butter ball and had eyes like bright brown beads. Rebecca Mary could honestly admire him, and Mrs. Klavachek beamed on "Olga's teacher lady."

Besides the new baby Olga showed Rebecca Mary her mother's new shoes and her father's new boots and the wonderful earrings her mother had brought from Serbia and the new broom she had bought up on Poplar Avenue and the flag her papa had got off the place where he worked, the Peter Simmons Factory, and the calendar which the butcher had given her and the picture of George Washington which she had begged from the grocer because George Washington was her father now that she was an American and George Washington was the father of America.

At last Olga had nothing more to show, and while she tried to think of some other way to entertain and surprise "teacher" Rebecca Mary told Mrs.

Klavachek again what a dear roly-poly baby she had, and Mrs. Klavachek caught Rebecca Mary's hand and said in her best Slavic that she would never forget her from-heavenly-goodness to Olga, and she kissed Rebecca Mary's fingers with warm grateful lips. No one had ever kissed Rebecca Mary's hand before, and the caress gave her an odd sensation quite as if she were a feudal lady with castles and steel uniformed retainers. She straightened her shoulders and lifted her chin and looked like a feudal lady as she said good-by to the Klavacheks and went up the street, a smile on her lips, a laugh in her eyes. She never would forget how funny the Klavachek baby had looked tied up in the big feather pillow.

She turned down Poplar Avenue where the broom had lived before it moved to the Klavachek kitchen and waited for her street car, thanking goodness that she was not Mrs. Klavachek. She would rather be a shabby worked-to-death teacher with a threatening old age which shows that she had already benefited from social intercourse. It so often makes one more satisfied with one's own lot to take a look at the lot of some one else. Rebecca Mary was still thanking goodness when a limousine drew up beside her. She stepped back as if she thought it intended to run right over her.

"I beg your pardon," called a soft voice through the open window. "But can you tell me where River Street is?" The owner of the soft voice must have thought that Rebecca Mary was a settlement worker or an Associated Charities visitor and so would know where any street was. "I am looking for a family by the name of Klavachek."

"Why, I've just come from Klavacheks'!" exclaimed Rebecca Mary. She could scarcely believe that it was the ungrandmotherly grandmother of the Waloo tea room who was leaning forward to speak to her. Involuntarily she looked for young Peter Simmons, but unless he had been transformed into a card board box he was not in that limousine.

"Then you can tell me exactly how to find them. I understand there is a new baby, and I am taking Mrs. Klavachek a few things. Mr. Klavachek works for my husband at the Peter Simmons Factory," she explained as if she could read the question which darted into Rebecca Mary's mind. "I am interested in all the new babies that come to our men."

Rebecca Mary looked at the few things. They filled the seat, and Mrs. Simmons had the grace to blush.

"I hope you are not a settlement worker who will scold me for indiscriminate giving? Perhaps it is dreadful, but it is good for me, and really I don't believe that it could be bad for Mrs. Klavachek. It can't be bad for a woman in a strange country to know that another woman is interested in her, can it?"

"Indeed, it can't!" exclaimed Rebecca Mary, as if she knew anything about it. "It would be splendid for any woman to think that you were interested in her!" she added impulsively as she looked into the sweet old face of Mrs. Peter Simmons. And she explained that if the limousine would turn the corner and go two blocks and stop at the little purple house it would surely find Mrs. Klavachek and her new baby. "The new baby is a love!" Rebecca Mary's eyes crinkled as she told how dear the new baby had looked tied in a big feather pillow.

"Thank you so much." Mrs. Simmons seemed very grateful for the careful direction. "Didn't I see you at the Waloo the other afternoon?" she asked suddenly. "Didn't you love that new fox trot?" She smiled as she drove away before Rebecca Mary could say whether she did or didn't love the new fox trot.

Rebecca Mary had time to gaze after her before a long yellow street car came and picked her up, and she thought again how very ungrandmotherly Mrs. Peter Simmons was with her twinkling face and her love of new fox trots. The grandmothers Rebecca Mary knew were staid, sedate women with aprons and knitting.

The second invitation to which Rebecca Mary had an opportunity to say "Yes, thank you" came the very next evening when one of the teachers in the Lincoln school offered her a ticket to a travel talk in an auditorium not three blocks from Rebecca Mary's "one room, kitchenette and bath." There must have been seven or eight hundred people there so that Rebecca Mary might be excused for looking for—old Mrs. Simmons, she told herself. But Mrs. Simmons was not there so far as Rebecca Mary could see, neither was her grandson. They were not at the school social, which was Rebecca Mary's next festal affair, nor at the concert to which she went with a woman who lived in the next apartment, and who was scared to death to go out after dark alone. Rebecca Mary began to lose faith in the crumpled clover leaf which she had put in an old locket and carried in her pocket, and no wonder. A talisman which was worth its salt should have brought better luck.

It was not as easy for Rebecca Mary to change

29

the point of view which she had carefully cultivated for so many years as it would have been for her to change a blouse. There were many times when it seemed as if she just couldn't say "Yes, thank you." It would have been so much easier if she could have wrapped her old point of view in brown paper and carried it to a clerk at Bullok's or the Big Store and explained that it didn't fit at all, that it was far too narrow and too tight, and she should like to exchange it for one that was much larger and broader and which had some mystery in its frills. It seemed such bad management on the part of some one that there wasn't an exchange department for points of view at one of the big stores. But as there wasn't she did her best, and she had to see that the second time was easier than the first and the third time was easier than the second.

"If I live to be a hundred," she told herself a little impatiently one day, "I shall probably say 'Yes, thank you' mechanically. But by that time I won't care what I say, and no one else will care. Oh, dear, I almost wish Cousin Susan hadn't taken me to the Waloo for tea that day and stirred me all up. What's the use of thinking about things I can't ever have?"

And then because Cousin Susan had stirred her

all up she threw out her little chin and clicked her white teeth together and murmured that she would have the things she thought about, yes, she would! She wouldn't be all stirred up for nothing. She just would have some good times to remember when she was an old woman and had nothing to do but remember the past.

In her eagerness to find the good times she forgot to frown and to scowl. Even the walk to school became interesting when she thought that romance might lurk around the corner, and as Rebecca Mary bravely struggled to forget her cares and see only her opportunities she began to look more like a real live girl, a girl who might have adventures. The sullen frown left her face, indeed, a little smile often tilted the corners of her lips as she let her imagination run riot. There was a new spring in her step because there was a new hope in her heart. Perhaps the four-leaf clover would bring something into her life besides taxes and insurance premiums.

At the Lincoln school where Rebecca Mary taught the third grade the principal believed firmly in a close relation between the home and the school, and to bring about this closer relation each teacher was expected to visit the family of each pupil at least once a term. Rebecca Mary was appalled when she discovered that it was the next to the last week of the term and she remembered how many calls she owed. While she was making out a list to be paid that very afternoon the principal came in to tell her that an urgent telephone message had just asked Joan Befort's teacher to come to Beforts' as soon as she possibly could.

"I said you would be down at once," went on Miss Weir. "Was Joan at school to-day?"

No, Rebecca Mary remembered that Joan hadn't been at school either that morning or that afternoon.

"Probably measles or mumps," prophesied Miss Weir, who had been made wise by years of experience. "Foreigners are so helpless at times. You will have to explain that the quarantine laws must be obeyed. What do you know about the Beforts?"

Rebecca Mary blushed, for when Miss Weir asked her she discovered that she knew very very little about the Beforts.

"Joan's mother is dead, and she and her father live with an old woman who keeps house for them." Rebecca Mary tried her best to make a complete garment out of her very small pattern. "Joan is devoted to her father. He took her to the Waloo for tea the other afternoon. It was Joan's birthday, and she gave me the violets her father had given her." Rebecca Mary's chin tilted a bit as she told her principal that she, too, had been at the popular Waloo for tea. "Joan is an odd child, different from the others. It isn't only that she is a foreigner, you know she has only been in this country a short time, and she has picked up a very American way of expressing herself, but underneath—underneath—" she floundered helplessly.

"Yes?" Miss Weir waited for her to explain that "underneath," and when Rebecca Mary just stammered on she said gently, but, oh, so firmly: "That is why I ask you to visit the homes, so that you can understand the 'underneath.'"

"Yes," murmured Rebecca Mary meekly, but when Miss Weir had gone with Disapproval shouting, "Fie, fie, Rebecca Mary Wyman," from her unbending back Rebecca Mary was anything but meek. She stamped her foot and threw a book on the floor and murmured rebelliously that the days would have to be three times as long as they were if she were to get "underneath" the forty children in her room.

She found the house, a modest frame cottage, in a block which held only one other house. Joan was sitting on the steps, and she looked very small and very forlorn until she saw Rebecca Mary. She jumped to her feet and stood waiting, her arms full of what Rebecca Mary naturally thought were playthings. She wore her hat and had a suit case on the steps beside her.

"Oh dear Miss Wyman!" she called joyously. "I thought you'd never come. Mrs. Lee, over there," she nodded toward the next house, "said you couldn't be here a minute before half-past three." She looked at the small silver clock which was one of the things she held and shook it for the clock said plainly that in its opinion it was a quarter to four. "This must be an ignorant clock," she decided with a frown, "for I know you wouldn't wait a minute when you knew I wanted you. It doesn't matter now, and I'm to tell you that I'm to be your little girl!" She was quite enchanted by the prospect, and she expected Rebecca Mary to be enchanted, too.

"My goodness gracious!" And Rebecca Mary frowned. Old habits are hard to break. "What do you mean, Joan?"

Joan was only too ready to explain. "You see my father has gone away for a long long time, we don't know how long, and Mrs. Muldoon, who keeps our house for us, has gone, too. She said I was to stay with you until she came back because at Mrs. Lee's they have scarlet fever upstairs and the mumps downstairs." Rebecca Mary could see for herself that Mrs. Lee had scarlet fever. A card on the house was actually red in the face with its efforts to tell her that Mrs. Lee had scarlet fever. "Mrs. Muldoon said she guessed my teacher was an all right person to leave me with, and so she's loaned me to you. Yes, she has!" as Rebecca Mary seemed unable to believe it. "I'm loaned to you until my father or Mrs. Muldoon comes home again. Aren't you glad?" Her lip quivered for Rebecca Mary looked anything but glad.

Rebecca Mary couldn't say she was glad, either. She seemed to have lost her tongue for she just stood there and looked down at black-haired, black-eyed Joan and wondered what in the world she would do if Joan's absurd story was true.

"Are you Joan's teacher?" called Mrs. Lee from next door. "Mrs. Muldoon was sure that you would look after Joan while she was away. Her son in Kansas City is sick. She went as soon as she got the telegram, and she said she didn't know a living soul who would look after Joan until she thought of you. I'd be glad to take her in here if the health officer would let me. If you can't look after her I suppose the Associated Charities could find some one," she suggested.

"Oh, no!" exclaimed Rebecca Mary. Joan did not seem at all like an Associated Charities case. Bewildered as Rebecca Mary was she could see that.

"That's what I thought, and Mrs. Muldoon thought so, too. Mr. Befort is away on business she said. They're nice people, used to much better days, I'd say. You won't have a mite of trouble with Joan."

"Not a mite!" promised Joan, winking fast to keep the tears in her black eyes. It wasn't pleasant to be loaned to a teacher who didn't want to borrow. "I'll be so good you'll never know I'm there!"

"Shan't I?" Rebecca Mary visualized the tiny apartment she had shared with a fellow teacher until Miss Stimson had been called home by the illness of her mother. At first Rebecca Mary had liked to be alone, but even before Cousin Susan talked to her as only a relative can talk to one, she had wished for a companion, not an eight-year-old companion she thought quickly as she looked at Joan. Goodness knows, she had enough of children during school hours. But what could she do? Plainly Mrs. Lee and Joan expected her to take Joan home and keep her indefinitely. It was absurd. But if she didn't take her there was only the Associated Charities.

A little hand clutched her arm. "You aren't h-happy because I-I'm loaned to you," faltered a trembling little voice.

Rebecca Mary was almost unkind enough to say she wasn't and to ask how she could be, but the sob in Joan's voice made her ashamed of herself and her frown. She dropped down on the top step and put her arms around Joan and her clock and a framed picture and a potato masher which she discovered made the odd collection in Joan's arms. The potato masher hit her nose and she frowned again.

Joan leaned against her with a tired sigh. "It's—it's very hard when no one wants you," she hiccoughed.

Rebecca Mary knew just how hard it was, but she didn't say so. Her back was toward the street so that she did not see a limousine coming toward them. It stopped in front of the cottage, and if it hadn't been for the four-leaf clover in her pocket Rebecca Mary would have been very much surprised to hear Mrs. Peter Simmons' voice.

"Does Mr. Frederick Befort live here? Upon my word!" as Rebecca Mary jumped up and faced her. "I wondered if we should meet again. Mr. Befort is one of the men at the factory so I have come to get acquainted with his family," she explained with a friendly smile.

"That's me!" Joan was on her toes with importance. "I'm all the family Mr. Frederick Befort has, but I'm loaned to Miss Wyman!"

CHAPTER III

FIFTEEN minutes later Rebecca Mary and Joan with Joan's suit case and the picture and the clock and the potato masher were driving away with Mrs. Simmons, while Mrs. Lee waved her apron and promised to let them know the very first minute that Mr. Befort or Mrs. Muldoon returned.

"This is the picture of my very own father and my very own mother," Joan explained as she showed Mrs. Simmons and Rebecca Mary the photograph of a man in a very gorgeous uniform and with an order on his breast standing beside a beautiful young woman in a smart evening gown, a long string of pearls about her neck. There was a coat of arms emblazoned on the silver frame, and Mrs. Simmons touched it with her fingers to call Rebecca Mary's attention to the splendor of it.

"This clock was my mother's, too," Joan chattered on. "And I've wound it myself every night since she went away so I had to bring it with me, and this," she looked at the potato masher doubtfully. "I don't know why I like it, but I do."

"Then I'm glad you brought it with you." Mrs. Simmons patted the small fingers which clutched the wooden potato masher and wondered if the pictured father was dressed for a costume ball or if his everyday clothes were so gorgeous. "Did you ever see her father?" she asked Rebecca Mary.

Rebecca Mary quite forgot the brief glimpse she had had of Mr. Befort's back as he was leaving the Viking room with Joan. "Never!" she exclaimed with an emphasis which made Mrs. Simmons laugh. It sounded so fierce, as though if Rebecca Mary ever had seen Mr. Befort she would have told him a thing or two.

"He has only been at the factory for a few months," Mrs. Simmons explained. "We'll stop at my house and telephone to the office. It will be interesting to hear where he has gone and why he has gone."

But when they stopped at Mrs. Simmons' house, a big sprawling mansion of brick and plaster and brown timbers, and telephoned to the office all they learned was that Frederick Befort had gone away on special business and could not be reached by any one—not by any one at all.

"Well, upon my word!" Mrs. Simmons was quite taken aback by the decisive answer from the office.

"I've half a mind to show that man that I can reach Frederick Befort if I want to. It's ridiculous, perfectly ridiculous, to think that any business is more important than his child. What will you do?" she asked Rebecca Mary.

"I suppose I shall have to keep her until her father comes back," sighed Rebecca Mary. "I really can't turn her over to the Associated Charities, but it seems to me that a good deal is expected of a teacher."

"She might stay here," suggested Mrs. Simmons. "One of my maids could look after her. How would you like that?" she asked Joan, who stood beside her.

"It would be like home." Joan looked about the big spacious rooms with their rich rugs and hangings, the attractive furnishings and beautiful pictures. "Our old home, I mean. But I wasn't loaned to you. I was—I was loaned to Miss Wyman." Her lips quivered and tears hung perilously near the edge of each black eye.

"So you were, honey." Suddenly Rebecca Mary realized that a great deal was being expected of Joan, too, and she hugged her. She felt almost as sorry for Joan as she did for herself. It couldn't be pleasant to be left on the door step with a picture and a clock and a potato masher. "It's ever so kind of you, Mrs. Simmons, but we'll manage some way."

"I'm sure she wouldn't bother me as much as she will you, and I have an obligation toward her as long as her father works for my husband. Don't go yet," as Rebecca Mary rose and took Joan's hand. "We'll have a cup of tea, and then I'll take you home in the car."

"I like to ride in cars," dimpled Joan, all smiles again. "I always used to."

Over her head Mrs. Simmons looked at Rebecca Mary and raised her eyebrows questioningly, but Rebecca Mary could only shake her head. Rebecca Mary began to see that there might be something in her principal's wish to have her teachers know more of their pupils than their ability to read and cipher. There was such a lot more about Joan that Rebecca Mary would like to have known that very minute.

"Where was your old home, my dear?" Mrs. Simmons did not hesitate to ask for any information she wished to have.

"Over the sea—at Echternach." Joan turned an eager face toward her, quite willing to talk of that old home where she had lived with her daddy and her mother until she had come to the United States with her mother. Her mother had died suddenly, leaving

Joan with a grandmother who had lived only long enough to give the little girl back to her father when he came a year later. And as she chattered Mrs. Simmons and Rebecca Mary looked at the coat of arms on the silver frame and at the photograph of the gorgeously uniformed man and the beautiful woman.

"Tell me about your father?" Mrs. Simmons asked as soon as she could slip a word in edgeways.

Joan looked up, a trifle puzzled by the question. "Daddy?" she repeated. "Why, he's just—daddy. He's like—well, his eyes always look at me so lovingly and his mouth talks to me so sweetly and his ears hear everything I say and his hands work for me and his feet bring him to me." She kept her eyes on the photograph to make sure she left nothing out. "That's my daddy!" she finished triumphantly, and she looked up as if she dared them to find fault with such a daddy.

Mrs. Simmons patted her shoulder, and Rebecca Mary hugged her.

"That's a very good working description of a daddy," smiled Mrs. Simmons. "And here is Sako with the tea."

When the Japanese butler had placed the tray on the low table beside Mrs. Simmons, Joan handed

43

cups and passed sandwiches quite as if she were accustomed to that pleasant task.

"I'm consumed with curiosity," Mrs. Simmons whispered to Rebecca Mary. "She is a most unusual child. You must tell me anything you learn about her. Echternach sounds German, doesn't it? And although the war is over and we're told we are to forgive our enemies, I can't quite forgive the Germans for all the dreadful things they did. Nor the Turks. Of course the children aren't to be blamed, but—That's my grandson," she told Joan, who was looking at a large framed photograph on the table. "Young Peter Simmons, and I'm sinfully proud of him. He was my first grandchild, and even when he was a fat bald-headed baby I knew that some day he would do wonderful things. I suppose all grandmothers think that, just as all mothers do. But I really didn't think Peter would do as wonderful things as he has," she went on more to Rebecca Mary than to Joan. "You know he has a *croix de guerre?*" She drew a quick breath and looked at Rebecca Mary with a smile which was not at all a laughing smile. "I'm apt to be a bit foolish when I talk of young Peter Simmons," she admitted as she wiped her eyes.

"I don't wonder!" Rebecca Mary drew a quick breath, too. "I should think you would be proud!"

44

She knew she should be proud if young Peter Simmons belonged to her. She didn't care if he had scowled at her.

"My daddy has one of those." Joan's pink finger pointed to the cross on young Peter Simmons' tunic. "Only his is an eagle." She showed it to them on her pictured father. "He doesn't wear it every day."

"Neither does my Peter," complained Peter's grandmother. "Listen! Doesn't that sound like Peter now?" For a car had stopped before the house, and there was a rush of young feet and a chatter of young tongues. "Don't you hope it is?"

Rebecca Mary must have hoped it was for she turned a deep crimson, and when young Peter Simmons did actually come in she gazed at him as if he were the most wonderful, the most amazing, man in the world. Rebecca Mary had never met a hero before and although Peter looked like any young man of twenty-three, big and brave and jolly, she knew that he was a hero and that the French government had given him a cross to prove that he was a hero. No wonder she drew a quick breath and that her eyes were full of awe as she looked at him. She quite forgot that once he had scowled at her, and she had scowled at him.

Peter was not alone, and Rebecca Mary and Joan

were introduced to Doris Kilbourne and Martha Farnsworth and Stanley Cabot. The girls rushed across the room to kiss Granny Simmons and tell her about their golf at the Country Club and to ask her if Peter wasn't a perfect brute to beat them.

And Peter chuckled. "You must expect to be beaten," he told them in a lordly manner. "Golf is no game for a girl, is it, Miss Wyman?"

Rebecca Mary colored to have him appeal to her, and she stammered a bit as she answered. "I thought it was a game for men, fat bald-headed old men."

The girls shrieked at that. "There, Peter Simmons! I reckon that will hold you for a while!"

"May we have some tea, Granny?" drawled Doris in her soft rich voice. "Or is it all gone?" She would have peeped into the tea pot to see but Granny kept her brown fingers in her soft white hands.

"Is it, Miss Wyman? Do you think you can find any tea for these thirsty children?"

Rebecca Mary was glad to pour tea. It gave her something to do while the others laughed and chattered of golf and tennis and the Country Club dances and a hundred other things about which she knew nothing. Doris and Martha wore smartly cut skirts of heavy white piqué. Doris had a green sweater and a soft green hat and green stockings while Martha wore purple. Rebecca Mary could scarcely decide which she liked the best as she sat back in her low chair, her hands loosely clasped on her knee. She wore a white skirt herself and a white blouse but they were a little rumpled from spending the day in school. But in her white hat and clothes and with a red rose in each cheek she had only a faint family resemblance to the girl in the shabby blue serge who had scowled at Peter that day in the Viking room. Peter looked at her curiously. There was something familiar about the rosy little face, but he could not remember where he had seen it as he refused tea and lounged back in a chair to smoke a cigarette.

"Hello, who's the chap in the Prussian uniform?" he asked suddenly, and he lifted the photograph of Joan's father and mother from the table where it lay beside the clock and the potato masher.

"That's my father!" Joan ran across to look at the picture with him. "And he has a medal, too." She pointed to it as she nodded at Peter.

"So he has, a real German eagle." Peter was as astonished as she could wish, and he lifted his eyebrows inquiringly at Granny as if he would ask where the German eagle came from.

"He showed it to me," Joan hinted delicately, and

47

when Peter only grinned, she went on not quite so delicately; "I love to see medals."

"Joan!" Rebecca Mary was mortified to death. What would Peter think?

"You'd like to see it, too. You told the grandmother you would," insisted Joan.

"Would you?" teased Peter, who had already discovered how easy it was to make Rebecca Mary blush, and what fun it was, also.

She blushed then, all the way from the brim of her hat to the V of her blouse, but she had to say, "Yes, thank you." Goodness, if she had imagined half the embarrassment her promise to Cousin Susan would cause her she never would have made it.

"All right, I'll show it to you, but it will be no treat to you, young woman," he pinched Joan's cheek, "if you have a German eagle in your family. Where is your father now?"

"He's gone." Her eyes filled with tears, and Peter imagined that he knew what she meant, that her father was dead, and he patted her shoulder sympathetically. "And I'm loaned to Miss Wyman!" The tears disappeared as she jubilantly announced what had happened.

"I hope Miss Wyman is as pleased as you are." Peter grinned at Rebecca Mary.

Rebecca Mary laughed softly and said that Miss Wyman was, and she only told the truth, for if it had not been for Joan she knew very well that she never would be in Mrs. Peter Simmons' lovely room with young Peter Simmons laughing at her.

Joan had to ask him again before young Peter pulled a small box from his pocket and showed her and Rebecca Mary the *croix de guerre*. Rebecca Mary had never seen anything which brought such a lump into her throat as that bronze cross on the red and green ribbon. She could not keep her voice steady as she said:

"How proud you must be of it!"

"Huh," grunted young Peter, closing the box with a snap and thrusting it back into his pocket. "It makes me feel like a sweep. Why, every man in the section deserved a cross more than I did!"

"The French general didn't think so!" Granny was indignant.

"It's true!" insisted Peter, red and embarrassed.

"Oh!" breathed Rebecca Mary. She liked to see Peter red and embarrassed. She hadn't supposed that heroes ever were that way, but she knew that school teachers were.

Stanley Cabot watched her face brighten. Stanley had been an artist before the war and now that the

49

war was over he was an artist again, and the vivid expression of her face held his attention.

"She looks as if she had just wakened up," he said to himself.

But suddenly the bright color faded from Rebecca Mary's cheeks. "We must go home," she said quickly. "Come, Joan."

"Not yet," begged Granny. "You can't stay? Peter, will you see if Karl is waiting? He will drive them home. Yes, my dear," as Rebecca Mary protested that it was not necessary, they could go home in the street car. "You have too much luggage," she laughed as Joan gathered her photograph and her clock and her potato masher. "The suit case is in the car, isn't it? I hope you will come very soon again," she said cordially, as she went into the hall with them. "I want to see more of you and of Joan. I love young people, and I love to have them with me. It makes me feel young. I hate to be old, but I am old, and the only way I can cheat myself is to have young people with me. You and Joan must come to dinner some night. Come Thursday. Perhaps we shall have heard something from Mr. Befort by then."

Joan, struggling with the potato masher and the clock, heard her. "My father's name," she said quickly, "isn't Mr. Befort. It's Count Ernach de Befort."

"What!" exclaimed Granny, who had no idea that she had been entertaining a young countess.

"Joan!" cried Rebecca Mary very much surprised, indeed, to learn that a young countess was in the third grade of the Lincoln school.

They were so amazed that Joan flushed and her fingers flew to her guilty lips. "Oh," she cried, "I forgot! I wasn't to tell. They don't have counts in this country."

"Ernach de Befort," murmured Granny in Rebecca Mary's ear. "That sounds like a queer Franco-German combination. I'd like it better if it were one thing or another, if it were French. Never mind, Joan," as Joan began to whimper that she had forgotten that she wasn't to tell. "We'll keep the secret, won't we, Miss Wyman? Do you believe her?" she whispered to Rebecca Mary.

Rebecca Mary shook her head. Not for a second did she believe that Joan's father was Count Ernach de Befort. She had met the active imagination of a child too often, and she whispered that Joan was only playing a little game of "let's pretend" before she said good-by to Granny and promised to come Thursday to dinner.

Peter was waiting beside the luxurious limousine.

51

"I hope I shall see you again soon, Miss Wyman," he said pleasantly, and Rebecca Mary devoutly hoped he would, too. "Good-by, Miss Loan Child." He grinned at Joan as she sat with her arms full of her treasures.

"Good-by." Joan released one hand to wave it at him as they drove away. "He's very nice, don't you think so, Miss Wyman? And awfully brave or he wouldn't have that cross. My father is as brave as a lion, too." And she held the photograph up so that Rebecca Mary could see how brave her father looked.

After Joan was tucked into Miss Stimson's abandoned bed Rebecca Mary sat by the window in the soft darkness and recalled the astonishing events of the day. How amazing they had been! And how jolly! She hoped she would see Peter Simmons again, but there wasn't much chance. He didn't go to the Lincoln school.

She laughed softly and jumped up and went to her desk to take out the insurance policy which was such a bugbear to her now and which was to be such a comfort to the old age that always had loomed so blackly before her. She read it over and then giggled as she took a sheet of paper and wrote across the top in large letters—"The Memory Insurance

52

Company." And below in smaller letters she copied and adapted the form of her old policy—"by this policy of insurance agrees to pay on demand to Rebecca Mary Wyman such memories as she may have paid into the said company." And below that she wrote in large letters again just one word—"Payments."

She pressed her fountain pen against her lips and studied that one word before she chuckled and began to enter her payments.

"Kitchen curtains.

"A four-leaf clover, origin unknown.

"One loan child of mysterious parentage.

"A hero and his *croix de guerre*."

What a lot there were! Why, it was only ten days since she had promised to take out a memory insurance policy. Cousin Susan would be pleased at the number of payments she had made on it already. Her whole face twinkled as she read the list. A hero and a *croix de guerre!* H-m! And that four-leaf clover! Where had it come from? That list—why, that list represented securities that she couldn't lose and which no one could take from her. So long as she could remember anything she would remember Cousin Susan's kitchen curtains which never would be bought now. She could scarcely wait to make another payment, and she felt in each of her two hundred and eight bones that there would be other payments,—many of them.

CHAPTER IV

THE very next day was Saturday so that Rebecca Mary was at home when the postman made his first round. He brought her a letter from her mother, and Rebecca Mary never suspected what a wonderful surprise was packed in the square envelope.

Mrs. Wyman's favorite aunt, a woman of some wealth and many years, had decided to give a few of her friends the legacies she had meant to leave them at her death so that she could hear how they were enjoyed. She had sent Mrs. Wyman a check for five thousand dollars and a check for a thousand dollars to each of the Wyman girls. Rebecca Mary's eyes fairly popped from her head when she saw her check and read the letter. She couldn't believe that it was her check.

I want you to spend at least a part of it on yourself," wrote Mrs. Wyman. You have been so splendid and unselfish in sharing everything with us that you have earned the right to be a little foolish with some of this money. You never expected to have it and so we never planned to use any of it for a new roof or a kitchen stove. Take a little trip in your vacation, dear, or buy some other pleasure. If you put it in the bank the interest would pay your insurance premium, but you have sacrificed so much to the future. Perhaps I have been wrong in making so much of it for after all you are young but once. I do want my girls to have some good times to remember. Write Aunt Ellen a little note, and tell her that you are going to buy a lot of pleasure which you will remember all of your life with her generous gift.

Rebecca Mary had to read that letter twice before she could quite understand it, and then she looked at her loan child.

"Joan," she exclaimed breathlessly, "let us give three rousing cheers for a four-leaf clover!"

And after they had given three of the rousingest sort of cheers they put on their hats and went down to the First National Bank, where Rebecca Mary deposited the most beautiful check that she ever hoped to see. And there they met Stanley Cabot, who was very much pleased to see Rebecca Mary again and who introduced her to his older brother, Richard Cabot, who was the youngest bank vice-president that Waloo had ever had. Rebecca Mary had never expected to know a vice-president of the First National Bank, and as soon as she saw him her eyes changed from saucer size to service plates, for she recognized him at once. He was the man who had been with old Mrs. Peter Simmons that afternoon at the Waloo, the man who had looked as if he could do things, the man who had made her cheeks burn and her heart thump. She had never thought that already he had done enough to make him a bank vice-president. He looked too young. Rebecca Mary had always thought of a banker, vice-president or president, as an old man with gray hair and plenty of figure. Richard Cabot hadn't a gray hair in his head and he was as slim and straight as an athlete. He seemed wonderful to Rebecca Mary, who gazed at him with a surprise and interest which amused and flattered him. He did not recognize her at all for she had changed her face. At the Waloo tea room she had worn a yellow brown scowl and at the bank she had on a pink smile. It was not strange that Richard did not recognize her until she had agreed that it was a gorgeous day and that Mrs. Simmons was a perfect old dear. Then it was Richard who opened his eyes wide.

"That's it!" he exclaimed, and the puzzled look in his face was chased away by a slight flush, which seemed rather strange to be on the face of a banker. "I thought I had seen you before, Miss Wyman. And it was at the Waloo the afternoon Granny took me there for tea. She would accept no refusal although I told her that bankers had no time and little use for tea. But I was glad I went."

He liked Rebecca Mary's pink smile and self-conscious manner. Richard knew any number of girls, all of those with whom he had grown up and all the relatives and friends of the older men with whom he was associated and who regarded him as Waloo's most promising young man, and those girls had always met him considerably more than half way. It was refreshing to meet a girl who blushed and hesitated over the first steps to his acquaintance. It made him feel big and mannish and important, which is exactly the way you like to feel if you are a man. That is why when he met Rebecca Mary at the bank door, after she had loaned that most beautiful check in the world to the cashier, that he said more impulsively than he usually spoke to a girl:

"If you have finished your banking, may I walk up the avenue with you?"

"My banking never takes long." Rebecca Mary was all in a flutter at the thought of walking up the avenue with Mr. Richard Cabot. Why, it would be like taking a stroll with the ten story bank building. "I just put a little in, and it seems to come out by itself," she explained sadly.

The walk up the avenue was a royal progress for Richard seemed to know every one. His hat was never on his head. Rebecca Mary was rather tongue-tied, but Joan's tongue was not tied. Before they were out of the bank she had told Richard that she had been loaned to Rebecca Mary and that they were going to dinner at Mrs. Simmons' house on Thursday evening.

"I've never been to a party dinner in all my life," she finished with great importance, "so I hope nothing will happen."

"What could happen?" asked Richard with a smile for Rebecca Mary, who gave him a shy smile in exchange.

"Lots of things. Scarlet fever or mumps or——"

"My goodness gracious, Joan! I hope you haven't been neighborly enough to take mumps or scarlet fever!" The mere hint that Joan might have been that neighborly was startling to Rebecca Mary.

"But I'm not going to think of them because they aren't going to happen, and there isn't any good in thinking of what never will happen, is there?" went on Joan.

"Not a bit," agreed Richard. "Are you going in here?" For Rebecca Mary had stopped before the very smartest shop in Waloo.

"We're going to buy clothes for the dinner," Joan whispered confidentially. "My father said that ladies, even as little ladies as I am, can't ever go anywhere without buying new clothes. He thinks it's very strange."

"So it is. No wonder their money won't stay in the bank. I am very glad to have met you, Miss Wyman, and I hope to see those new clothes some time soon." He looked straight into Rebecca Mary's gray eyes as he told her what he hoped to do before he said good-by and went on up the avenue.

"Joan, you are an awful chatterbox," rebuked Rebecca Mary.

"I only talk because my head is so full of words that they just tumble off my tongue. Don't the words want to tumble from your tongue?" Joan asked curiously as they went into the smartest shop.

Rebecca Mary looked at the beautiful frocks about her. Oh, Cousin Susan was right, and her clothes were a disgrace. They weren't clothes at all, they were only covering. She sent a little thank you message to Aunt Ellen by telepathy before she began that easiest of all tasks for a woman, to spend money.

She had an odd feeling that she was not herself as she went up Park Terrace with Joan on Thursday evening, and she surely did not look like her old shabby self. How could she when she wore a smart white Georgette crepe frock under a smart beige cape and her big black hat had been designed by a real milliner and not copied by a "make over person?" Rebecca Mary had spent an hour with a hair dresser that afternoon after school so that from the wave in her yellow brown hair to the sole of her white pumps she was absolutely new. She felt as new as she looked, for there is nothing which will take the tired discouraged feeling from a woman, or a man either, quicker or more effectively than new clothes. Festal garments had been found for Joan in the suit case which Mrs. Muldoon had packed so that any one who saw Rebecca Mary and Joan walk up Park Terrace knew at once that they were going out to dine.

They were early, and Rebecca Mary was dreadfully mortified. It looked so eager, so hungry, she told herself crossly, to be early. Joan was not mortified at all for in her small mind a guest could not go to a party too early. Mrs. Simmons joined them in a very few minutes. Joan curtsied prettily and kissed Granny's wrinkled white hand.

"Did you teach her to do that in the Lincoln school?" Granny asked Rebecca Mary after Joan had gone into the sun room to see the gold fish in their crystal globe. "Have you heard anything from her father yet? If Mr. Simmons were here we would soon know all about Mr. Frederick Befort, Count Ernach de Befort," she corrected herself with a chuckle of amusement. "But he isn't here, and I don't like to make trouble at the office. I hope Mr. Befort comes back soon for your sake. Here is Richard Cabot. He asked himself," she explained as Richard came toward them. "He called me up and asked if I would give him some dinner. He often drops in when Mr. Simmons is away to keep me from being lonesome. I'm glad he came to-night."

Richard looked a trifle conscious himself as he took Rebecca Mary's hand and told her that he was very glad to see her again.

"And her new clothes, Mr. Cabot," whispered an anxious little voice at his elbow. Joan was desperately afraid that Richard would not see Rebecca Mary's new frock. "You said you wanted to see her new clothes soon, and here they are. Aren't they beautiful? And they were marked down from sixty-nine fifty! Doesn't she look like a princess?"

"I've never seen a princess," laughed Richard, his eyes telling Rebecca Mary more than his lips how very much he liked her marked down frock.

"Haven't you?" Joan looked quite surprised and sorry. "I have. I've seen the Belgian princess and some of the English ones and, of course, all of the German ones."

Rebecca Mary and Granny looked at each other as Joan spoke of the many princesses she had seen. They couldn't help it. And Rebecca Mary began to think that perhaps Joan had too much imagination.

It was a very gay little dinner, and before they had finished their coffee young Peter Simmons and his mother ran in to ask what Granny had heard from grandfather. They were followed almost at once by Sallie Cabot and her husband, young Joshua Cabot, and close on their heels came young Mrs. Hiram Bingham with her adoring father-in-law. Richard drew Rebecca Mary to the other side of the grand piano and told her how Sallie Cabot had eloped with her great aunt and found a husband and of the jam rivalries which had threatened the romance of Hiram and Judith Bingham. It was like reading two volumes from the public library to hear Richard, and Rebecca Mary's eyes sparkled. So there really was some romance in the world. She had been afraid there wasn't any left. She had thought it must all be shut up in books.

"You ask Sallie," advised Richard, when she said

that. "She'll tell you that there will be romance in the world as long as there are people in it. I used to laugh at her but, by George, I'm beginning to think that she is right!"

"Of course, I'm right," declared Sallie, who had strolled near enough to hear herself quoted. "Wherever did you find that child?" she asked Rebecca Mary with a nod toward Joan. "Granny said she was a mystery, but she is also a darling. She talks like an American kiddie, but she doesn't act like an American. She acts more like a—like a French child," she decided. Sallie Cabot had been at a French convent so she thought she knew what French children were like.

"Her mother was an American, from New Orleans." Rebecca Mary didn't know what Joan's father was so she couldn't tell Sallie. "She is a dear, isn't she? When she told me she had been loaned to me I was scared to death and furious, too, but she really is fun. I expect I was in a rut," she confessed with a shamed little face and voice which quite enchanted Richard.

"A rut? What an unpleasant place for a pretty girl to be. May I tell you that I love your frock?"

Rebecca Mary glowed with pleasure to hear young Mrs. Joshua Cabot admire her marked down frock.

Every one in Waloo knew that Mrs. Joshua Cabot could have a new frock every day and two for Sunday if she wanted them.

"I like it," Rebecca Mary admitted with adorable shyness.

"So do I!" Richard did not speak at all shyly but very emphatically.

Sallie smiled as she moved away. "Any new fox trots, Granny?" she asked. "I depend upon you to keep me up to the minute. Put on a record, Peter, and let us jig a bit. You like to trot, don't you, Miss Wyman?"

Rebecca Mary admitted that she did, and Richard asked her to have one with him as if he were afraid that some one would claim her before he could. He was a perfect partner for he extended just far enough above her five feet and three inches to hold her right, and their steps suited perfectly. Rebecca Mary had never enjoyed a dance more, she thought breathlessly, when at last they stopped because the music stopped.

"Here's your next partner," announced Peter, when he had changed the record and another fox trot called them to dance.

If Rebecca Mary had been thrilled to dance with Waloo's youngest bank vice-president you may imagine how bubbly she was inside to fox trot with Waloo's hero. Peter smiled as he looked at the flushed face so near his own. Lordy, but he hadn't realized what a jolly little thing Granny had found. Nothing school marmish about her with her shining gray eyes, which were almost black now, and her yellow-brown hair and her pink cheeks and her smart new frock. Absolutely nothing.

Looking up to make a little remark about the call of the fox trot, Rebecca Mary caught the admiration in Peter's face, and she was so astonished that she lost the step. That made her furious, and she frowned impatiently.

"By thunder!" exclaimed Peter in quick surprise, and he stopped dancing to look at her. "Now I know where I saw you before! It was at the Waloo, and you scowled at me like a pirate. I was scared to death for fear you didn't like me."

"You scowled at me first!" Rebecca Mary's defense of her scowl was more emphatic than logical.

"Oh, come now!" Peter wouldn't believe that he had been that culpable. "I couldn't scowl at you. My old Granny was quite broken hearted to see you frown. She said if you were her daughter she'd lock you up until you had learned to smile. Granny's strong for the grins. Give one and you'll get one

66

is her motto. You can see for yourself how it works. You scowled at me,—sure it was that way!—and I scowled at you, although I don't see now how I ever did it."

"It's a very bad habit," Rebecca Mary told him severely. Her mouth was as sober as a judge's mouth ever was, but her eyes crinkled joyously. "You should break yourself of it."

"I shall," Peter told her promptly. "Just how should I go to work? You seem to have broken yourself of it." His eyes were full of boyish admiration.

"Not entirely." Rebecca Mary sighed, "I wish I could. A frowning face is horrid. If you ever see me scowl again I wish you would shout 'Pirate' at me as loud as you can. I'm afraid I do it unconsciously." And sure enough her eyebrows did begin to bend together unconsciously.

"Pirate!" shouted Peter instantly. "I can see it's going to be some work to be monitor of your eyebrows," he chuckled.

Rebecca Mary was sorry when the dance with Peter was over although she turned politely to Joshua Cabot when he spoke to her.

"Peter's a lucky chap," he said as he swung her out into the room. "All girls love a hero, and he's a hero all right. I'd like a decoration myself, but I don't know as I'd care to be kissed on both cheeks by a hairy French general. That duty should have been delegated to fat Madame General or better still to pretty Madamoiselle General. Peter is a good old scout, and modest. He blushes like a girl when any one speaks of what he has done."

Rebecca Mary nodded. She had seen him blush. She colored delicately herself, and Joshua looked wisely over her head to his wife. Hello, another victim for old Peter, his glance seemed to tell Sallie Cabot.

Joan danced, too, with old Mr. Bingham, who was not as light on his feet as he had been once.

"I do it for exercise," he explained to Granny. "Judy thinks it's good for me."

"You needn't make any excuse to me, Hiram Bingham. I take exercise myself, don't I, Peter? And if old Peter Simmons comes home in time we shall dance nothing but fox trots at our golden wedding."

"A golden wedding!" Joan had never heard of such a thing. "What does that mean, dear Granny Simmons? Would I like one?"

Granny patted her rosy cheeks. "If you have any kind of a wedding I hope you will have a golden

68

one, too. It stands, Joan, for fifty years of self-control and unselfishness and forbearance and——"

"And love," interrupted Sallie Cabot quickly. "Don't leave out the love, Granny. No man and woman could live together for fifty years without love."

"I reckon you're right, Sallie," agreed Granny meekly.

"I've never been to a golden wedding," ventured Joan, playing with the black ribbon which kept Granny's glasses from losing themselves. "I've never been invited to one!"

"You are invited to mine this minute," Granny told her with beautiful promptness.

"Oh!" Joan balanced herself on her toes and exclaimed rapturously: "A golden wedding! What good times I've had since I was loaned!"

"I suppose you young people think you are having good times," murmured Granny wistfully, "but they aren't a patch on the good times we had, are they, Hiram? I like to take my memories out and gloat over them when I hear you young people talk. I have a lot of them, too. Why, Joan, if I should take all my memories out and put them end to end I expect they would reach around the world, and if they were piled one on top of the other they would be higher than the Waloo water tower." She named the highest point in Waloo.

Joan was not the only one impressed by the vast number of Granny's memories.

"Imagine," Rebecca Mary turned to Richard, who was at her elbow, "having so many things you want to remember. Most of my experiences I want to forget." And she shivered.

"Have they been so unpleasant?" Richard had never imagined he could be so sympathetic. "But I've heard that the hard experiences are the very ones that people like best to remember."

Rebecca Mary shook her head. "How can they?" She didn't see how any one would want to remember unpleasant experiences.

"But you aren't going to have any more disagreeable times," promised Richard confidently, as if he knew exactly what the future had in store for her. "You are going to walk on Pleasant Avenue from now on."

"I hope so." But Rebecca Mary was not so confident, although she looked up and smiled at him. "I surely have been on Pleasant Avenue this evening, but now I must run back to Worry Street. I'm like Cinderella, only out on leave." And she laughed at his prophecy before she went over to tell **Granny** that she had never had such a good time.

"Must you go?" Granny held her hand in a warm friendly clasp and thought that the child looked as if she had had a good time. "Wait a minute. Peter——"

Rebecca Mary's heart thumped. Was Granny going to ask Peter to take her home? But if Granny was she didn't for Richard interrupted her.

"Let me take Miss Wyman home. I have my car."

"I have mine, too," grinned Peter.

"But you have your mother. I'm alone."

Beggars cannot be choosers and although she would far rather have gone with Peter it was pleasant to ride with Richard in his big car, Joan tucked between them. Richard bent forward.

"Tired?" he asked gently.

"I'm glad to be tired to-night." Rebecca Mary spoke almost fiercely. "I've been dead tired from work and from disappointment, but it hasn't been often that I've been tired from pleasure." And then she amazed herself and charmed Richard by telling him something of her life, which had been so full of work and disappointment and so empty of pleasure. She even told him of Cousin Susan and the price she had paid for their tea at the Waloo, and Richard,

71

banker though he was, had never heard of kitchen curtains buying tea for two.

"You were there that afternoon," she reminded him after she had decided that she would not tell him about the four-leaf clover. It would sound too foolish to a bank vice-president.

"I know," Richard said hastily before he went on in his usual matter-of-fact voice. "You modern girls are wonderful. You are as brave as a man, braver than lots of men I know."

"That's because we have to be brave," Rebecca Mary explained. "I don't know why I've bored you with my stupid past," she said, rather ashamed of her outburst. "I've never spilled all my troubles on any one before."

"I'm mighty flattered that you told them to me. It means that we are going to be friends, doesn't it?" He bent forward to see as well as to hear that she would be friends with him. It was not often that Richard had asked for a girl's friendship.

Rebecca Mary felt that in some occult feminine fashion, and she offered him a warm little hand and said indeed she should be glad to be friends with him. If her voice shook a trifle when she said that it must have been because Richard was such a very important young man in Waloo.

Before she went to bed Rebecca Mary took out her memory insurance policy and entered another payment.

"A fox trot with the hero of Waloo."

So far as her memory insurance went the most promising young man in Waloo did not seem to exist although she liked him very very much. But Rebecca Mary was like everybody else, she would rather have what she wanted than what she could get.

CHAPTER V

I CAN'T blame any one but myself because I don't know all about Joan." Rebecca Mary was an honest little thing and she made no attempt to shift the blame to any one else. She packed it all on her own slim shoulders. "If I had been a good teacher according to my principal I should have called at the house long ago and heard the whole story from Mrs. Muldoon. But I didn't. I kept putting it off, and so I don't know much."

Granny had stopped at the Lincoln school at the close of the afternoon session to inquire if Rebecca Mary had learned anything more about Joan's father. But Rebecca Mary hadn't learned a thing. Joan was an odd mixture of frankness and reserve. There were times when Rebecca Mary thought that she must have been forbidden to speak of her old life in the town with the German name. The whole situation was puzzling. Rebecca Mary could not understand it at all.

If you imagine that Joan's company was a constant joy to Rebecca Mary you imagine all wrong.

74

Rebecca Mary liked to have Joan with her well enough at times, but there were other times when she was perfectly indifferent to her guest and still other times when Joan was almost an irritation, and Rebecca Mary could not see why of all the teachers in the Lincoln school she should be the one to have to borrow a child whether she wanted one or not. She had not had a chance to say "Yes, thank you."

"I've learned that Frederick Befort is on the factory pay-roll and as Frederick Befort," Granny said slowly. "There is no record of any Count Ernach de Befort. Of course now that the war is over I don't suppose it matters if he is a German. There wouldn't be any secrets for him to learn. Germany wouldn't be interested now in what is being done at the factory."

"But de Befort sounds French," objected Rebecca Mary, who could not see that Joan bore any resemblance to any German child she had ever taught. "Joan was born in Yokohama but that doesn't tell us anything. She certainly isn't a Japanese. It's funny but she doesn't seem to want to tell me what country she did come from. I was stupid enough to lose her nativity card, and when I made out another and asked her what nationality her father was she said he was going to be an American. I told her

75

I wanted to know what he was now and she said he had told her that they would forget what they were before they came to this country. That seemed rather queer. But Joan talks of Paris as much as she does of Berlin. I wish I spoke French half as well as she does."

"She speaks very good German, too. And as you say there is something suspicious in the way she avoids any reference to her nationality. It does seem as if she had been told not to speak of it. I suppose I am a silly prejudiced old woman, but I should rather have Joan and her father almost anything but German. Are you through? Don't you want to take a spin down the River Road before you go home? It's perfect out, a real June day. Do come with me."

Rebecca Mary had no trouble at all to say "Yes, thank you" to that invitation. She called Joan, and they went with Granny to the limousine which was waiting at the curb.

"I wonder if Cinderella's coach went as fast as this?" Joan said as they flew toward the River Road. "We read about Cinderella this very day," she explained to Granny. "It would be more interesting to have rats than engines, wouldn't it? I'd like a pair of glass slippers, too, even if they would break

76

so easy. Wooden ones would be the strongest. That's what they wear at home, you know, wooden ones."

"In Germany, you mean?" asked Granny quickly.

Joan wriggled. "Yes, in Germany they wear wooden ones," she said as quickly. "I've never seen glass slippers, not in London nor Paris nor Vienna nor anywhere. Aren't they any place but in fairy land?" she twisted around to ask.

"Nowhere. No matter how much money you have you can't buy Cinderella's slippers anywhere but in fairy land," Rebecca Mary told her with a sigh as if she, too, would like to find glass slippers somewhere else.

For a while Joan was silent, meditating perhaps on the shoe shops in fairy land with their glass slippers of every size and color.

Granny and Rebecca Mary were silent, also, but they were not thinking of glass slippers as the car swung into the River Road, which is quite the prettiest drive about Waloo. Never before had Rebecca Mary driven over it in a smart limousine with a liveried chauffeur at the wheel. She had walked there times without number, but walking is not like riding in a pneumatic-tired machine, and Rebecca Mary did enjoy the change. She was afraid that

77

there was the making of a snob in her for she did like to ride with Mrs. Peter Simmons better than she liked to walk with a teacher as shabby as she had been. Yes, she was a perfect snob. She laughed as if she found it funny to be a snob. Joan looked up and laughed, too.

"I like you best when you laugh." She squeezed Rebecca Mary's fingers. "Of course I like you always, days and nights and every minute, but when you let your face break into little holes," she reached up and touched Rebecca Mary's one dimple, "why I just love you!"

"So do I," said Granny. "And it makes my old face break into little holes, too. Dear me, that makes it very serious, doesn't it? It is our own fault when people frown at us. Don't ever forget that, Joan. If you smile at people they will smile at you."

"Will they? But I like to have people frown at me sometimes. It makes me shiver all down my back. Don't you like to have your back shiver?"

"My back is too old to like to shiver. It's far too old and too stiff."

Rebecca Mary caught the note of sadness in Granny's voice and ventured to touch her hand. "It's the heart not the back which should be young," she said softly. "I read that somewhere so it must be true. And your heart, dear Mrs. Simmons, will never in the world be old. Gracious, I should say it wouldn't!" she added emphatically as she remembered how far from old Granny's enthusiasm was.

"Don't call me Mrs. Simmons," begged Granny, and she took Rebecca Mary's hand in hers. "I'm Granny to all of my young friends. I'd like to be Granny to you."

Rebecca Mary caught her breath. Just imagine calling Mrs. Peter Simmons,—Mrs. Peter Simmons of Waloo—, Granny!

"I'm not going to let my heart grow old either," exclaimed Joan before Rebecca Mary could tell Mrs. Simmons how glad she would be to call her Granny. "I want to keep it young for ever. But how can I when it gets older every year? To-day my heart's eight and next May it will be nine! How can I keep it young for ever?" Joan's voice was a wail.

"Yes, Miss Wyman, how can we keep our hearts young when there is always a birthday before us?"

"You know. No one can give a better rule than you can."

But Granny shook her head. She declared that there wasn't any rule, that was why there were so many old hearts. People didn't know how to keep their hearts young. They weren't taught in any school she knew of.

"I'll ask daddy," promised Joan. "I expect he'll know. I'll ask him just as soon as I see him. But I hope he won't come for me before the golden wedding." She turned pale at the mere thought of missing a golden wedding.

"The golden wedding won't be until July," Granny told her. "Imagine any one being married in July. It was the most scorching day. I thought I should melt and that old Peter Simmons would melt and there wouldn't be any one left to be married. We went to New York and the sea shore on our wedding trip, and Peter ate too many lobsters and was ill. Such times as we had!" She smiled at their memory. "The twenty-second of July," she said dreamily. "Will you keep Joan until then, Miss Wyman? Oh, I have a plan! This is the last week of school, isn't it?"

Rebecca Mary nodded to the last question before she answered the first. "I'll take Joan down home with me, to Mifflin, if Mrs. Muldoon doesn't come back."

"No, I want you both to come to me. Please," as Rebecca Mary looked at her in surprise. "I'm so lonely in that big house by myself. Mr. Simmons

is away so much, I never know when he will be home.
It would keep my old heart young," she hinted, "to
have two young things in the house again. Do,
please take pity on a crabbed old woman."

"You're not a crabbed old woman!" Rebecca
Mary said fiercely.

"I shall be if you don't come and stay with me.
We might motor up to Seven Pines, that's our country place, for a few days. Most people think it's
very pretty there. You want to come, don't you,
Joan?"

"Yes, I do." Joan did not hesitate a breath. "I
want to help you keep your heart young. Don't
you want to help too, Miss Wyman?" She didn't
see how Miss Wyman could refuse to help.

"But my mother and sister will expect us in
Mifflin."

"We can run down Saturday and tell them," suggested Granny. "We can motor down and back in
a day. I know your mother will be willing."

But still Rebecca Mary hesitated although it
would be fun to go rolling into Mifflin in the big
limousine, and it would be fun, too, to stay with Mrs.
Simmons in her big house, but—— Her fingers
touched her pocket and felt a hard round object,
the locket which held the four-leaf clover. The

81

locket reminded Rebecca Mary that she couldn't refuse Granny Simmons' kind invitation if she kept her promise to Cousin Susan. She blushed and stammered a bit as she said "Yes, thank you." And then impulsively she showed Granny the locket and told her what a mystery it contained.

"Well, upon my word!" Granny seemed as surprised and interested as Rebecca Mary could wish. "How romantic! We must find who gave it to you. I do hope it wasn't that fat old waiter who sniffs. Haven't you any clue? Who was in the tea room that afternoon?"

"I was there with daddy, wasn't I, Miss Wyman?" Joan pulled her sleeve. "But I gave you violets. I didn't give you any lucky clover."

"Did you see her father?" Granny asked immediately. She was surprised that Rebecca Mary hadn't told her she had seen Frederick Befort.

Rebecca Mary shook her head. "You can't really say you have seen a man when you have had only a fleeting glimpse of a back. You were there, Mrs. Simmons. And your grandson!" To save her soul Rebecca Mary could not keep the crimson wave from her cheeks when she just the same as put a wish in words.

But Granny shrieked with delight. "If it was

Peter!" she chuckled. "If it only was Peter! He is such a matter of fact old boy. I'd love to think he went around giving girls four-leaf clovers."

"Matter of fact!" Rebecca Mary stared at Granny. Peter was anything but matter of fact to her. Her voice told Granny so.

Granny stopped in the very middle of another chuckle. "Perhaps my eyes are as old as my heart," she admitted. "You'll have to come and help me see Peter as you do, help me change my old eyes."

"Can you do that?" Joan wanted to know at once. "Can you change your eyes and your heart if you don't like the ones you have, like Mrs. Muldoon changed the bread one day? She said it was stale."

"Indeed you can change a stale heart, Joan. It is wrong and foolish to keep such a useless thing as a stale heart. You should change it at once."

"Where?"

Granny looked helplessly at Rebecca Mary. Joan's endless questions were sometimes hard to answer. Rebecca Mary laughed and answered for her.

"Wherever there is anything to love," she suggested.

CHAPTER VI

WHEN Richard heard that Granny was going to take Rebecca Mary and Joan to Mifflin in her limousine he discovered that he had to call on the Mifflin National Bank, and he suggested that they should make the trip together.

"I'll drive you in my big car," he said. "We could stop at the River Club for lunch and come home by way of Spirit Lake for dinner. You'll like the River Club," he told Rebecca Mary. "It's on an island in the Mississippi and the dining room hangs over the river. You can catch your lunch from the window."

"What fun!" dimpled Rebecca Mary. "It sounds like a most beautiful pink plan."

"Pink plan?" Richard didn't understand what she meant, but he thought she looked rather beautiful and pink herself as she stood beside him.

"Whenever I hear of anything that is absolutely all right," Rebecca Mary explained, "I seem to see it as the most lovely rose color. And so I always think of absolutely all right things as pink. How lucky it is for us that you owe the Mifflin Bank a call."

"It's lucky for me," insisted Richard with a smile.

So on Saturday Richard brought his big car to Rebecca Mary's door, and Joan and Rebecca Mary ran down from the window where they had been watching for him for hours. Rebecca Mary wore another portion of Aunt Ellen's gift, a new motor coat—to tell the truth it was the only motor coat she had ever had—and a fascinatingly small hat demurely veiled. She looked just exactly right for a motor trip, and Richard told her so with his eyes while Granny, who was already in the tonneau, admired her with her lips as well as her eyes.

"That's a very smart and becoming coat and hat, Rebecca Mary," she said at once. "Suppose you sit in front with Richard? Riding in an open car always makes me sleepy and if you are back here you will talk to me and keep me awake."

"Won't I talk to you?" Joan didn't know how she was going to keep from talking all the way from Waloo to Mifflin, but she obediently nestled down beside Granny.

"I rather think you will." Granny smiled at her and patted her fat little hand. "But before you begin to talk you must help me plan how we shall persuade Mrs. Wyman to loan us her daughter. That will take a lot of thinking, and you can't talk very well while you are thinking."

On the front seat Rebecca Mary laughed joyously. "It sounds as if this was going to be a very important expedition," she said.

"It is," Richard told her with a flash of his eyes. "All ready? Quite comfortable?"

And when Rebecca Mary had said she was quite ready and comfortable he took the seat beside her and did something to buttons and levers and they were off.

Rebecca Mary felt like one of the princesses Joan talked about so intimately as they rolled down the street, through the suburbs and into the real country. Richard called her attention to this old house, a relic of pioneer days, or to that new public library, and to the white sign boards which told them that they were on the Jefferson Highway. The name was between a palmetto and a towering pine to show them that New Orleans was at one end and that Minnesota was at the other end of that ribbon-smooth road. Richard seemed to know the way and there was nothing which Rebecca Mary should have seen which he did not show her.

86

"Want to go faster?" he asked when she leaned forward to look at the speed indicator. He touched a button again and they went faster.

"It's like flying!" she exclaimed with shining eyes. "Oh, I do think there are such wonderful things in the world! Aren't you glad that you are living now!"

He laughed at her enthusiasm. What a jolly little thing she was! And he told her that he most certainly was glad to be living that moment in a way which deepened the vivid color in Rebecca Mary's cheeks.

"Of course it's an old story to you," she went on quickly. "But this is the very first time I ever motored from Waloo to Mifflin. I've always gone in a stuffy day train and had cinders get into my eyes. Once the train was held up four hours by a wash-out on the road and an old Norwegian gave me some cookies. They did taste good," she assured him for he seemed as interested in the cakes as if he were a baker instead of a banker.

"Norwegian women are good cooks, and Norway is a beautiful country."

"I suppose you've been there? Every country will be beautiful to me unless I am so old when I start on my travels that I can't see. My favorite castle is a railroad ticket. I've never been farther than Waloo in all my life. I don't know why I tell you that for of course you know it. Any one can see that I've never been anywhere nor seen anything."

"Yes." Richard agreed with her so promptly that she felt as if he had pinched her for naturally she had expected that he would say that any one to see her would think she had been everywhere and seen everything. The sting was taken from the pinch when he went on: "If you had been everywhere you wouldn't be so jolly and enthusiastic as you are. Girls who have been everywhere and seen everything aren't satisfied with anything."

"I wonder," meditated Rebecca Mary. "Then you think it's better not to have and want than to have and not care for?"

"Much better. Very much better!"

"M-m," murmured Rebecca Mary doubtfully. "I don't believe you know a thing about it," she exclaimed suddenly. "You've had all of your life!"

"Not everything," Richard insisted. "There is at least one thing I've never had." But he did not tell her what that one thing was, and she did not ask him.

The River Club was all that Richard had said it

would be. They crossed a bridge to the island at one end of which was the rambling shingled club house which really did overhang the river. Richard was quite right, and Rebecca Mary could easily have fished from the window of the big dining room, but she preferred to let Richard order her lunch from the club pantries. A dozen or more men were lunching at the little tables, and Rebecca Mary heard scraps of their talk—"fifteen pounds"—"the brute got off with my best fly"—"that darned pike couldn't have weighed less than six pounds." She looked at Richard and laughed.

"I suppose more lies are told in this room than anywhere in the state," she whispered.

"I expect you are right," he whispered back.

They had a most delicious luncheon of black bass fresh from the river, of new potatoes and peas and salad and strawberries from the club garden. Many of the fishermen who had nodded to Richard came over to speak to Granny, and Richard introduced them to Rebecca Mary, and told her in an undertone that this one was a lumber king and that one was an iron king and the other one was a flour king. Rebecca Mary had never been in a room with so many kings in her life, and she looked after them curiously as she said so.

"Yes," Granny murmured. "They call this the millionaires' retreat, don't they, Richard?"

"I prefer the River Club, myself," was all Richard would say.

The club with its royal members seemed to make Richard even more important to Rebecca Mary, and she looked at him a trifle oddly as they left the island and went on to Mifflin. She had known that Richard was very clever and important—Granny had told her that old Mr. Simmons considered Richard Cabot quite the most promising young man in Waloo—but she hadn't thought these elderly kings of lumber and iron and flour would listen to him as they had listened. Richard seemed too young to belong with those bald-headed white-haired pudgy kings and yet they had greeted him as if they were very glad to see him. Rebecca Mary stole a shy glance at Richard. He was looking at her instead of twenty feet in front of his car as a motor driver should look, and he smiled.

"Like it?"

"Love it!" And she smiled, too, and forgot all about kings. How splendid it was to have Richard for a friend. And if he hadn't been a friend he never would have smiled at her like that. It gave her such a warm cozy little feeling to have a man like Richard for a friend. "Oh, isn't this the most wonderful day that was ever made out of blue sky and golden sunshine!" she cried suddenly. "And we're coming to Mifflin. There's Peterson's farm!"

And now it was Rebecca Mary who pointed out the points of interest, the old mill, the spire of the Episcopal church and the new starch factory, which was going to make the fortunes of the farmers, she told Richard with a serious little air which he liked enormously.

"What do you know about starch?" he teased.

"Lots. I know that the farmers have planted loads of potatoes, and they are going to sell them to the starch factory for enormous prices."

"Farmers always expect to sell for enormous prices, but if they have all planted enormous crops some of them will be disappointed. There is a little old law of supply and demand which regulates that sort of thing, you know."

"That's just it," Rebecca Mary exclaimed triumphantly. "The demand for Mifflin starch is going to be so great that there will be a huge demand for potatoes. I have a tiny bit of money that I might invest myself now," she told him a little proudly as she remembered how much was left of

Aunt Ellen's gift. "I might become a starch queen," she giggled.

"You might. But you might become a starch bankrupt, too. Don't you put any of your money into anything until I have a chance to look into it," he said firmly.

"I never should have dared to ask you for advice," she began, but he interrupted her.

"You haven't asked, I've offered, and I want you to promise you won't buy shares in anything until you have talked to me. I've had more experience in picking out good investments than you have."

Rebecca Mary laughed. "You couldn't have had less. It's awfully good of you, Mr. Cabot, to be willing to bother about my pennies, and when I have enough to do anything with I'll remember your very kind offer. Turn down this street if you want to find my home. Perhaps you would like to know whom you will see there. There is only my mother and sister. Mother is a dear, and she has had an awfully hard time. Grace is a dear, too. She is a year and a half older than I am and looks after the public library for Mifflin. There is the house, the big frame one on the corner. "Why——" for the big frame house on the corner had just been treated to a coat of fresh white paint, and Rebecca

Mary scarcely knew it when it shone forth so resplendent with its green-blinded windows.

"What an attractive place!" Granny woke up to lean forward and tell Rebecca Mary how much she liked her old home. "It looks as if it had been a home for more than one generation."

"It has!" Rebecca Mary twisted around to tell her its history. "My grandfather built it when he brought my grandmother here a bride just after the Civil War. It's grown since then, of course; that wing on the right and the L. It's really too big for mother and Grace but we couldn't sell it if we wanted to. I'd hate to sell it if we could." Rebecca Mary really loved the old house and she loved it more than ever now that it was repaired and painted. It really looked imposing. She had no reason to be ashamed of her home, and she was very grateful to Aunt Ellen as she slipped her arm through Granny's and led her up the bricked walk as Mrs. Wyman and Grace hurried out to meet them.

Rebecca Mary's eyes widened as she saw the pretty summer frocks which her mother and Grace were wearing and when she kissed Grace she whispered in her ear: "Hurrah for Aunt Ellen!" They all stood talking and laughing on the wide porch.

"So this is where you grew to be such a big girl?" Richard looked at the ample lawn which the white fence enclosed. He seemed to find it of great interest.

"Yes," nodded Rebecca Mary. "That is where I made mud pies, and there is the apple tree I climbed. I pretended it was a ship which was taking me to the Equator. I had the wildest interest in the Equator when I was ten. And that is the gate I was always running out of until mother tied me to the apple tree."

"Why, Miss Wyman!" Joan's very foundations seemed to totter. "Were you ever a bad little girl?" She couldn't believe it. Miss Wyman was her teacher and teachers,—could they ever have been bad little girls?

"Very bad!" Rebecca Mary's laughing answer did not sound at all convincing. "At least that is what my mother said, and she should know."

Joan might have carried her investigation of this startling statement further if Grace had not called to her to come and see the new brown cocker puppy and help choose a name for him. Richard and Rebecca Mary were left alone to talk of the days when Rebecca Mary had to be tied to the gnarled old apple tree.

94

"Richard!" It was Granny who interrupted them. "If you are to call on the Mifflin Bank don't you think you had better go?" Granny's voice almost sounded as if she didn't quite believe that Richard owed the Mifflin Bank a call.

Richard jumped up and looked at her in a dazed sort of a way for he had completely forgotten the business which had brought him to Mifflin. Rebecca Mary walked to the gate with him and gave him careful directions as to how he should find the Mifflin Bank. When he had driven away she went with Grace to the kitchen, where she mixed sprays of mint, fresh from the garden, with sugar and lemons and ice and ginger ale until she had a most delicious drink. Grace arranged the little cakes she had made on one of Grandmother Wyman's old plates.

"A new recipe of Anne Wellman's," she said, giving one to Rebecca Mary to sample. "An after the war recipe. There is nothing conserved in these cakes. Rebecca Mary, do you know what mother and I planned last night? Neither of us has ever seen the Atlantic Ocean. I suppose you will think we have lost our minds but we are going to take a part of Aunt Ellen's present and go to the sea shore."

"I don't!" exclaimed Rebecca Mary quickly. "I think you've just found your minds. As a family we should have lost the art of spending if Aunt Ellen hadn't sent her present just when she did. I'm glad you and mother are going to have some fun. Good old Aunt Ellen! You must send her a post card. Send her two post cards!" And the two girls laughed joyously. "That's all right," Rebecca Mary went on more soberly, "but just let me tell you what her present has done for me. I wrote you that I'd met the wonderful Peter Simmons, didn't I?"

"Seven pages. You do have the luck, Rebecca Mary! Why didn't you bring the wonderful Peter with you to-day instead of the First National Bank?"

Rebecca Mary chuckled. "The First National Bank is really splendid," she insisted. "And awfully important. He's been perfectly corking to me. But Peter Simmons, Grace, Peter Simmons!"

"M-m," murmured Grace enviously.

Granny was enthusiastic over the old mahogany and walnut furniture which filled the house and which Grandfather Wyman had brought from his grandfather's old home in Pennsylvania.

"It's beautiful," she exclaimed. "You don't seem to have anything but old mahogany and walnut, Mrs. Wyman. This is a real museum piece." And

96

she ran her fingers over the smooth surface of the old Sheraton sideboard and looked at the old Chippendale chairs.

Rebecca Mary had come in with her big crystal pitcher and she placed the tray on the old Chippendale table. "And the reason we have nothing but old stuff," she confessed frankly, "is that we never could buy new. I suppose it is lucky we couldn't, but it just about broke my heart a few years ago that we didn't have anything but four post beds and gate legged tables. I yearned for a davenport upholstered in green velours instead of that ancient sofa. I wanted less old mahogany and more new clothes. Is that Mr. Cabot?" The sound of a motor car drew her to the window. "I hope he found the Mifflin Bank at home."

It was Richard, and when he came in he had a big box of candy under his arm. He gave it to Mrs. Wyman.

"This isn't Mifflin candy," Grace exclaimed when she saw the tempting contents. "You never found this in Mifflin!"

And Richard had to confess that he hadn't, that he had brought the box from Waloo for Mrs. Wyman, and Grace looked at Rebecca Mary signifi-

97

cantly. "Very thoughtful of your First National Bank," she seemed to say.

Mrs. Wyman drew Rebecca Mary from the little group to ask her if she wouldn't rather go east and be introduced to the Atlantic Ocean than accept Granny Simmons' invitation. She and Grace would love to have Rebecca Mary with them, but they wanted her to do exactly as she wished.

"I think I'll stay with Mrs. Simmons," Rebecca Mary said after a moment's frowning thought. "You see there is Joan. I couldn't take her east very well. And, anyway, the Atlantic Ocean will keep. It has been there for some years, and Mrs. Simmons may never ask me again. I should like to visit in a big house like hers, and she said she would take us to her country place, Seven Pines. I can board at a sea shore hotel whenever I have the money, but I can't always visit an old dear like Granny Simmons."

"That is true. I hope you don't think we are foolishly extravagant, Rebecca Mary? Aunt Ellen said we were to use the money for pleasure. And then you wrote me what Cousin Susan said to you about memories. I do want Grace and you to have some good times to remember. I hope it isn't foolish," Mrs. Wyman repeated, for deep down in her heart she was almost sure it was foolish to spend Aunt Ellen's present for a trip when she could buy a mortgage with it.

"If I told you what I honestly think we'd never save another cent, and we'd have to take our memories to the poor house some day. Really, mother, it is the wisest thing to do. Cousin Susan convinced me that sometimes you can pay too big a price when you save and scrimp. Do get some pretty clothes, lots of them. They make you feel all new and— and efficient," she laughed at her choice of a word. "That's a love you have on now. You never got it in Mifflin. And if Joan's father comes for her and Mrs. Simmons gets tired of me I'll come east and join you. I should like to meet the Atlantic Ocean. I've heard quite a lot about it."

Her mother looked at her and smiled. The last time Rebecca Mary had been home she had not laughed like that. She had frowned over the bills and talked of the future as of a barren desert. If taking out a memory insurance policy would change a girl as Rebecca Mary had changed, Mrs. Wyman was going to advocate memory insurance policies for every one.

Granny was delighted that no objections were made to her invitation, and she asked Mrs. Wyman and Grace to spend a few days with her on their way east. But Mrs. Wyman thanked her and said that they had planned to do their shopping in Chicago and it would be out of their way to go to Waloo. Altogether it was a very satisfactory visit, and every one was sorry when it was over and Granny and Joan were once more in the tonneau of Richard's big car.

"I like your mother and your sister and your home so much, Rebecca Mary," Granny said when they had waved a last good-by before they turned the corner.

"So do I!" exclaimed Richard heartily.

"I do, too," repeated that echo, Joan. "Am I to talk to you on the way home, Granny, dear?"

"If you think it will make the ride pleasanter," Granny obligingly told her. "But you must not be surprised if I doze in the middle of your story. Motor riding does make me sleepy."

The way to Mifflin had led them down the river and the way to Spirit Lake took them back through a rich farming country. Richard astonished Rebecca Mary by the ease with which he could distinguish young wheat from oats and oats from barley or buckwheat when he was passing a field at the rate of thirty-five miles an hour. The fields

were only a green blur to Rebecca Mary. They
reached Spirit Lake just at sunset and were pleasantly surprised to find Stanley Cabot perched on
the railing of the hotel veranda smoking a cigarette.
He jumped up and threw his cigarette away as he
came to meet them.

"How pretty it is!" Rebecca Mary looked around
with shining eyes. "What is that down by the
lake?" And she nodded toward a screened pavilion
which wore a gay necklace of colored lanterns.

"That's the dancing pavilion," Stanley told her
eagerly. "Want to run over and have a fox trot?
There's just time before your dinner will be ready."

Rebecca Mary's eyes sparkled. "Shall we?"
But she said it to Richard instead of to Stanley.

"Sure. Come along." And Richard held out his
hand.

"The dickens!" Stanley looked after them as
they ran to the pavilion. "I thought I issued the
invitation. She seems to have made an impression
on old Dick, Granny? I thought he was immune
to girls. What is it?"

Granny, comfortably settled in a big rocking
chair, looked mysterious. "I expect it was her
scowl. She frowned at Richard, and Richard, you
know, Stanley, isn't used to frowns. Girls have

always smiled at him. I expect Rebecca Mary's scowl interested him."

"That might be. A girl has to offer a man new stuff to interest him. You may be right."

"Of course I'm right. What are you doing here, Stanley?"

And while Stanley told Granny and Joan about the sketching trip which had brought him to Spirit Lake, where he had found some corking effects, Rebecca Mary and Richard danced on a floor which was far from smooth and to the music of a piano and a violin which were not as harmonious as you would wish a piano and a violin to be, but both Rebecca Mary and Richard said that it was the jolliest dance they had ever had when it was over, and hand in hand they ran back to the hotel and the waiting dinner. It seemed the most natural thing in the world for them to go hand in hand, but Rebecca Mary was quite breathless when she came up the steps after she had pulled her fingers from Richard's hand.

"I hope we haven't kept you waiting," she cried. "But it was such fun."

"Much you care about us when you scorned my invitation and went off with my brother," Stanley said, as if cut to the very quick. "I don't know what reparation you can make unless you sit beside me and talk exclusively to me."

"Oh!" Rebecca Mary was pinkly embarrassed. "I didn't hear you deliver any invitation," she stammered, but her explanation only made matters worse.

"Granny heard it and so did Joan." Stanley quite enjoyed teasing Rebecca Mary into pink embarrassment. Perhaps he wanted to see the scowl which had interested Richard, but if he did he was disappointed for Rebecca Mary never frowned once. She was too happy and too contented. She could only laugh and smile as she promised to sit beside him and talk exclusively to him. That wasn't so easy to do as to promise for there were other girls on the screened porch where the dinner tables were arranged, and they smiled and nodded to Richard until he had to go and speak to them.

"My brother Richard is very popular with the girls," Stanley told Rebecca Mary with a twinkle. "He's quite a boy, is my brother Richard."

"M-m," was all that Rebecca Mary would say to that, but she watched his brother Richard out of the tail of her eye.

Although Stanley was jolly and Richard was as devoted as those other girls would permit, Rebecca Mary was glad when they were in the car again and

103

had said good-by to Stanley and the other girls and were speeding over a road which was quite as perfect as the Jefferson Highway.

"You drive awfully well!" Rebecca Mary told Richard.

"Want to learn? It wouldn't be any trick at all to teach you."

"You shan't teach her now," exclaimed Granny, who was not so drowsy but she had overhead him. "This is no time to teach any one. You can hold your automobile class, Richard Cabot, some time when I'm not with you."

"All right. Miss Wyman, I'll hold a class limited to one, in motor driving some other time. Want to be the one?" He smiled down at her.

"Do I?" Rebecca Mary was almost speechless. She could only look at Richard until he flushed and murmured that he knew it would be no trouble at all to teach her, absolutely no trouble at all.

"It's been the most wonderful day!" Rebecca Mary was almost at a loss to tell them how wonderful it had been when at last they stopped at her door again. Words seemed too inadequate.

"As pink as you expected?" asked Richard.

"Pinker. The most beautiful shade imaginable. I'll never forget how pink it has been."

"If you liked it so much we'll go again," promised Richard, eager to give Rebecca Mary another good time. Her enthusiasm made him feel very generous. "And don't forget that motor class of mine!"

"Forget!" Rebecca Mary stared at him. How could she ever forget. She expected to remember his motor class as long as she lived, but she didn't tell him that. She just thanked him sedately and told him to let her know when his motor class would meet and she would try to be on time. She did dislike tardy scholars.

CHAPTER VII

REBECCA MARY could never believe that the next two weeks really happened. They were far too wonderful. They couldn't have happened to her for nothing but influenza and moths and insurance premiums had come to her. She felt as if she were in the middle of the very nicest dream a girl could have when she stood in the most attractive bed room she had ever seen and looked around her. It certainly was going to be jolly to perch in the lap of luxury for a while.

No wonder Rebecca Mary liked Mrs. Peter Simmons' guest room. It was so very different from the dingy rectangle which was her sitting room by day and her sleeping room by night. Mrs. Simmons' guest room, with its flower strewn chintz whose roses were repeated in the garlands on the ivory bed and dresser, overlooked Mrs. Simmons' garden from which the roses seemed to have strayed. A white bathroom opened from this rose bower and beyond it was a blue room among whose forget-me-nots and bachelor buttons Joan had found a place for her family portrait, her clock and her potato masher.

And Rebecca Mary's days were as different as her bed room. Instead of going to school Rebecca Mary went about with Granny and met a lot of pleasant people of all ages. Granny was a favorite with the young people, and as there was no end to what she would do for them she was always the center of a jolly little group.

"It's the prescription I'm trying to keep my heart young," she told Rebecca Mary wistfully.

So there were luncheons and teas with girls Rebecca Mary had never imagined she would ever know, and informal dinners and dances at the Country Club and long automobile drives. One morning Granny took her guests to see Mrs. Hiram Bingham's small sons, and Joan hung enraptured over the dimpled twins.

"Horatio and Hiram!" How Granny laughed at the names. "What should you have done, Judith, if there had been but one baby? Which father would you have honored?"

"Thank goodness I didn't have to make a choice!" Judith shivered at the mere thought of honoring but one father. "Providence was mighty good to send me two sons. Horatio and Hiram are dreadful

names, aren't they? But I just had to name the
boys for my daddy and for Father Bingham."

"If there had been but one you could have named
him for the jam which brought you and Hiram together," suggested Granny with a twinkle.

"They name babies for kaisers but do they ever
name them for jam!" Joan could not believe that
a jar of preserves would furnish a suitable name for
any child. "My daddy was named for a kaiser,
not this kaiser but another one. His name is Frederick William Gaston Johan Louis," she announced
proudly.

"Mercy me, what a mouthful! What does he
do with so many?" Granny had emphasized each
name with a squeeze of Rebecca Mary's arm.
Surely Joan could never have imagined such a
combination.

"He doesn't use them all now." Joan was almost
apologetic. "In Waloo he only uses the Frederick
one. Isn't it funny how your names change? In
Germany I'm Johanna. '*Ein gutes Kind, Johanna,*'
the kaiser said I was himself, and in France and
America I'm Joan. Oh, did you see that?" For
young Horatio had seized a handful of Joan's black
hair. "Isn't he a darling! He's—he's a lot better
than a potato masher, isn't he?"

They all laughed, and names were forgotten for the moment although Granny gave Rebecca Mary an extra hard squeeze when she heard what the kaiser had called Joan.

"They must be German," Granny said, when she and Rebecca Mary were alone. "I thought so all the time. No one but a German would go away and leave a little girl as Joan was left. I shouldn't be surprised if Count Ernach de Befort never came back," she added cheerfully.

"Oh!" Rebecca Mary was stunned at such a thought. "Of course he will come back. And Joan didn't say she was a German."

"Joan doesn't say she is anything. I don't believe she knows even if she did say she was from Echternach. Never mind, Rebecca Mary, if she is left on your hands I'll help you take care of her. She amuses me with her contradictory statements. I like a mystery now that the war is over."

"I'm not sure that I do," murmured bewildered Rebecca Mary.

She really didn't have much time to wonder about Joan for Granny's friends seemed to have entered into a delightful conspiracy to make much of Rebecca Mary. Sallie Cabot gave a dinner dance for her and Rose Horton, who had been Rose Cabot, gave a tea and even Madame Cabot, who was Richard's great aunt, gave a theater party, after which she took her guests to the Waloo for supper and to dance. You can't really blame Rebecca Mary for rubbing her eyes and wondering if she could be Rebecca Mary Wyman.

Stanley Cabot was at several of these affairs, and he watched Rebecca Mary with an amused smile.

"I thought you said she scowled at old Dick," he said to Granny. "Perhaps I don't know a scowl when I see one, but I didn't think it was like that." And he nodded toward Rebecca Mary, who was smiling at Richard Cabot.

"Dear child," murmured Granny. "When you are my age, Stanley, you will hate to see anything but smiles on young faces. I hope Rebecca Mary has forgotten how to frown. But it was a scowl, Stanley, I know it was, which first attracted Richard."

It almost seemed as if Rebecca Mary had forgotten how to do anything but smile, and young Peter had no occasion to shout "Pirate." He was in and out of the house at all hours and so had every opportunity to see what Rebecca Mary was doing. It was not often that she could persuade him to talk to her of his experiences in France.

"Of course a man can't get it out of his thoughts," he did say one day, "but it isn't anything he wants to talk about. It was just luck that got me up to the front. If I hadn't been lucky I shouldn't have gone any farther than Dick Cabot. You know he tried to get into the service, any service? Yep. But he broke his arm when he was a kid and it's a little stiff. The doctors wouldn't pass him. Then he tried for the Red Cross and Uncle Sam said, 'No, you're a banker, Dick Cabot, and the work you can do is to sell Liberty bonds.' I'd hate to tell you how many bonds Dick did sell. It was owing to him that this district went over the top as soon as the sales were on. He's a corker, Dick Cabot, all right, all right. And he did as much at home to win the war as I did in France."

"Oh!" breathed Rebecca Mary, trying to grasp this point of view which Peter was offering her. It was splendid of Peter to talk that way but she couldn't really think that Richard at home had done as much as Peter in France, and she said so.

"That shows what an ignorant little girl you are," Peter retorted. "But don't let's talk about the war. There are a lot of pleasanter subjects."

"Such as?" If he wouldn't talk about the war he could choose his own subject.

"You," Peter told her as she should have known he would tell her. And he chuckled when she flushed as he had known she would flush. Peter loved to make Rebecca Mary blush and stammer although it was not as easy as it had been. Rebecca Mary was acquiring poise.

Richard's class in motor driving met as he had planned, and his one pupil would never forget the first time that she had her hands on the wheel and felt the pull of the sixty horses harnessed under the hood.

"It makes you feel like a—like a god!" she gasped, not daring to take her eyes from the road.

"It makes you look like a goddess," laughed Richard. "You're going to make a good driver, Miss Wyman. You can follow instructions and keep your mind on what you are doing. You don't try a dozen things at once."

"That was what I was trained to do. A school teacher has to keep her mind on her work, and, goodness knows, she is given plenty of instructions to follow."

"You won't be a school teacher long," prophesied Richard, reaching over to show her something, and his hand covered hers.

A thread of fire seemed to start from his fingers

112

and run all over Rebecca Mary. She couldn't speak for a second, and when she did speak her voice was not as steady as she wanted it to be.

"Gracious me, I hope not," she stuttered. "Who would want to teach school for ever?"

"You won't do it for ever!" Richard said again, and no seventh daughter of a seventh daughter could have been more emphatic about the future. He smiled at Rebecca Mary as she sat beside him, her cheeks pink, her eyes black with excitement, her hair blowing about her face. She wore another small portion of Aunt Ellen's present, an old rose silk sweater, and it was wonderfully becoming.

"I'd like to do this for ever," she murmured. "I've at last found an occupation which suits me right down to the very ground."

"Would you like to do it for me for ever?" The question did not surprise Rebecca Mary half as much as it did Richard. It was not often that he uttered soft nothings to a girl. He was more accustomed to talk of stocks and bonds, and he thought it was strange that he never wanted to talk of stocks and bonds to Rebecca Mary. "You must have another lesson very soon," he went on in a more matter of fact voice as she did not tell him whether she would like to drive for him for ever. "Practice is the

only thing that will make you perfect. You must
have a lot of practice."

When Peter heard that Richard was teaching Rebecca Mary to drive his big car he pretended to be
vastly indignant.

"Why didn't you tell me you wanted to learn?"
he demanded.

"I didn't have to tell Mr. Cabot," she answered
triumphantly.

"Great old mind reader, Dick Cabot is, isn't he?
Well, if you're learning to drive his big car you
had better let me teach you how to manage a roadster
and Granny's small car and the limousine."

"And then I can stop teaching school and open
a garage," dimpled Rebecca Mary. "Very well,
bring out your roadster."

"You drive very well," Peter was good enough to
say when Rebecca Mary had demonstrated what she
could do. "A little more practice and you can
drive anywhere."

"Really!" Rebecca Mary liked his words so
much that she wanted to hear them again.

"Really."

And then Rebecca Mary killed her engine and
couldn't remember how to start it again. Peter
put his hand on the button at the same moment she

114

did, and his five fingers closed over Rebecca Mary's five fingers. Rebecca Mary quivered to her toes, but she tried to be very matter of fact.

"Granny said I might have to drive for her," she said quickly. "Karl is going to leave, and she hasn't found a new chauffeur yet."

That evening she actually did drive Richard through the traffic which surged around the pavilion where the weekly band concert was given. If Peter had been there he would have had to shout "Pirate" several times for Rebecca Mary did scowl yellow brownly, but that was because she was so anxious to drive well.

"Aren't you shaking in your shoes?" she asked when they were held up at a very busy crossing. "No one can question your bravery now. You've certainly earned a medal."

Richard looked at her sparkling eyes, and his staid invulnerable heart gave a flop which startled him, and a flash appeared in his dark eyes.

"I'm a man who always collects what he earns," he told her in a way which made her heart thump a bit, too, although she would not let him know that, not for worlds. "There isn't a better collector in all Waloo than I am."

"My goodness gracious AND my gracious goodness!" Rebecca Mary seemed much impressed by Richard, the bill collector. "But you must not read the future by the past," she cautioned gravely. "I seem to remember that at college I was told that even Napoleon had his Waterloo."

"We are not discussing Napoleon Bonaparte but one Richard Deane Cabot," Richard reminded her severely.

"Vice president of the First National Bank of Waloo," she nodded as if to make sure that they were talking of the same Richard Deane Cabot. "That sounds very important, doesn't it? Important and rich and—and solid. How does it feel?" she asked with a certain gay insouciance which was as new to Rebecca Mary as it was becoming.

He laughed. "Just at present it feels mighty good. I'm very grateful to the First National Bank. I owe my present job as a motor teacher to that same bank."

Rebecca Mary's sober face made a desperate attempt to conceal her amused smile. "That's true," she said, but her voice was as much of a failure as a disguise as her sober face. "The two most important buildings in Waloo are undoubtedly the First National Bank and the Waloo Hotel. At last!" as the traffic policeman gave them the right of way.

116

"I hope I don't do the wrong thing now and mortify my teacher as well as myself. You never can tell what a pupil will do."

"I'm not afraid of my pupil." Richard was stimulatingly confident.

"I told you that you were a brave man. There!" Rebecca Mary drew a long breath. "We are on our way again." She turned impulsively to Richard and exclaimed from the very depths of her heart: "I can't ever tell you, Mr. Cabot, how happy you have made me!"

"I'm glad," was all Richard said, but his eyes flashed again. "It doesn't take much to make some little girls happy."

"Don't belittle your own generosity," scolded Rebecca Mary. "You've given me a lot and you know it."

Joan ran out to meet them when they returned.

"Granny is going to let me have a party!" she cried, scarcely able to believe her news herself. "I'm to choose the guests and the dinner and everything. I'm going to have you and the Bingham twins and Mr. Peter. And I can't think whether to have little pig sausages and waffles like we did the other morning for breakfast or nightingales' tongues like in the story you read me, Miss Wyman. Granny said

117

sausage and waffles didn't belong to dinner, but if we had them for dinner they would, wouldn't they? And she said she was afraid there weren't any night-ingales' tongues in the market, and if there were did I think the Bingham twins could eat them. Once at home we had a swan with all its feathers on, and another time, at Echternach, when the kaiser came, we had a boar's head. Do you think you'd like one of those?" doubtfully.

Rebecca Mary looked up quickly to see Richard's face when Joan spoke of the kaiser as a dinner guest at Echternach, but he only looked amused so Rebecca Mary stooped and kissed the flushed little face. "What I should like best would be a little spring chicken," she said.

"Odd little thing, isn't she?" Richard said when Joan had danced away to ask Granny if the three months' old Bingham twins could eat spring chicken. "Have you heard from her father?"

"Not a word. Nor from Mrs. Muldoon. We drove over yesterday, but Mrs. Lee hadn't heard anything."

"It was mighty good of you to take her in." Richard spoke as if no one in the world but Rebecca Mary would have taken charge of a child who

118

had been left on the door step with a clock, a portrait and a potato masher.

"What else could I do?" Rebecca Mary would like to be told how she could have done anything else. "She was—loaned to me." And she laughed. It was so easy to laugh at the loan now.

"All the same it was mighty good of you." He wished she would laugh again. Like Joan, Richard did admire Rebecca Mary's face when it "broke into little holes." "I don't know many girls who would have taken care of a child who had no claim on them."

"But she did have a claim on me. I was her teacher." And Rebecca Mary did laugh again.

Granny was just hanging up the telephone receiver when Rebecca Mary went into the house.

"I've been talking to Seven Pines," she said. "Is there any reason why we shouldn't drive out there to-morrow, Rebecca Mary? Mrs. Swanson just called me up to tell me that Otillie is going to be married and she wants me to come out and see her wedding things."

"A wedding!" Joan jumped up and down on delighted toes. "You'll take me, Granny Simmons? You'll never leave me in Waloo? You know I've never been to a wedding. I've only been to church and school and a moving picture show."

"Then you certainly shall go to Otillie's wedding. We'll start in the morning and take our time," Granny suggested to Rebecca Mary. "What do you say!"

"I say goody, goody!" exclaimed Rebecca Mary. "You have told me so much about Seven Pines I'm crazy to see it."

That night when she went to her room she nodded merrily at the radiant face of the girl in the big mirror.

"Well, Rebecca Mary Wyman," she murmured joyously. "You certainly have turned over a new leaf—a real four-leaf clover leaf. You're having the time of your young life. You must send Cousin Susan a testimonial for her memory insurance company!" For she remembered to give the credit for her new leaf to where credit was due. "You've had more fun since you took out one of her policies than you ever had before. Gracious, I should think you had!"

She was still looking at the happy face in the mirror and dreamily wondering about the bright new leaf she had turned over when the door opened and there stood Granny Simmons. She wore her hat and her motor coat dragged from her arm. In her hand she held a yellow telegram.

"Come, Rebecca Mary," she said impatiently. "Put on your hat. We'll go to-night!"

CHAPTER VIII

"TO-NIGHT!" Rebecca Mary swung around to look at her. It was almost midnight, time to go nowhere but to bed, but Granny was not dressed for bed. What on earth did she mean?

"I promised Mrs. Swenson I'd come and see Otillie's things," Granny spoke almost fretfully. "I know what time it is, Rebecca Mary, but if we don't go before old Peter Simmons comes we'll never leave. He'll want us to stay at home until he can go with us, and he can never go. He's always too busy."

Rebecca Mary's eyes opened wider. She didn't understand why Granny should want to leave for Seven Pines in almost the middle of the night if old Peter Simmons was coming home. Rebecca Mary did not know old Peter Simmons, she did not know very much about him except that he was the head of a big manufacturing plant and that he was to have a golden wedding on the twenty-second of July. Granny had always spoken as if she adored her husband. It seemed strange for her to leave for Seven Pines if he was coming home.

"Just put a few things in a suit case," ordered Granny. "We shan't be away more than a couple of days."

Rebecca Mary only stared harder. There was an expression on Granny's face which she did not understand.

"We'll go to Seven Pines to-night for several reasons," went on Granny impatiently. "First because I want to go to Seven Pines before my golden wedding for a special reason, and I promised to take you and Joan there, and because Otillie Swenson wants us to see her wedding things. If we don't go before old Peter Simmons comes we won't go at all, as I said. When he is in Waloo he wants me to be in Waloo. I can gad as much and as far as I please when he's away but when he is in town I must be home. I know very well the way he'll stamp in here and say: 'Hello, Kitty! How are you?' and kiss me and go to bed and sleep like a log until seven in the morning and then he'll eat his breakfast and go to the factory and I shan't see him until dinner time. I might as well be at Seven Pines. And then—I suppose you'll think I'm crazy, Rebecca Mary, but I never was saner in my life. You would understand perfectly if you had been married to old Peter Simmons for almost fifty years." The twinkle died

123

out of her eyes as she spoke of those fifty years, and she borrowed a frown from Rebecca Mary.

Rebecca Mary caught her breath and wondered if there could be any trouble between Granny and old Peter Simmons. Granny had always talked so proudly of her husband and what he had done to help win the war, quite as proudly as she talked of young Peter.

"Oh!" was all she could say, but Granny seemed dissatisfied with that startled exclamation.

"Read that!" She thrust the crumpled telegram into Rebecca Mary's hand.

" 'Will be home on the 11.55 what do you want for the jubilee?' "

Even after she had read the telegram and mechanically divided it into two sentences, Rebecca Mary did not seem able to understand.

Granny took the message from her and read it aloud with an indignant snort.

"You see?" She looked at Rebecca Mary as if she defied her to say that the situation was not spread out before her as clearly as the green vegetables at the grocer's. " 'What do you want for the jubilee?' " she read scornfully. "If that isn't just like old Peter Simmons! For almost fifty years, Rebecca Mary, I've told that man what I wanted for anniversary and birthday and Christmas presents. I've even had to tell him when the anniversaries and the birthdays were. Never once has old Peter Simmons remembered them for himself. He has never brought me a present without first asking me what I wanted. He can't even remember whether I like white meat or dark when we have chicken for dinner. He asks me every single time just as if it were the first time. And I'm tired of doing his thinking for him. He knows very well what I want. We've talked of it often enough. But I feel in my bones that if I see him to-night and he asks me what I want for my golden wedding I'll say something that will make trouble. And I don't want any trouble that will interfere with my golden wedding. I've earned that, and I'm going to have it. I'm not going to take any chance of an argument to-night. And the safest way to avoid an argument is to run away from it. We'll go out to Seven Pines and look at Otillie Swenson's wedding clothes and then I may feel different. Put on your hat, Rebecca Mary. I know Peter does a lot of this only to tease me, but I don't feel like being teased now. Isn't there something else you should take with you?" she asked, and she looked vaguely around the

125

room when at last Rebecca Mary was hatted and packed.

Rebecca Mary stopped feeling anxious and giggled. It did seem so absurd for her to run away with Granny from old Mr. Simmons' frantic question. She could visualize just how frantic old Mr. Simmons was, and she felt sorry for him. At the same time she didn't blame Granny. It was irritating to be asked continually what you wanted a person to give you. Rebecca Mary's mother was something like old Peter Simmons. For weeks before Christmas she wrote and asked Rebecca Mary what she wanted when all the time she knew that Rebecca Mary would have to take what she needed.

"Isn't there something else you should take?" Granny asked helplessly as Rebecca Mary put her in her motor coat and straightened her hat.

"There's Joan?" suggested Rebecca Mary, trying to keep her face from breaking into the little holes Joan liked.

"Of course." Granny pulled herself away before Rebecca Mary could button her coat. "We can't leave Joan until we find her father. You call her, while I explain to Pierson."

Joan was an interrogation point when she was wakened and told that she was to go to Seven Pines at once. She caught the picture of her father and mother from the table but Rebecca Mary was glad to see that she left the potato masher where it was.

"I don't care as much for it as I did," Joan confessed, a little ashamed of her fickleness. "But I just have to take the picture and the clock, too."

"Aren't you ready?" called Granny. "It's half past now." And as if to prove that she was right Grandfather clock in the hall boomed the half hour. It sounded very solemn, and Joan slipped her free hand into Rebecca Mary's hand. "It is fortunate you have learned to drive the car, Rebecca Mary," Granny said as they went down the stairs. "Karl left this morning, you know, and the new man isn't to come until to-morrow. We'll take the small car, the five passenger. You can drive it, can't you?" she stopped on the last step to ask.

"I hope so." That was as much as Rebecca Mary could promise for it was one thing to drive a car over a smooth boulevard in broad daylight and with a helping hand at her elbow, and a vastly different thing to drive a car over an unknown country road in the moonlight and without a helping hand. Rebecca Mary was really scared to pieces, but Granny was so confident that Rebecca Mary didn't like to confess how scared she was.

She looked to see that there were gasoline and water for Richard had told her never to take out a car without seeing that it had plenty of food and drink. "You'll save yourself a lot of trouble in the end," he had promised, and, goodness knows, Rebecca Mary didn't want any trouble.

"You're taking a lot of time," fretted Granny from the tonneau where she sat with Joan. "And we haven't a minute to waste. It's a quarter to twelve now. If old Peter Simmons finds us in this garage we'll never see Otillie Swenson's wedding things."

"I'm ready now." Rebecca Mary wiped her hands on a piece of waste and slipped in behind the wheel.

They had to stop at the house for Pierson was waving a small basket.

"I put up a few sandwiches for you, Mrs. Simmons." She was breathless from the haste she had made. "You'll be hungry before you get to Seven Pines."

"That's very thoughtful of you, Pierson," commended Granny as Pierson put the basket on the seat beside Rebecca Mary. "Now, remember, you are not to tell Mr. Simmons when we went. Just say that I am on a motor trip with a couple of young friends. And don't tell him we are at Seven Pines.

If he doesn't know where I am he can't keep asking
me irritating questions. Now, my dear, straight
ahead until you come to the end of the boulevard.
Yes, Joan, it is very wrong to run away from home
in the middle of the night and you are never to do
it until you are sixty-eight years old and not then
unless your husband will annoy you by asking what
you want for a golden wedding present."

"I won't, Granny." Joan promised solemnly, although she knew that she would never live to be
sixty-eight. Why, it would take years and years and
years. But it was enough to make a little girl feel
solemn to be wakened in the middle of the night and
told to get up and run away from a question. No
wonder Joan shivered. "And I know why you are
running away," she went on eagerly. "It isn't from
any question, is it? It's to find the young heart
you are always talking about. I'm going to look
for my father. Why are you going, Miss Wyman?"
she leaned forward to ask.

Alone on the front seat Rebecca Mary laughed.
"I reckon I'll find a payment on my memory insurance," she said, and over her shoulder she told
Granny of the policy which Cousin Susan had persuaded her to take out and which was to be payable
at any time during her old age. And Granny, who

had reached her old age, thought that it was a most wonderful and business-like arrangement.

"Your Cousin Susan is exactly right. Young people begin all their thoughts with 'I shall,' but old people think 'I did' or 'I had.'"

"I'm young then," Joan announced with much satisfaction, "for I always think I shall."

"So do I!" Rebecca Mary was quite astonished to find that she did. "How far is it to Seven Pines, Mrs. Simmons?"

"Sixty-three miles from our front steps. Listen— is that the train? I reckon we are safe now." And she leaned back with a sigh of relief.

"Sixty-three miles!" gasped Rebecca Mary, who never had driven one mile by herself. But there is always a first time, and she remembered that she would have to drive only a mile at a time, and anyway it would be Granny who would be responsible for what would happen.

They did not talk much after the first few miles. Joan fell asleep and even Granny dozed although she really couldn't sleep for Rebecca Mary had to ask her every few minutes the way to Seven Pines. Long before they reached the end of the boulevard Rebecca Mary forgot to be frightened or nervous. She found it rather thrilling to run away from old

Mr. Simmons' question in the moonlight. They seemed to have the world to themselves for they met no one. Rebecca Mary thought she should like to go on for ever and ever.

She would never forget this ride, and she chuckled to herself. When she was as old as Granny she would remember how they had fled from old Mr. Simmons' irritating question. And thinking of old Mr. Simmons, whom she had never seen, made her remember young Mr. Simmons, whom she admired so much. What would he think when he came to-morrow, no, to-day, and found her gone? And Mr. Cabot? She had promised to drive out to the Country Club with Richard that very afternoon after banking hours. Richard was going to teach her to play golf. She was sorry that Granny had not given her time to write a little note, to write two little notes.

But she would not be away long. Granny had said only a few days. And she could telephone to Richard and to Peter from Seven Pines the very first thing, before she even looked at Otillie Swenson's wedding things. She hoped Peter and Richard would miss her for she knew that she would miss them. A month ago she had known neither of them. And now——

Young Peter Simmons was the most fascinating man. She flushed as her thoughts strayed back to young Peter, and she wondered if the day ever would come when he would ask his wife what she wanted for a birthday or an anniversary present. She knew that Richard Cabot would never ask. He would never have to ask for he would make a note of the date in his memorandum book and would be ready with his gift on the proper day. Young Peter and Richard were as different as a vanilla ice and a cherry pie. She liked them both. She couldn't think which she did like the best. Peter had fascinated her ever since she had seen him eating fresh tomato sandwiches with such gusto at the Waloo, and Richard did give her such a comfortable, well cared for, warm feeling. It was like being wrapped in a down comforter on a winter night to be with Richard. Hello, here they were at another cross road. Should she turn to the right or the left or keep straight ahead? She would have to ask Granny.

But when she turned she saw that Granny was fast asleep beside Joan. Joan's sleek little head was on Granny's shoulder and Granny's gray head was resting on Joan's black hair. They looked so comfortable cuddled close together that Rebecca Mary had not the heart to disturb them. And anyway what difference did it make when they reached Seven Pines?

"She'll be awake in a few minutes," she thought lazily. "And in the meantime I'll stretch myself and take a sandwich."

She slipped from her seat to draw a rug over the two sleepers and then stretched herself luxuriously before she took the place beside the wheel where she would have more room to stretch while she ate her sandwich.

"Chicken salad," she murmured approvingly when she opened a package.

What a strange world it was, she thought as she lounged back in Mrs. Peter Simmons' car and ate Mrs. Peter Simmons' chicken salad sandwiches. A month ago and she would have hooted at the person who would have suggested that she ever would do either. She never would have had the chance to do either she acknowledged if it had not been for Joan the young Countess Ernach de Befort, she laughed. Joan was a dear if she was sometimes a nuisance. How cross and horrid she had been when Joan had announced that she had been loaned to her. Why, if it had not been for Joan she would be fast asleep this minute in her old walnut bed in her shabby little room in Mifflin. She would never in the world be eating chicken salad sandwiches in Mrs. Peter Simmons' car, with Mrs. Simmons and Joan asleep in the tonneau. She was sleepy herself, and she yawned. But she could not go to sleep. She was on guard and—and what happens when sentries go to sleep at their post?

CHAPTER IX

I'M hungry!"

Joan's plaintive wail woke Rebecca Mary, and she opened her eyes and then sat up very straight.

"Why—why——" she stammered, rubbing her sleepy eyes to make sure that they were telling her the truth. "Where are we?"

For they were no longer under a star-studded moon-illumined sky. They were in a rough shed with a roof so close to Rebecca Mary's head that she could have touched it if she had stretched up her arm. She looked at hungry Joan and then at Granny, who was rubbing her eyes, too, and feeling for the glasses which should hang around her neck.

"This isn't Seven Pines!" Granny declared crossly, as one occasionally speaks when roused from sound slumber. "Where have you brought us, Rebecca Mary?"

Rebecca Mary's bewildered face turned a lovely pink and the corners of her red mouth tilted up. "Then it wasn't a dream," she said softly. "It wasn't a dream!" she told Granny triumphantly.

"What wasn't a dream?" Granny's voice still had a bit of an edge to it. "Don't ask conundrums the first thing in the morning, Rebecca Mary. What wasn't a dream?"

"Well," began Rebecca Mary, and her voice sounded as if she wasn't quite sure of her story herself. "You know you went to sleep in the car last night, and when we came to a cross road I didn't know which way to turn. I hated to waken you, so I ate a couple of sandwiches while I waited for you to waken yourself. Suddenly I heard some one laugh and say: 'Hello, I thought I knew this old boat. Where do you think you are going?' And there was Mr. Simmons——"

"Not old Peter Simmons?" exclaimed Granny excitedly. "It couldn't be! He was to be in Waloo at eleven-fifty-five. He couldn't have been at the cross roads!"

"It was young Mr. Simmons," Rebecca Mary hastened to explain. "He was in a roadster with another man. I told him we were going to Seven Pines, and he wanted to know why we were going at night, why we didn't wait for morning. And I said it would be so warm in the morning. I didn't know whether you wanted him to know——"

"Indeed he may know. I don't care who knows," declared Granny generously.

"And he said he knew the way to Seven Pines, and he got in our car and took the wheel, and we started again. But the road was so long and so white and the car ran so smoothly and we didn't talk much of any, and I was so glad to have him drive that I must have dozed off, too. Anyway, I just remember that we turned in at a big gate where Peter talked to a man. I thought of course that it was Seven Pines. And then we went a little further, I suppose into this shed, and Peter got out and said he would see about something and—That's all I remember," she finished abruptly.

"But that's perfect nonsense," insisted Granny. "What would Peter be doing at the cross roads at that time of night? You must have been dreaming, Rebecca Mary. And I wasn't asleep all the time. I was awake off and on, and I remember now, that at one time I thought I heard you talking to some one. But it couldn't have been to Peter. You must have been dreaming, Rebecca Mary!"

She was so very positive that she made Rebecca Mary wonder if she could have gone to sleep at her post. It didn't seem possible that she would have closed her eyes when she had the responsibility of

Granny and Joan on her hands but sleep can sometimes be a wily enemy. It isn't always a helpful friend. But if slumber had stolen insidiously over her how had they reached the old shed? Her story furnished the only possible explanation, and yet Granny frowned and said that her story was nonsense.

"Are you afraid?" whimpered Joan, suddenly clutching her arm. "Shall I be afraid, Granny? Are you afraid, Miss Wyman?"

"I'm scared to death!" But Rebecca Mary laughed softly, and she put her arm around Joan. "But it is because I went to sleep on guard. Granny said I did. I should have stayed awake to watch. But you needn't be frightened, Joan. There is nothing to be afraid of, is there, Granny?"

"Nothing at all." Granny made the endorsement strong and prompt. "But we might as well look around and make sure."

But when she stepped from the car she had to catch hold of the door or she would have fallen for her limbs were cramped and stiff from spending the night in the tonneau.

"If you live to be sixty-eight, Joan," she explained a little impatiently as she straightened herself, "you will have learned that there is nothing in

138

the world to be afraid of. Come and let us see if we can find some breakfast. I don't suppose whoever brought us here plans to starve us to death."

They presented rather a disheveled and crumpled appearance as they stood in the open doorway of the shed and looked across the green grass which ran without stopping to the green hedge a half of a mile away. What was on the other side of the hedge was kept a secret by the arbor vitæ. Near the shed the grass was marked by many wheel tracks. There was no one to be seen, and Granny went bravely forth with Rebecca Mary on her right and Joan clinging to her left hand.

"The grass is wet." Granny looked down at her shoe. "Was there any rain in your dream?" And she laughed at Rebecca Mary's puzzled face.

"I don't know." Rebecca Mary's voice was as puzzled as her face.

They passed a huge stone barn and several small sheds but there was no one about them. From somewhere they could hear the sound of a gasoline engine. Puff—puff it said, but the silly words conveyed absolutely no information to Rebecca Mary.

When they rounded the corner of the barn they faced a great stone house which might have begun its existence as a giant's bandbox, it was so very big and square. But some one had added wings on either side so that now it looked like a home and sprawled so hospitably among the shrubbery that it seemed to call: "Come in, come in."

Granny gave a funny little exclamation when she saw it, and she hurried around to the front, where she stood and stared at the house and then at the formal garden with its pool and borders and its pergola, which ran all the way from the west wing to the river bank. The barn and sheds were on the other side of the house and, at some distance. In front the trimly shaven lawn was broken by a driveway which slipped in from the high road half a mile away to encircle and say "howdydo" to a huge flower bed which flaunted its red cannas before the wide front terrace. There were two tennis courts on one side of the driveway, down near the secretive hedge.

"God bless my soul!" gasped Granny, as she looked around her. The wind blew her gray hair about her face, which looked a bit pinched in the strong morning light. "Whose place do you think this is?"

"The beautiful princess's!" Joan jumped up and down in delight. "It's too pretty to belong to an ogre."

"It's Riverside, Rebecca Mary!" But as that

name conveyed nothing to Rebecca Mary, Granny gave her more information. "Joshua Cabot's grandfather's old home. Did you ever! It must have been Joshua instead of Peter who came along and found us. But we certainly haven't anything to be afraid of now. We'll go right in and ask Joshua for breakfast, and then we'll scold him for bringing us out of our way, and then we'll go on to Seven Pines."

Rebecca Mary did not think that she could have confused young Peter Simmons and Joshua Cabot, but she did not say so as she followed Granny and Joan up the steps and in through the open door. There was no one in the broad hall but Joshua Cabot's great grandfather and grandmother and they hung quietly on the wall in old gilt frames. No one was in the big dining room to which Granny turned, but some one had been there for the table was laid for breakfast. Covers were placed for three. Granny drew a chair from the table and sat down before a plate of tempting strawberries.

"I'm old enough to take privileges," she said. "I hope there are more strawberries, but if Joshua Cabot has been playing a practical joke on an old lady he should pay for it. Come, children, and eat your breakfast."

141

Joan obeyed with hungry alacrity, but Rebecca Mary hesitated, wondering if she dared. But the strawberries looked so delicious, Granny and Joan enjoyed them so heartily that Rebecca Mary found that she did dare. In a very few minutes there was not a strawberry left on that table. Then Granny rang the bell for what was to follow, but no one answered it. She rang again, and when again there was no response Joan jumped up and ran into the kitchen. She came back in a minute, big-eyed and important, to report that there was no one, no one at all, in the kitchen. Granny pushed back her chair.

"The maid has probably gone out for the eggs," she said with unruffled serenity. "I expect Joshua insists that they shall be perfectly fresh. While we are waiting, Rebecca Mary, come into the parlor. I want to show you a portrait of Joshua Cabot's great-grandmother. She was Richard Cabot's great-grandmother, too, you know."

Rebecca Mary rose obediently and followed Granny and Joan across the hall and into the parlor, which ran the full length of the house and whose many French windows opened on the formal garden and furnished many charming pictures of the river

142

and the low hills beyond. And the sweet-faced young girl in a gauzy white frock and with a pink rose in her long slender fingers was Richard Cabot's great-grandmother. Rebecca Mary quite forgot that the sweet-faced girl was also Joshua Cabot's great-grandmother as she gazed at her. There were several other pictures to which Granny called Rebecca Mary's attention, but always Rebecca Mary's eyes strayed back to the portrait. It seemed to call to her in some strange fashion. Suddenly they heard a clatter, and a door slammed.

"There are the eggs!" exclaimed Granny with a sigh of relief. "I suppose they will be ready in three minutes. Dear, dear, it is very plain that Sallie isn't here. She would never put up with such careless service, not for a minute."

She was interrupted by a roar, a very bellow, which made them draw close together.

"Here!" cried a harsh voice which sounded for all the world like the voice of the Big Bear. "Who has been eating my strawberries?"

The words rang through the hall and came into the big parlor with inhospitable roughness. There was a startled, an awed silence.

"That," whispered Rebecca Mary, as Joan huddled against her, "doesn't sound a bit like Mr. Cabot."

"It sounds like an ogre," Joan was sadly disappointed because it hadn't sounded like a prince. "It sounds exactly like an ogre!"

CHAPTER X

ALMOST immediately there were steps in the hall, and a man stood in the doorway. He did not look unlike an ogre for he was short and fat and had a round red face which was topped with a shock of grizzled hair and bisected by a bristling grizzled mustache. Between the hair and the mustache were two piercing blue eyes which seemed to bore right into Granny and Rebecca Mary and Joan. Behind the short fat man were two tall slim young men, who seemed very much surprised and pleased to find that guests had arrived so unexpectedly. The short fat man looked angry as well as surprised, and he showed no pleasure at all.

"My country!" he growled, still playing very realistically the rôle of Father Bear. "Where did you come from? How the dickens did you get in? And what the deuce do you want?"

Granny did not answer him because she never had been spoken to in quite that tone and manner. Men always approached Mrs. Peter Simmons of Waloo with courteous deference, and this isolated case of

145

gruff rudeness left her speechless. Rebecca Mary could not speak because a hot indignation clutched her by the throat and made it impossible for her to utter a word. It was Joan who mastered her tongue. She looked fearlessly up at the frowning ogre and answered his last question to the best of her knowledge.

"We want a young heart and a big payment on a memory insurance and my daddy," she announced clearly and somewhat peremptorily, as if she were accustomed to receive what she wanted.

If Joan had not mentioned her daddy the ogre would have thought they were all three mad, but he could understand a daddy if he could not comprehend a young heart or a big memory insurance payment.

"My country!" He breathed heavily and looked first at the young man at his right shoulder and then at the young man at his left shoulder. But they never looked at him at all. They were staring at Rebecca Mary in her crumpled white frock and her pink sweater.

"How did you get in here?" demanded the ogre, and it was plain to each one of them that he would have an answer, an intelligent answer, at once or know the reason why.

146

Granny drew herself up and looked at him with cold disdain. She did not like his manner, and as he wore big round glasses he must have seen that she didn't.

"We don't know," she told him in a very frigid voice.

"Don't know?" he repeated, almost sure now that they were mad. Surely an old woman and a young woman would know how they had entered a house if a child didn't. He excused Joan on account of her age but he did not excuse Granny nor Rebecca Mary. "You must know!" he told them with that unpleasant dictatorial impatient voice, although the man at his right touched his arm suggestively.

"Don't say 'must' to me!" Granny rather lost her temper. There is no doubt that bad manners are contagious. "Where is Mr. Cabot? I will make my explanation to him, although I think he owes me an apology." The ogre might have been but a speck of dust on the threshold from the way she looked beyond him.

"Mr. Cabot isn't here." The ogre's high and mighty manner began to slip from him.

"This is his house," began Granny, as if a man were always to be found at home.

"Not now——"

147

"He hasn't sold it?" Granny couldn't wait for him to put a period to his sentence. "Joshua Cabot never would sell his great-grandfather's house." She was so sure that he wouldn't that she stopped being indignant or cold and was just frankly curious.

The ogre looked as if he were not sure that it was any of her business what Joshua Cabot would do before he made a grudging explanation. "No, Mr. Cabot hasn't sold Riverside, but he has turned it over to us. We are making a very important experiment for the government and we cannot be disturbed."

Granny's manner changed at once. It became quite friendly. "In that case I shall tell you how we happened to disturb you." And she did tell them that she and Rebecca Mary and Joan had left Waloo in their automobile the night before and this morning they had found themselves in a shed at Riverside. But she never said a word of Rebecca Mary's dream.

"But that's a ridiculous story," objected the ogre. He didn't believe a word she had said, for he had his own reasons for being suspicious of strangers at Riverside. "You must know who brought you here. Why should any one bring you? How did you pass the guard at the gate?"

148

Granny looked at Rebecca Mary questioningly, but as Rebecca Mary only seemed bewildered, she shrugged her shoulders. It was not for her to explain the whys of other people. "I am Mrs. Peter Simmons of Waloo," she said with great dignity. "And people believe what I tell them."

"Mrs. Peter Simmons!" The ogre found it hard to believe that was who Granny was. "My country!" he muttered under his breath. "Mrs. Peter Simmons—of Waloo?" Granny nodded stiffly. "Mrs. Peter Simmons!" He didn't seem able to make himself understand that she was Mrs. Peter Simmons, and his voice grew more like the voice of a human being with every word. "My country! Mrs. Simmons, of course. I don't doubt the truth of what you say," he stumbled on, "but this is strange, very strange. I can't understand why——" He stopped abruptly and no one said a word. It was so very plain that he could not understand. "I am surprised to see you, Mrs. Simmons," He made a fresh start, and no one questioned the truth of that statement, either.

"Have you had your breakfast? Ben will make you some fresh——" His voice choked again and he had to swallow hard before he could bring it up from his boots. "I am Major Martingale of the

149

engineer corps of the United States Army," he announced explosively. That was the only fact he was sure of just then, and he made the most of it.

Granny was not of the type which bears malice and the strawberries had not conformed to her old-fashioned idea of what a breakfast should be nor satisfied her appetite, so she accepted the white flag which he was holding out so ungraciously.

"Thank you, we should like some toast and coffee and perhaps a fresh egg. I rather think we ate your strawberries. We should have eaten the rest of your breakfast if Ben had answered the bell."

"Ben went over to the farmhouse with a message to Erickson," ventured the young man at the left of Major Martingale, glad to have a chance to speak. "You didn't find any one to answer the bell, did you?" He seemed quite grieved that he had not been there to answer it.

"Not a soul. It was most mysterious. I dare say it was all right but I should never approve of leaving unlocked a house with as many valuable things in it as this house has." Granny glanced around the room with its many souvenirs of pioneer days. "The front door stood wide open. I am sorry if we disturbed you, but if you will give us some-

150

thing more substantial than strawberries to eat we will go on and leave you to your experiment."

Major Martingale tugged at his mustache and looked at her in surprise. "That's the trouble, you know," he rumbled. "You can't go on."

"Can't go!" Rebecca Mary found her tongue, and the men behind Major Martingale smiled pleasantly. They liked Rebecca Mary's voice as soon as they heard it. They thought it harmonized with her eyes. "Why can't we go? Is there anything the matter with the car?" She wouldn't be surprised if there was. She never had driven a car alone by moonlight over a country road before. Perhaps she had done something to it.

"I don't know anything about your car," fussed Major Martingale unhappily. "But you should have known, the guard at the gate could have told you, that no one is allowed to enter Riverside now without a permit, and no one who enters is allowed to leave. No one!" He exploded again.

Granny and Rebecca Mary stared at him and then at each other. They didn't believe him. It sounded too ridiculous.

"Do you mean to tell us that we can't go when it isn't our fault we're here? We didn't mean to come here. We wanted to go to Seven Pines!" exclaimed Rebecca Mary when she could speak, which wasn't for a full second.

"I mean just that." Major Martingale's voice sounded as if it were made from the best adamant and was warranted to withstand any pressure. It would be useless to coax or to cry. "I told you we are making a most important experiment here for the government." Surely they could understand the government. "A most important experiment," he repeated, swelling proudly. "One that will mean a great deal to the whole world. Germany has heard something about it and has been trying, is still trying, to get hold of the inventor and his idea. If she could it would go a long way toward giving her back her place in the commercial world, for it will be a vital necessity for every country. And we don't propose to let Germany have it. That is why we came down here to work and why we have a guard at the gate and why we forbid any one who comes here to go away. German propaganda hasn't stopped. Any one who employs labor will tell you that, and the socialists, the I. W. W. and the other agitators are fighting a new war for Germany. We chose a few loyal workmen, men whom we could absolutely trust, and brought them down here where they can't be influenced and coaxed away by any agitator or German spy. You are an American, I suppose, Mrs. Simmons, but your companions, what are they?"

Granny was about to exclaim indignantly that they were Americans, too, when she glanced at Joan. Just what was Joan? Joan answered for herself.

"I must be an American," she said slowly, "for I'm honest and brave and true and free and equal. And that's what Americans are. My daddy said so."

"And he's dead right," murmured the man behind Major Martingale's right shoulder.

Major Martingale only snorted. "We shall try and make you comfortable as long as you are here," he promised with a groan. "But you can see we aren't going to take any chance of a leak. You'll have to stay until we are through with our work."

"Fiddlesticks!" exclaimed Granny with more force than elegance. "We'll finish our breakfast, and then I'll telephone to Joshua Cabot and ask him if we can't go to Seven Pines."

"You can't use the telephone," Major Martingale told her sharply. "Evidently you don't understand that Riverside is cut off from the world at present."

Granny stopped on her way to the dining room.

"Does he actually mean that? Is he telling us the truth?" She appealed to the two young men, but they only nodded their heads. "Mayn't I even telephone to my maid for clothes?" Granny asked almost feebly.

"You may not." Major Martingale was glad that she was beginning to understand. "You may give me any message, and if I consider it safe and necessary I may send it on. While you are not actually prisoners you can't leave Riverside, and you can't communicate with any one. It isn't my fault," he added hurriedly. "I didn't bring you here. I don't want you here! Mr. Simmons shouldn't have let you come!"

"Mr. Simmons doesn't know anything about it."

"He doesn't!" The major was all suspicion again. "I'll send him word. I'll——"

Granny caught his sleeve. "No, you shan't send him word!" she exclaimed quickly. "He'd—he'd laugh at us," she explained stumblingly, and a red flush crept into her cheeks. "You see we started for our country place. Mr. Simmons always said women couldn't be trusted and he'd tease us so. Please don't tell him. We'll be model prisoners if you won't, won't we?" She appealed to Rebecca Mary. "If you do tell him you may wish you had

154

"DO YOU MEAN TO TELL US THAT WE CAN'T GO?"

never been born," she prophesied with a smile, but there was something behind the smile which made Major Martingale mop his brow and look unhappy.

"So long as you obey orders I'll keep still," he promised unwillingly. "I can't say more than that. Mr. Marshall, will you see that these ladies have breakfast. I can't waste any more time. I shan't wait for breakfast. I've lost my appetite." And he waddled away before any one could say a word.

Granny looked after him all ready to say several words if he would only stay and listen to them, but as he never looked back, she dropped into the nearest chair and laughed until the tears stood in her eyes. Rebecca Mary was frightened and ran to her.

"There, there," she said soothingly. She was sure that Granny had hysterics, and she did not know what to do for hysterics. She wished she had taken the First Aid last winter when she had a chance. "It's all right," she insisted, although she was not at all sure that it was all right.

Granny pushed her away. "It's—it's——" she began, and stopped to wipe the tears from her eyes. "Oh, my old heart!" And she put her hand to her side and looked at them helplessly.

Joan ran to her. "Is your old heart getting younger, Granny?" she asked anxiously.

Granny patted her cheek. "I expect that is it. My old heart is getting younger. No wonder I have a queer feeling in it."

"Better have some coffee," suggested Mr. Marshall. He was young enough to regard food as a panacea for every ill. He introduced them to Mr. George Barton, an electrical engineer, and explained that he was an engineer, too, a chemical one, before he persuaded Granny to return to the dining room, where Ben brought fresh coffee and eggs and toast.

And while they ate their breakfast Mr. Marshall and Mr. Barton told them that Major Martingale was quite right, most important things were being done at Riverside.

"We're all here until the experiment is proved a success or a failure," went on Mr. Marshall. "It may be for a week and it may be for two months. No one goes out but the Big Boss. He went away last night."

"What is this great experiment?" asked Rebecca Mary between two bites of soft boiled egg.

"I'm sorry but we can't breathe a word about it. We scarcely speak of it among ourselves," regretted Mr. Marshall. He looked as if he would be glad to tell them if he only could. "The Major is right, old

156

Germany is moving heaven and earth to get it from us."

Granny sniffed. "H-m," she murmured. "And you think we are going to stay here indefinitely while this Major Martingale—Major Cross would be a better name—finds out whether he is a fool or a genius?"

George Barton laughed joyously. "That isn't exactly the way I'd state it, but it's the way it is, isn't it, Wallie? You see the thing is frightfully important. We're scared to death for fear the Germans may get a hint. We all took an iron clad oath, but the Huns are so devilishly clever you never can tell how or when they will reach your workmen. It isn't so bad here. We don't have such worse times, good quarters, fine eats, plenty to read, a victrola and a grand piano and tennis. Do you play tennis?" he asked Rebecca Mary, who was staring at him with big round eyes. She couldn't believe yet that it was true, that she and Granny and Joan were prisoners in Riverside.

"You may call yourself prisoners if you wish," it almost seemed as if Wallace Marshall had read her thoughts. "But we shall think of you as honored guests. And, believe me, I'm glad you came,"

157

he said fervently. "You've no idea how you will be appreciated."

Granny pushed back her chair and regarded him with a strange glance. Evidently she did not care for his appreciation.

"Oh!" Rebecca Mary pushed back her chair, too. She did not know what she feared Granny might do or say.

"Rebecca Mary," to her great relief Granny chuckled as she turned to her, "did you ever hear of such a thing? I reckon I've managed to get away from that question better than I planned. No one can come here to ask me what I want for a jubilee present." And she laughed before she turned to Wallie Marshall and George Barton. "We'll stay for a while," she went on quite as if she were at the seashore arranging dates with the manager of a popular hotel instead of in prison talking to an assistant jailer. "But you will have to finish your experiment by the twentieth. I have an important engagement on the twenty-second. A very important engagement. We can't stay a minute after the twentieth. And Major Martingale will have to explain to Mrs. Swenson why we didn't come to see Otillie's wedding things."

CHAPTER XI

WITH a broad smile Ben led the way up the stairs, talking all the time.

"Ah suah will be glad to hab ladies about agin," he chuckled. "Genelmen is all right in der way. Ah hain't got nothin' to say agin genelmen as genelmen, but no one can say they is so picturefying as de ladies. You better take the fambly rooms, Mrs. Simmons. There hain't nobody been usin' of 'em an' you'll find 'em mighty pleasant whether you looks out or in. An' they's allus ready."

He opened the door of the suite which occupied the west wing, and Rebecca Mary gave a little exclamation of delight. She quite agreed with Ben. The rooms were mighty pleasant in their pretty furnishings, while from the windows one looked over the formal garden to the river which flowed so peacefully between its two banks.

"How perfectly beautiful!" she murmured.

"Yes, they are very good cells," agreed Granny. "I'm sure we shall be as comfortable as prisoners should be. Bring in our suit cases, please, Ben.

Doesn't it seem restful and quiet, Rebecca Mary? I believe it will be good for us to rest here for a few days. It is too bad we won't see Otillie's wedding things, but that isn't our fault as I shall explain to Mrs. Swenson. You heard me tell that young man that we might stay until the twentieth? That was just a blind. We'll only stay until we want to go and then we'll slip away."

"How?" laughed Rebecca Mary, still hanging enchanted over the garden. "Shall I twist a sheet and lower you from the window?"

"I don't think it will be necessary to spoil good sheets," Granny laughed, too, perhaps at the picture Rebecca Mary had painted of a golden wedding bride dangling by a twisted sheet from a second story window. "I shall find a more comfortable way. You know, Rebecca Mary," she said in an undertone so that Joan, who was trying all of the faucets in the bathroom, would not hear her, "I'm not just sure about things here. That story may be all right, it may be true that Major Martingale has brought a lot of men down here to work out some experiment for the government and he may be afraid that some hint may leak out to the Germans, but it sounds very queer to me. I can't imagine what the experiment could be. And Joshua Cabot has never hinted to me that he has loaned Riverside to any one. So I think we had better not make any fuss but just stay quietly until we can learn something definite, and then if the story isn't true we can slip away and warn Joshua that queer things are happening here."

"Why, Granny Simmons!" Rebecca Mary had never thought that Major Martingale's story could be anything but true. "How shall we find out?"

"We shall keep our eyes and ears wide open. First we must make them trust us and then—and then, Rebecca Mary, we can learn the truth. Don't ask me how again," as she saw the question trembling on Rebecca Mary's lips, "for I don't know. But we shall, and until we do we'll just forget about it. I declare I feel younger than I have for years. But I'm tired. I didn't sleep well last night. If you take my advice now, children, you'll try these beds and see how soft they are. I am sure I feel the need of at least forty good winks."

"Oh, I couldn't sleep now." Rebecca Mary was too excited even to think of sleep. She would rather go down to the garden where the big pool showed the blue sky how becoming the fleecy white clouds were. The garden was far more alluring to her just then than the softest of beds.

"I couldn't, either!" exclaimed Joan. "Must I?"

161

Granny did not insist, and after she was tucked under the silken comforter Rebecca Mary and Joan went down the stairs hand in hand. They ran through the open door and found a surprise on the other side, a surprise over six feet long.

"Hello!" exclaimed the surprise, all a-grin.

"Hello!" replied Rebecca Mary somewhat feebly, and then she laughed for the surprise was young Peter Simmons. If Rebecca Mary's fingers had not been in her pocket with the four-leaf clover locket she would not have believed her two gray eyes. "Then it wasn't a dream!" she said triumphantly.

"Wasn't it?" Peter looked at Rebecca Mary as she stood before him in her crumpled white frock and pink sweater. Peter never saw that the frock was crumpled. He only saw the two shining gray eyes, the smiling red mouth and the two pink cheeks which helped to make Rebecca Mary's radiant face.

"I told Granny that you found us last night and she said I was dreaming," she explained more soberly. "Have you come to rescue us again?" It would be so romantic if the four-leaf clover had sent young Peter Simmons to their rescue a second time.

"Rescue you?" He looked puzzled, for Rebecca Mary did not look as if she were in any danger as she stood there in front of the door. "I want to

162

apologize for leaving you in the old shed," he went on. "It started to rain just before we turned in here last night and the shed was the nearest place. Yes, I picked you up, it wasn't any dream. Granny was wrong. I had received a hurry up call to come out at once and was on my way in my little gas wagon with a man from the factory when at the cross roads, a mile and half back, I came across two women and a half——"

"Was the half me?" demanded Joan, dancing up and down. "Do you mean me when you say half a woman?"

"I certainly do," smiled Peter. "One woman and a half were sound asleep and the other woman was just about asleep. The cross roads didn't seem the safest place for a nap so I left my machine to the mechanic and took the wheel of yours. I didn't dare take you to the house until I spoke to old Martingale but when I met him he wouldn't listen to my story but marched me off to the shop for a minute. The minute grew into sixty before I could get away, and when I went back to the shed you had gone. How is Granny? The idea of a child of her age going to sleep in a motor car thirty miles from home. Any one could have come along and carried you off!" It almost sounded as if Peter was scolding them.

163

"I said you brought us here. I remember perfectly now, but Granny wouldn't believe me. Did you know that we would have to stay for ever?"

"For ever?" Peter didn't understand.

With Joan's assistance Rebecca Mary explained that no one who came to Riverside could leave, and Peter threw back his head and laughed and laughed.

"Good work," he chuckled. "I guess I've eliminated old Dick Cabot for a while. He always was in the way in Waloo. But why in the dickens were you and Granny and this half woman," he pinched Joan's cheek, "going to Seven Pines in the middle of the night?" Evidently he had forgotten the explanation Rebecca Mary had given him in the middle of the night.

"Your grandmother decided rather suddenly to leave home," Rebecca Mary dimpled as she remembered how suddenly Granny had decided, "and she asked me to drive her to Seven Pines. I was scared to pieces but I couldn't refuse."

"That's very good as far as it goes, but it doesn't explain why Granny had to start in the middle of the night, why she couldn't wait until morning?"

Rebecca Mary hesitated until she remembered that Granny had said she didn't care if Peter knew, she didn't care if every one knew.

164

"I suppose I may tell you," the corners of her mouth tilted up. "She wanted to run away from a question."

"A question?" Peter looked hopelessly bewildered. "Why should any one, least of all an old woman of sixty-eight, run away from a question?"

Even when Rebecca Mary had explained what question it was which had made Granny abandon her comfortable home in Waloo at midnight Peter didn't seem to understand, and he said so.

"That's because you're a man!" Rebecca Mary was very scornful of a man's power of comprehension. "I understand perfectly, and I don't blame Granny a bit. It must be perfectly maddening to have your husband ask you whether you want light meat or dark every time a chicken comes to the table or what you want for a birthday or a Christmas present. I don't blame Granny," she repeated for fear he had not heard her the first time she said it.

"Neither do I when you say it like that," Peter agreed amiably. "Although I can't see why she didn't go to grandfather and tell him how she felt. My grandfather, Miss Rebecca Mary Wyman, is the best old scout in the world. Don't think for a minute that he is a crabbed selfish old dub because he isn't. He's the head of a big manufacturing plant which he had ready to turn over to the government before the war because he saw it coming, and it's been no joke to get it back to a peace basis since the war. I don't know anything about this chicken meat proposition, but I do know that granddad has so much on his mind that it isn't surprising if he has forgotten a little thing like an anniversary——"

"Little thing!" Anniversaries were not little things to Rebecca Mary. They aren't little things to any woman. "A golden wedding a little thing!" It was perfectly clear to Peter that a golden wedding with all its tributes and attributes would never be a little thing to Rebecca Mary.

"She's going to ask me," Joan broke in excitedly. "I've never been to one, and I can't think what it will be like. What will be golden? The bride can't be, can she?"

"No," Rebecca Mary put an arm around Joan as she explained. "No, honey, the golden part will be the beautiful memory the bride and bridegroom will have of the fifty happy years they have spent together." She stopped suddenly as she remembered that was what Cousin Susan had said, that memories were golden. "What a long time that is!" she murmured dreamily. "Fifty years!"

"Not too long for two people who love each other," suggested Peter in a voice which sent the ready color to her cheeks. "When you are married you will want a golden wedding, won't you?"

"I wonder," her lips murmured perversely, although her heart told her with one big beat that she would, she most certainly would, want a golden wedding.

"I know," insisted Peter. "Come on in and help me find some breakfast. I haven't had a thing to eat since last night," piteously.

"We have!" Joan was triumphant. "We had strawberries and toast and eggs and coffee!"

"Greedy!" Peter made a face at her. "I hope you didn't eat all the strawberries, nor all the eggs, nor all the toast?"

CHAPTER XII

REBECCA MARY and Joan sat beside Peter while he ate his strawberries and his eggs and toast and bacon. Rebecca Mary poured two cups of coffee for him in a demure little way which Peter found quite enchanting, and his eyes told her so as they followed her to the other side of the table. But there was nothing sentimental to Joan in the fact that Rebecca Mary had poured Peter two cups of coffee. She found it only interesting, and her eyes grew big when Peter broke a third egg.

"Gentlemen hold a lot more than ladies, don't they?" she asked with frank interest. "Granny only ate berries and toast and drank half a cup of coffee, and you, dear Miss Wyman, had an egg with your toast and coffee and so did I, but Mr. Simmons already has eaten——"

"Spare me the list of my victories," begged Peter. "And bear in mind, Friend Joan, that men are hard working creatures who have to be well stoked to do their job."

"But ladies work, too." Joan objected to such

168

sex discrimination. "I've seen them, haven't I, Miss
Wyman?"

"You have unless you kept your eyes shut, which
is what so many of our busy gentlemen do,"
twinkled Rebecca Mary. "If you are quite sure you
won't have another cup of coffee, Mr. Simmons, I'll
run up and see if Granny is awake and tell her the
surprise that is waiting for her."

But Granny was still asleep under the rose strewn
coverlet, and Rebecca Mary slipped out as quietly
as she had slipped in.

Peter had finished his breakfast when she returned to the dining room, and they all walked out
to the garden where he smoked a cigarette.

"But you know Granny can't stay here without
sending word to grandfather," insisted Peter.

"Why can't she?"

"Why can't she?" Peter stared as if Rebecca Mary
should have known better than to waste words on
such a question. "My grandfather adores my grandmother, Miss Wyman, although he does tease her to
death, and he'll worry his old gray head off if he
doesn't know where she is."

"Mrs. Simmons left a message with Pierson."

"That she had gone to Seven Pines. When grandfather calls up Seven Pines Granny won't be there. No, she must send him a message at once."

"You can't send any messages from Riverside. Major Martingale told us so most emphatically."

"I rather guess we could get a word to old Peter Simmons if we went about it in the right way." Young Peter seemed much amused to hear that she imagined that they couldn't. "Don't you know——" he began, and then he laughed and stopped short.

Rebecca Mary knew, of course, that he had meant to tell her what an important man his grandfather was, and she liked him the better for breaking his sentence off in the middle and not boasting. He chuckled to himself several times as he walked with Rebecca Mary through the garden which was such a riot of gorgeous color, around the flower-bordered pool, by the old lichen-studded sun dial and through the green wreathed pergola to the river bank, where Peter forgot his grandparents as he remembered his history and told Rebecca Mary the legend the Indians had written on the big rock on the other side. It was a gruesome tale, and Joan shook in her small shoes. Rebecca Mary would have shivered in her larger oxfords if she had not remembered that the gruesomeness was some two hundred years old. They had a most delightful morning and strolled back

170

when they heard the clang of a big bell, a bell which Peter told Joan talked of absolutely nothing but food.

"The mechanics are quartered in the farmhouse," he explained.

There was one word in his sentence which reminded Rebecca Mary that she was a member of Granny's detective bureau, and she looked up quickly.

"Just what is this experiment which is going to mean so much to the world?" she asked with serpent guile. The minute she had seen young Peter Simmons she knew that Major Martingale's story was true, but she should like to know more of his experiment. She had no doubt Peter would tell her more.

Peter squirmed uneasily. He wanted to tell her what he knew but a man's tongue is sometimes tied.

"I'm sorry," he said as Wallie Marshall had said earlier in the morning. "But we aren't allowed to breathe a word. We're under oath, you know. Can't run the risk of any leak."

"You don't trust me?" For just a second Rebecca Mary threatened to be injured or indignant. Peter held his breath. "Never mind!" She decided to smile, and Peter drew a sigh of relief. "It must have something to do with aëroplanes——"

"I'm not here as an aviator," Peter told her quickly, and then seemed sorry that he had spoken.

"You're not?" But as Peter refused to say in what capacity he was at Riverside she went on rather scornfully; "I suppose it has nothing to do with chemistry or electricity, either, although Mr. Marshall told me he was one kind of an engineer and Mr. Barton was the other."

"The dickens he did!" Peter grinned at her powers of deduction.

"I dare say I'll know all about it in time." Rebecca Mary tossed her head with a fair show of indifference. "That is if there is anything to know. Come, Joan, I'm sure Granny is awake now."

"I say, you're not angry with me?" Peter did not see why he should be intrusted with secrets which would make Rebecca Mary angry with him. He caught her hand.

She looked down at the five fingers which rested on Peter's broad palm and then up at his face, and to his delight there was no anger in her eyes, nothing but the most innocent surprise.

"Why should I be angry?" And when he didn't tell her she went on lightly: "Of course, I should want to know anything I shouldn't know, any girl would, and equally, of course, you must keep your

172

oath, but———" She shrugged her shoulders and took her fingers away from Peter.

"I see," muttered Peter ruefully as he followed her. But he didn't see at all.

They found Granny awake and on the terrace. She was surprised to see Peter for she had not believed a word of Rebecca Mary's dream, and she asked him at once if Major Martingale's story were true or should she and Rebecca Mary run away and warn Joshua Cabot that queer things were taking place at Riverside? There was no beating about the bush with Granny. She did not hesitate a second, and she looked very crestfallen when Peter told her that Major Martingale had told nothing but the truth.

"You'd never believe how important the experiment is nor how much Germany wants it," he said. "Old Martingale has to be suspicious and careful. He can't trust any one who isn't on oath. You were lucky you weren't shot at sunrise. No, you can't do a thing but stay until the Major lets you go. I'm glad you're here. It will make it pleasanter for me," he explained with a grin. "Although I'll confess that I didn't realize that things were on quite such a military footing. I didn't bring you here to be locked up but because I thought it was

173

safer than to leave you on the high road. I didn't know you would have to stay," he insisted. "Better send a message to grandfather," he told his grandmother.

She shook her head. "I can't. I'm not allowed to send messages to any one."

"I'm sure I can get old Martingale to let you write a letter." There was a funny twinkle in Peter's eyes as he told what he could do.

But Granny just shook her head again. "It won't do your grandfather any harm to worry about me for a while. He has been too sure of me, and I've been too good-natured. You know yourself, Peter, that we never would have left Waloo if we hadn't gone before he came home. I made allowances for him during the war, but that is over. No, Peter, I'm just full of things it wouldn't be safe to say to him now. I want a peaceful golden wedding, so I'll just stay where Fate has put me. If he were to come here and ask me what I want for a golden wedding present I'm afraid I should lose my temper. Why, we've talked of it hundreds of times and he should know. Perhaps it is a little thing, Peter, but you're old enough to know that life is made up largely of little things and they must be right. The big things

174

come so seldom that we can overlook the wrong in them."

"Grandfather's an awfully busy man just now," Peter began, but she would not let him finish.

"That's what I've been told for fifty years, and I've overlooked a lot because he was so busy and so important. But I rather think I'll be important for a while now. No, Peter Simmons, and if you say anything to Major Martingale I shall be cross. I don't know why I feel this way, I never did before, but I do feel that I can't be teased now. There is no use arguing with me. You might as well save your breath."

"It's all wrong," Peter grumbled to Rebecca Mary the minute they were alone. "Grandfather shouldn't have this private worry when he has so much public responsibility. Women have no sense of proportion."

"How can they have any when men have so much?" Rebecca Mary spoke as if there was just so much sense of proportion in the world and the men had taken it all. She showed how sarcastic she could be in a few words. "I don't blame Granny a bit, but I'll give you a little advice. If you leave her alone she will agree with you a lot sooner than if you argue with her. That's the way I manage the children and it succeeds nine times out of ten."

"I'll bet it does!" Peter was all admiration as he heard her method. "All right, I'll stop badgering the old dear—for a while anyway. Come and have a try at tennis. I'll wager you play a good game."

Rebecca Mary did not play a good game,—how could she when she had had so little practice?—but she obediently followed Peter to the court and let him knock balls toward her. She made up in effort what she lacked in skill.

She jumped up to hit a ball, which flew high above her head and struck it in such a way that it bounded from the court and went off at a tangent to strike the shoulder of a man who was hurrying to the house. He stopped and swung around to throw the ball back to the court.

"Oh!" Joan gave a shriek. "It's my father! It's my own father!" And she dashed to him as fast as her two feet would take her. He met her half way and caught her in his arms.

Rebecca Mary and Peter drifted toward each other.

"I thought her father was dead!" exclaimed Peter.

"Oh, no!" Rebecca Mary was dying to turn and look at Count Ernach de Befort but she was with-

176

held by a fine delicacy from staring at Joan's father.

Joan brought him across the court at once, clinging to his hand.

"I've found him!" She was tremulously triumphant. "I'm the first to find what we came for. This is my own father, dear Miss Wyman."

Her own father took the hand which Miss Wyman offered him and clasped it warmly. Now that she could see more than his back, Rebecca Mary felt rather than knew that Joan had not drawn him from her imagination. He was very different from the father in the photograph, older and more serious. There was a tired, worn look in the face which showed where Joan had found her black eyes and broad forehead and he had an absent-minded, detached air which explained how he had been able to leave his little daughter alone in Waloo with a housekeeper. He drew his heels together as Rebecca Mary had seen German officers draw their heels together in the movies, and Rebecca Mary caught her breath for she remembered the Prussian uniform he had worn in his photograph, the German eagle on his breast, and she remembered also that Major Martingale had said no Germans were to be at Riverside.

"I cannot understand," he said, bewildered and surprised as he tried to follow Joan's incoherent explanation, and although his English was quite correct there was a foreign intonation which Rebecca Mary found fascinating for it told her that Joan might be right and her father might really be Count Ernach de Befort. Counts of any nationality were a novelty to Rebecca Mary. She had not met one of them in the third grade of the Lincoln school.

She assisted Joan to explain that Mrs. Muldoon had been called away by the illness of her son and had left Joan with her teacher.

"She loaned me, daddy," emphasized Joan. "I'm so glad she did."

But Joan's father frowned as if he were not glad that his only daughter had been loaned to any one, and the explanation went on to state how they had come to Riverside.

"And we're prisoners!" exclaimed Joan. "Are you a prisoner, too, daddy?"

"The same kind of a prisoner that you are. Isn't that right, Mr. Befort?" laughed Peter.

Rebecca Mary breathed easier. If Peter laughed that way it must be all right for Frederick Befort to be at Riverside.

Frederick Befort smiled as if he thought it would

178

be very pleasant to have his daughter and her teacher fellow prisoners at Riverside before he said that he was one of the men working on the great experiment.

"I am surprised at Mrs. Muldoon," he went on with a frown. "She has been so honest and faithful that I was sure I could trust her to take care of Joan until I returned. My work here I could not leave to another. You know——" He looked at Peter.

Peter nodded. "Sure, I know." And he put his hand on the older man's shoulder. Yes, decided Rebecca Mary, it must be all right. "Funny I never connected you with the kid, for Befort isn't a common name. I guess I was so interested in your job I never thought of you as a father."

"I have," confessed Rebecca Mary impulsively. "I've thought of you a lot. Because we knew so little," she hastened to explain when Frederick Befort looked surprised to hear that he had occupied so many of Rebecca Mary's thoughts. "Granny Simmons and I have searched the map of Germany for Echternach, the place Joan said you came from, but we couldn't find it anywhere. We began to think that Joan had made up the name."

"You searched all Germany?" asked Frederick Befort, putting his fingers over Joan's lips as she

179

tried to tell them that she hadn't made up the name
of Echternach. "No wonder you could not find it.
It is a small place, Miss Wyman, but old, very old.
One of your English saints, Willibrod, came there
in the seventh century as a missionary. You should
have looked down in the southern part of Germany"
—Rebecca Mary was conscious of a feeling of disappointment. So Granny was right and he was a
German—"to the very edge of Rhenish Prussia until
you found the river Sure, and on the other side of
that river you would have discovered Echternach.
But it is not in Prussia, it is in the Grand Duchy of
Luxembourg." He drew himself up proudly as he
told her where Echternach was.

"Oh!" Rebecca Mary could not say another word
to save her soul. She could only look at him with
the pinkest of cheeks. "I was so afraid that you
were a German!" she told him honestly.

The laughter left his lips and a grave light took
the place of the smile in his eyes.

"No, Echternach is not in Germany. It is not
strange that you thought it was, Miss Wyman. And
if you traveled in our duchy you often would be
puzzled to know whether you were in Germany or
in France. German is spoken almost as much as
French and we used German money. But a German

regiment was garrisoned in Luxembourg for fifty
years and we have not forgotten. Germany tried to
swallow us as she tried to swallow so many prin-
cipalities, but Luxembourg would not be swallowed.
Can you repeat for Miss Wyman our national hymn,
ma petite?" he said to Joan. "The words the Cathe-
dral bells ring out every other hour for fear we shall
forget them. Now then." His voice prompted Joan's
as they repeated the Luxembourg anthem:

> *"Mîr welle jô kê Preise gin;*
> *Mîr welle bleime wat mor sin!"*

"That means we shall never become Prussians.
We shall remain what we are," he translated, and his
eyes flashed.

Rebecca Mary's eyes were larger than any saucer
as she gazed at him. She had known Russians and
Italians and Bohemians and Roumanians and Ser-
bians, she had taught children of almost every nationality, but she had never met a Luxembourger
before, and she tried to remember something of the
grand duchy. But she couldn't remember a thing.

"Joan should have told you." Frederick Befort
did not understand why she should look so pleased.
"You have been away from your native country

many months, *mignonne*, but you have not forgotten which side of the Sure was your home?"

"No," wriggled Joan. "But no one knows of Luxembourg and the grand duchess, and every one knows of Germany and the old kaiser."

"Alas, that it is so!" Frederick Befort shook his head sadly before he looked at Rebecca Mary and said, oh, so feelingly: "I cannot understand how Mrs. Muldoon could desert my little girl, but I am grateful to the good God that he sent her such a friend in you. I cannot thank you for your heavenly kindness to my little daughter." And before Rebecca Mary realized what he was doing he had taken her hand and kissed it.

If it had thrilled Rebecca Mary to have her fingers kissed by fat Mrs. Klavachek you may imagine how shaken inwardly she was to have them kissed by Count Ernach de Befort.

"It wasn't anything," she stammered, wishing for goodness' sake that she could think of something clever to say.

"It was everything!" he insisted, gazing into her eyes.

"Aren't you glad I found my daddy, Miss Wyman!" Joan was jumping up and down as she clung to her father's hand. "But I'm sorry you haven't

182

found any payment for your memory insurance," she went on regretfully.

"Oh, but I have!" Rebecca Mary forgot to be shy because a Luxembourg count had kissed her fingers, and she laughed. "I've found a tremendous payment!"

CHAPTER XIII

GRANNY was very much surprised when they trooped in to tell her that a tennis ball had just found Joan's father, and that he was not a German but a good Luxembourger. The width of a river had kept him from being a German. Granny knew little more of Luxembourg than Rebecca Mary, but she "oh'd" and "ah'd" before she looked at Frederick Befort and said slowly:

"You are quite sure you are from the Luxembourg side of that river?"

Frederick Befort's eyes never wavered as he looked at her. "Quite sure. There was a time when I regretted that I did not belong on the other side of the river. You know I went to school in Germany, in Bonn, and I had many German friends. The old emperor was a friend of my grandfather's. I was named for him; and the present emperor has visited us at Echternach."

"That is why he made you an eagle, isn't it?" Joan broke in, eager to have a share in these interesting explanations.

184

"Indirectly, yes." He smiled at her as she stood beside him. "I was able to arrange a very successful wild boar hunt and the kaiser was so pleased that he decorated me. He was with us for several days and made excursions all over the duchy. It was as if he wished to learn every road and mountain path. We thought nothing of it then, fools that we were! I even put on the Prussian uniform of one of the officers and wore it at the costume ball that my wife gave in his honor." So that was why he had been photographed in a Prussian uniform. Rebecca Mary's eyes crinkled. "There always has been a close relation between Luxembourg and Germany," he went on, and a frown chased the smile from his face. "Before our present grand duchess came to the throne German influence was supreme, most of our trade was with Germany, our railroads were developed with German money and by Germans, but in our hearts we had no love for Germany. And then came the day when the German army would have marched through the duchy and our grand duchess, brave little Marie Louise Adelheid, motored out to forbid them to use her country as a thoroughfare. She had her car turned across the road to bar their entrance, and the German officers laughed at her. Laughed at her, madame! They told her to go home. What could

185

Marie Louise Adelheid do? We had an army of three hundred, only a palace guard and a military band," he laughed bitterly. "We were not soldiers, we were farmers. Germany knew that. And our little grand duchess had to go home. It would have been useless to resist. Germany would have devastated Luxembourg as she devastated Belgium. But I have it in my heart to wish that we had resisted, that we had fought and died as the Belgians did. The Germans have used Luxembourg as they pleased. For fifty years our capital was garrisoned by German troops. They left an odious memory and the German soldiers who have swarmed over the duchy since 1914 are even more odious. No, madame, you need not ask. No people hate Germany as do we of Luxembourg."

His words sounded brave and true, and his face looked brave and true. His eyes flashed fire. It was easy to believe that he would rather have fought and died than to have yielded to the German hordes.

"We are small," he said more quietly, "but we are rich. Germany wanted us, she wanted our iron, our factories, but she did not get them. No! You see, madame, I have changed my mind. I no longer believe that I was born on the wrong side of the

Sure. I thank God now that there is no German blood in my veins!"

"You should," nodded Granny. "Men of German blood, and women, too, will have to pay a fearful price for their nationality, the price of a world hatred. That is a dreadful thing, to be hated by a whole world." She shivered as she thought what a dreadful thing it would be.

"How can it be otherwise?" Frederick Befort shrugged his shoulders. "If you had seen what I have seen——" He broke off with a shudder.

Granny leaned forward and put her hand on his. "It is strange that we should find you here," she said after a moment. "Providence has queer ways of bringing people together. It would have seemed easier to have introduced us that afternoon we were all in the Viking room at the Waloo."

"On my birthday," Joan whispered to her father. "Miss Wyman was there and Granny Simmons and young Mr. Simmons, and, oh, everybody."

"It might have been easier but would it have been as thrilling?" Rebecca Mary was almost faint from the thrills of the afternoon. "We might never have had such wonderful times if we had met that day at the Waloo." She drew a long breath as she thought

187

of the wonderful times which had followed that tea hour.

Granny smiled at her, so did young Peter and Frederick Befort, and unconsciously they all promised Rebecca Mary more wonderful times. Enthusiasm does make people so much more generous than quiet acceptance.

"Then, perhaps Joan is right and you are really Count Ernach de Befort?" laughed Granny. "We thought the child was romancing."

"Yes, in Luxembourg I am a count but in America I like best to be just Mr. Befort." And Mr. Befort looked almost apologetic.

For the first time in her life Rebecca Mary knew what it was to be a popular girl. As she had told Granny, since she had been in Waloo she had known no men over eight years of age and while the boys in her third grade were interesting and dear they were young. Here at Riverside, where she was a prisoner, Rebecca Mary found three most attractive men of exactly the right age, Peter Simmons, Wallace Marshall and George Barton, and one very fascinating older man, Frederick Befort, who was a count in his own country, a country which Rebecca Mary scarcely knew by name.

Busy as the men were over the experiment which

was to be such a boon to the world, they found many hours in which to walk with Rebecca Mary, to play tennis with her, to talk with her, to dance with her while the victrola played a new fox trot, or to ride with her around the farm on the fat horses which Peter borrowed from the farmer. Each one of them showed Rebecca Mary very plainly that there was no other girl in his world, as indeed there wasn't just then, and Rebecca Mary, to her undying astonishment, discovered that she could flirt and play one man against another as well as any woman. She scarcely had time to record the payments on her memory insurance policy she was so busy making them.

And if the three younger men admired her for her youth and sex and gay enthusiasm, Frederick Befort revered her for her kindness to Joan. When he was not absorbed in the experiment or at the shop, where he worked with a detached interest to the world around him, which would have made Granny and Rebecca Mary understand many things about Joan which they had not understood, he had to think of what might have happened if Rebecca Mary had not accepted the loan of Joan. His gratitude was sometimes embarrassing and always thrilling to Rebecca Mary, who often had to pinch herself to make

189

sure that she really was Rebecca Mary Wyman. She told herself a dozen times a day that, of course, it was because she was the only girl at Riverside that every one was so perfectly wonderful to her, but she liked to pretend that it was because she was so beautiful and fascinating. At heart Rebecca Mary was not a bit conceited. Her life never had let her accumulate enough vanity to balance on the point of a pin. And if you had told her that really she was very pretty and very charming she would have laughed at you.

She liked them all, even old Major Martingale, whom she had identified as the short, stout, red-faced man who had consumed such quantities of hot buttered toast that afternoon at the Waloo. She discovered that Wallie Marshall and George Barton had been in the tea room on that memorable afternoon also and it did seem strange, as Granny had said that Fate should bring them together again in this fashion. Never for a moment did Rebecca Mary suspect that Major Martingale had slipped the four-leaf clover into her hand, but she did wonder if one of the others had. She did not want to ask them outright, that would have ended, perhaps spoiled, the delightful mystery. She would have to wait and the waiting was proving very enjoyable. Once Rebecca Mary had hoped that it was Peter who had given her the talisman but now she wished it was Frederick Befort. It would be so romantic when she was sixty to remember that it had been Count Ernach de Befort. Dear me, but Rebecca Mary was glad that Cousin Susan had been so foolish as to spend her kitchen curtains for two cups of tea.

And while Rebecca Mary was the belle of Riverside, Granny took the rest cure.

"It's a heaven sent chance," she told Rebecca Mary and Peter. "I was in such a whirl all through the war that I'm still wound up in a hard knot. I'm sorry we didn't get to Seven Pines but I'll just rest here for a few days and perhaps I'll be in a good condition to enjoy my golden wedding."

"Grandfather——" began Peter, but she cut him short.

"Don't say grandfather to me, Peter Simmons. When you've been married fifty years less a few weeks you'll understand more than your grandfather ever understood if I know anything of the modern girl. Won't he, Rebecca Mary?"

"I don't know how much his grandfather understands." Rebecca Mary was proving every day what a help she would be to a diplomatic corps.

191

"He doesn't understand anything about women," grumbled Granny.

She did not come down to breakfast but let Rebecca Mary take a tray to her room and after she had eaten her berries and toast and drunk her coffee she exchanged her bed for a couch in the sun room, where she dozed until luncheon, when she appeared in the dining room to be received like a queen. A nap over a novel filled the afternoon, and after dinner she always played three games of double Canfield with Major Martingale, who frowned blackly over the first game, was puzzled at the second and smiled broadly at the third, which Granny always let him win.

"That keeps him in a good humor," she explained to Rebecca Mary. "Men have to be managed even over a game of cards."

She took Rebecca Mary over the house and showed her the original part which had been built by the great grandfather of Richard and Joshua Cabot.

"He was one of the big pioneers of the northwest," she said. "He came from Pennsylvania in the early forties as an Indian trader. Later he went into the transportation business. He used wagons first, those queer Red River carts. You've seen

192

them at state celebrations?" Rebecca Mary nodded. She remembered the quaint two-wheeled squeaky carts if she didn't remember the Cabots. "Old Mr. Cabot built here when the state was still a territory, and from an historical standpoint I suppose there isn't a more interesting house in the northwest. Councils of war, political rallies, balls, celebrations of every sort were held in these rooms. He entertained all the important people who came to the northwest. His wife was the daughter of a rival French trader, and Joshua Cabot's grandfather was prouder of his French blood than he was of what his father had done to open up a new country. I think Richard is like the old Pennsylvanian," she went on thoughtfully. "More so than Joshua or any of the others. I expect he will do something big some day."

"I should say he has done something big already," exclaimed Rebecca Mary, rather surprised to find herself championing Richard Cabot. "There aren't many men of his age who are vice-presidents of a bank like the First National. And Peter told me how splendid he was at selling Liberty bonds."

"That's true," admitted Granny soberly, and she carefully hid the twinkle in her eyes from Rebecca Mary. "And banks and bonds are not the only things that interest Richard. I used to think they were. But they're not."

"Yes?" questioned Rebecca Mary politely, but she was too polite, and too unconcerned. Granny refused to tell her what, with stocks and bonds, shared Richard's interest. Rebecca Mary had to guess what Granny meant. It was astonishing how often they talked of Richard, or would have been astonishing if they had not been prisoners in Richard's great-grandfather's old house.

No one came to Riverside as one day ran after another. They were quiet and restful days for Granny, but far from quiet or restful to Rebecca Mary and Joan. Joan made friends with the farmer's wife and the farmer's eight months' old baby and a maltese cat, and she deserted Rebecca Mary for the farmhouse. There were chickens at the farmhouse which Joan was allowed to feed if Mrs. Erickson did not have to say "don't" too many times, and a shaggy dog and a flock of young turkeys as well as the baby, which Joan was permitted to hold if she was sure that her hands were clean.

Bread and milk may be a healthy change from lobster à la Newburg and chiffonade salad, but to a palate accustomed to the rich food a simple fare soon palls. Before many days Granny began to feel so rested that she was not satisfied to lie in the sun room and doze. She began to wonder what old Peter Simmons was doing, what he had said when Pierson delivered her message the night he came home on the eleven fifty-five and found her gone, and to wonder last of all if she had been wise to run away. Her conscience began to prick and prick hard. At last she went to Sallie Cabot's pretty writing table.

"My dear old Peter," she began, "of course Pierson told you that I had left for Seven Pines with a couple of young friends. I did not wait to see you for several reasons. If you take time to think you will know why I felt that I had to go to Seven Pines just now. Do take care of yourself. I shall die if anything should happen to spoil our golden wedding. I've looked forward to it for over fifty years."

She signed herself "Your affectionate wife," with a little grunt and sigh and then she carefully tore the "Riverside" mark from the paper. She folded her letter and put it in a plain envelop, which she inclosed in a second envelop, which was addressed to the housekeeper at Seven Pines. She gave the letter to Peter and told him that as he had bothered

her so unceasingly she had written to his grandfather and the letter could be sent if it could go by
way of Seven Pines.

Peter seemed quite sure he could have it sent that
way. "Good work, Granny!" He patted her shoulder approvingly. "You won't be sorry," he promised.

"I hope I shan't," sighed Granny.

"She's a good old sport," Peter told Rebecca Mary
when he had his turn for a dance or a walk and they
chose a walk down by the river. "I honestly didn't
think she'd do it, but she did. Of course——" He
stopped suddenly and called her attention to the
hollyhocks, like pink and white sentinels.

Rebecca Mary was not to be diverted by pink
or white hollyhocks. "Yes? You were saying——"

"Nothing, that is, nothing of any consequence,"
he told her hurriedly. "I say what was old Wallie
telling you before dinner that made you both howl?
I haven't heard a good joke for some time and that
must have been a scream from the way you two
chortled."

But if Peter wouldn't tell her she wouldn't tell
him. "I don't feel at liberty to repeat Mr. Marshall's
jokes," she said very loftily.

"Now you're testy and it isn't my fault. I say,

196

you know, you're not the girl you were in Waloo," reproachfully. "You wouldn't have exploded at nothing in Waloo," he complained.

It was only the truth. Rebecca Mary was not the same girl she had been in Waloo. She knew it as well as he did and laughed triumphantly. She was so glad she was not that old scowling shabby Waloo girl. The soft low laugh rather went to Peter's head. He put out his hand and took Rebecca Mary's fingers in his warm palm.

"I say," he began a bit huskily, "you shouldn't look at a fellow like that. You—you——"

"Yes?" Rebecca Mary dared him with a racing heart.

"Hi there, Simmons! Miss Wyman!" shouted a voice behind them and there was Wallie Marshall, all indignation. "You think a fat lot of yourself, don't you?" he said to Peter with some heat, "to run off with all the partners at this dance. What do you think you are? Come this way, Miss Wyman. I found a corking place among the willows this afternoon when I was fishing. Let us see how it looks by moonlight."

"It looks beautiful," Rebecca Mary told him when they had found the corking place. She had been rather glad to run away with him from Peter. As soon as she had dared Peter she was sorry, afraid, for a girl never knows what will happen when she dares a man. "All shined up with the best silver polish. It should be inhabited by fairies."

"I guess there isn't any fairy that has anything on you," stammered Wallie. "You make a fellow like me feel so clumsy and rough."

"Clumsy! Rough! You!" The three exclamations told his scarlet ears that Rebecca Mary did not think he was either the one or the other.

He drew closer. "I say, you're a wonder, all right. My word!" He drew a deep breath. "But I'm glad you dropped in here. Just imagine if we had never met!" He couldn't imagine it. It was too horrible.

"We might have run across each other somewhere else," suggested Rebecca Mary. "The Waloo tea room perhaps. Strange things have happened there." She giggled as she remembered one of the strange things.

He shook his head. "No other place would be like this, where I can see such a lot of you. I hope you don't think it's too much?" He was seized with a sudden fear. "I don't bore you, do I?"

She assured him that he didn't. He hadn't bored

her for a second. He beamed, but he could not leave well enough alone.

"Then you like to be with me as much as with Simmons?" he asked jealously.

"Don't incriminate yourself, Miss Wyman," advised George Barton, who had come up behind them. "Cut along, Wallie. You're through."

"Through!" shouted the indignant Wallie.

George turned away from him. "Strange effect the moonlight has, Miss Wyman. See that bush over there? Doesn't it cast a shadow like a fool's-cap on the head of our friend, Wallie?"

She laughed, she couldn't help it, and when he heard her Wallie groaned and walked away.

"This is better." George twisted himself on the garden seat so that he could look up into Rebecca Mary's dimpling face. "Gee, but we have had a day!"

"Didn't things go well?" Rebecca Mary knew no more about the work which took the men over to the shop and sent them back to her than she did the day she had come to Riverside, but she always was interested to hear them mention it.

"Oh, yes, well enough, but don't let's talk about that now that I have found the girl and the time and the place. Moonlight is awfully becoming to you, Miss Wyman, you should always wear it. It makes you shimmer and sparkle."

"Too bad I can't buy a few yards to put away."

"You don't really need it. I've seen you sparkle quite fetchingly in the sunlight. You know you're different from any girl I ever knew," he went on with a curious wonder that he had found Rebecca Mary so different.

"In what way?" Rebecca Mary always had thought that she was different and, oh, how she wanted to be like other girls.

"In what way?" he repeated as if it should be as plain to her as it was to him. "Why, other girls—other girls are just nowhere beside you!"

"Oh!" Rebecca Mary was quite willing to be unlike other girls in the way described by his deep drawn breath and flushed face, but she looked at him provokingly and murmured sadly: "That might be taken in two ways."

Before he could tell her that it most certainly could be taken in but one way, Joan pushed through the shrubbery to announce excitedly that Ben had made some ice cold lemonade and if they wanted any they had better run, for Mr. Marshall said he was thirsty from his head to his heels, and Mr. Marshall was six feet three inches tall and the lemonade pitcher wasn't more than eighteen inches. Mr. Marshall had said so. A scant eighteen inches, he had said.

"Mercy, mercy, Joan!" Rebecca Mary caught her hand. "Let's fly!"

And away they dashed by the snapdragons, by the foxgloves and the hollyhocks, by the pool to the rose tangled terrace where the six-foot-three Mr. Marshall waited triumphantly beside the scant eighteen inch lemonade pitcher.

Frederick Befort waited there, too, and when Rebecca Mary, pink and breathless, murmured something about the roses, he drew her into a fragrant corner to tell her of the wonderful roses which have made Luxembourg famous, for there are roses everywhere, climbing the garden walls, the houses, the battlements and the towers. It made her flush and sigh to hear of the beauty of that rose garlanded city, and suddenly he flushed, too, and began hurriedly to talk of the eight hundred primary schools in which education is compulsory, for education is much thought of in the little duchy. And later, oh, much later, as Rebecca Mary brushed her hair before the mirror, she told her smiling reflection that she never had realized what a fascinating subject education could be.

CHAPTER XIV

"DO you know what I am going to do?" Peter demanded gloomily when he found Rebecca Mary in the pergola overlooking the river at the foot of the garden.

Rebecca Mary was reading a book which she had found in one of the big cases in Joshua Cabot's grandfather's library. She flushed guiltily when Peter discovered her and put her book hurriedly behind her, which was no way to hide it from him. Peter immediately wanted to know what was the matter with her book that she should put it behind her back when he came in sight, and what was her book, anyway? A minute later Rebecca Mary had yielded to brute force, and Peter read the title of the thick volume—"The Grand Duchy of Luxembourg," and then he took up a small volume which was on the bench beside Rebecca Mary and read the title of that—"French Grammar."

Then and there Peter had taxed her with giving more of her time and thoughts to Frederick William Gaston Johan Louis, Count Ernach de Befort, than she did to him, plain Peter Simmons, a former private in the Lafayette escadrille.

"You are always talking education with him. Education!" he sneered. "Or reading about his blamed little country or studying his blamed,—no, I can't call the language of the French names. But you know, Rebecca Mary, that you give him more of your company than you give me." And when Rebecca Mary just sat there flushed and guilty, Peter went on with great determination, "Do you know what I am going to do?"

Rebecca Mary could truthfully say that she didn't, she hadn't the faintest idea what he was going to do.

"I'm going to take this many-named count out and drown him. Oh, yes, I know we're forbidden to go on the river and that Befort is needed at the shop, but I'm going to drown him just the same. Yes, Rebecca Mary Wyman, that is what I shall do, I'll take him out on the river and drown him. What does he mean by butting in, anyway? Doesn't he know that I brought you here to get you away from old Dick Cabot?"

"Oh!" Rebecca Mary was all in a flutter when he spoke of old Dick Cabot.

"Doesn't Befort know that you are my girl?"

went on Peter with a frown, although there was a grin lurking around the corners of his mouth.

"Am I?" dimpled Rebecca Mary, pink to her hair to hear that she was Peter's girl.

"Aren't you?" Peter could answer one question with another as well as any Irishman, and he leaned closer to see if Rebecca Mary agreed that she was his girl. "And I'm not going to let another fellow cut me out," he went on sternly. "Marshall and Barton are bad enough, but I can manage them."

"How?" interrupted Rebecca Mary, eager to hear how Peter was going to manage Wallie Marshall and George Barton.

"I'm a bigger man than they are and a better," Peter explained promptly. "They don't worry me, but this Befort—I'm bigger than he is, too, but he's romantic, and all girls fall for romance. I can see that he might have quite a drag with you. Most girls would rather have a diamond already cut and polished in their platinum ring than one in the rough. I like old Befort myself, but I'll have to drown him just the same. Godfrey!" he jumped to his feet and looked down at her. "There's no time like the present. I'll hunt him up and ask him politely to come for a little row on the river, and then I'll drown him."

Rebecca Mary laughed. "There used to be an old saying that ran something like this—'First catch your hare.'" Her eyes danced. It was such fun to hear Peter run on. Not one of the eight-year-old men she had known in the third grade of the Lincoln school had ever talked to her like this.

Peter grunted scornfully. "Oh, I'll catch him," he promised confidently. "I have only to stay here with you, and I'll catch him and drown him."

Neither of them knew that just behind the vine wreathed pergola Joan was playing with the farm-house kitten which she had borrowed without permission. She had hesitated between the baby asleep in a chair on the porch and the kitten asleep on the step and then had wisely chosen the kitten.

When she first heard Peter talking to Rebecca Mary she had not listened to him for the kitten was so cunning as it played with the string Joan held just out of reach of the four paws, but when Peter kept on insisting that he was going to drown some one she had to listen. When she heard who Peter was going to drown she jumped to her feet, almost on the borrowed kitten, and gasped. Her first impulse was to rush to Peter and tell him that he couldn't, he just couldn't, drown her father for liking to talk to Rebecca Mary. If he did that he would have to drown himself and every one at Riverside and a lot of people at Waloo, for almost every one liked to talk to Rebecca Mary. He even would have to drown her. And then another plan slipped swiftly into her startled brain, and her slim legs scarcely touched the ground as they carried her around the pergola and up through the garden.

It was the greatest luck that just as she passed the tall clump of larkspur she should see her father coming leisurely toward her. If Joan had been older and in less haste she would have seen that her father had changed since the day the tennis ball had found him. He did not look as haggard nor quite as absent-minded and his shoulders did not sag. He looked just then as if he had come from the hands of a very good valet.

"Eh, Joan," he called when he saw the flash of her bare knees. "What now? Where are you going in such haste?"

Joan threw herself against him, clasping his legs in her arms, and gasped, "You won't let him drown you, will you?" she begged.

Frederick Befort dropped on the grass beside her and took her in his arms. "Indeed, no one shall drown me, *ma petite*. Why should they?"

"Then when he asks you to come for a row on the

river you won't go, will you?" Joan went on. "Say you won't?" She gave him a little shake. "I—I don't want you to be drowned."

"And I don't want to be drowned." Frederick Befort laughed gently as he wiped the tears from her eyes. "Some one has been teasing you, *mignonne*."

"It wasn't to me he said it. It was to Miss Wyman. He said he could manage Mr. Marshall and Mr. Barton, but that you were too romantic and he would have to drown you."

To Joan's surprise her father threw back his head and laughed and laughed. "So," he murmured as he hugged her, "I am romantic, am I? Miss Wyman——" An odd expression crossed his face as if an odd thought had just crossed his mind. "You like Miss Wyman, don't you, Joan?"

Joan nodded as she clung to his hand. If Peter drowned her father he should drown her, too. Even if she did love Miss Wyman she did not want to live without her father.

"He said you were a cut and polished diamond set in platinum," she hiccoughed. "And he said he was in the rough. That was why he would have to take you in a boat and drown you, because you were a cut and polished diamond. So I ran just as fast as I could for I knew if I told you he never could drown you, could he?"

Frederick Befort put his fingers under the eager little face and tipped it up so that he could kiss the trembling lips. "I don't think Peter wants to drown me, Joan," he explained gently. "He was speaking figuratively."

"What's that?" The new word had to be explained at once. "What's figure speaking?"

Frederick Befort searched his brain for the right words with which to explain it. "When you ran races with Miss Wyman and Peter last night you called out that you were flying because you ran so fast. But you really weren't flying, you know, you just felt as if you were. Peter Simmons doesn't really want to drown me, he just wants to pretend that he does."

"Oh!" The explanation proved satisfactory, and Joan's lips stopped trembling to smile. "It won't hurt to do it that way, will it?"

Frederick Befort smiled ruefully. "I'm not so sure. You know, Joan, that Peter Simmons is young and life is all before him. My life is behind me, the best part of it." He jumped to his feet as Rebecca Mary and Peter rounded the larkspur.

Peter was carrying the "Grand Duchy of Luxembourg" and the French grammar.

Joan jumped to her feet, too. "I heard what you said," she called triumphantly, "and I ran to tell my father. Yes, I did, and so you can't drown him now only in your mind."

Peter looked surprised and crestfallen before he laughed. "You saved his life," he said, tickling Joan's neck. "If you hadn't told him I'd take him right out now and drown him."

Joan shivered and looked quickly from Peter to her "cut and polished" father, who didn't shiver at all.

"Only figuratively, *mignonne*," he reminded her.

"But he could do it truly, perhaps," she said tremulously, for Peter did seem so big and resourceful. "He has a war cross for being brave, you know."

"He received that for saving people, not for drowning them," Frederick Befort said swiftly. "I envy you that, Peter," he added gravely.

Peter nodded. "I hadn't thought of it like that. It is good to think that I helped save, but when you get down to brass tacks that's what all the fellows were doing," he went on quickly. "They saved the world, ideals, freedom, everything that makes life worth while."

"Yes, you are right. Have you been studying your lesson, Miss Wyman?" Frederick Befort took the French grammar from Peter's hand. "Are you ready to recite it? Let us go down by the river."

And before Peter could say "booh" he had taken Rebecca Mary and the grammar both away from him.

Peter looked after them and his jaw dropped. "Well, I'll be darned!" he muttered. "You bet I'll have to drown that man."

CHAPTER XV

REBECCA MARY had walked over to the farmhouse for Joan, but Joan was feeding the chickens and just couldn't come at once, so Rebecca Mary sat down on the steps and talked with Mrs. Erickson until the last downy chicken had been given its dinner.

"My, Miss Wyman, I expect you'll be glad when they're through their work here and you can leave," Mrs. Erickson remarked sympathetically, as she offered Rebecca Mary a plate of crispy flaky gooseberry tarts. "It must have been pretty hard to start for a wedding and find yourself in jail. I know how it is with me. I never was much of a gadabout, but, land knows, I'll be glad enough when the guards are taken off, and I can come and go as I please."

"It is rather horrid," Rebecca Mary carelessly agreed as she ate a gooseberry tart. "But I'm not having such a bad time really, Mrs. Erickson. It might be a lot worse."

"I wish I could look at it like that. But I ain't one to dwell much on the cheerful side of things.

What's the use, I say, when there's so much that ain't cheerful. I suppose the old Major knows what he's about, but there's queer things going on in Riverside, or I miss my guess."

Rebecca Mary looked up quickly. "What do you mean?" she wanted to know at once. Mrs. Erickson looked as if she meant such a lot.

Mrs. Erickson drew a sigh from the sole of her stout shoes and moved closer to Rebecca Mary, quite ready and willing to tell her what she meant.

"Well," she said in a whisper which blew a lock of Rebecca Mary's yellow brown hair across her face, "as I understand it, Major Martingale brought all these men down here to work on his experiment and locked us up with them so he wouldn't be disturbed or interrupted and so he wouldn't have any Germans nosing around. Wouldn't you think, then, that he wouldn't want any Germans here? But last night her father," she nodded to Joan, who was vainly trying to divide the dinner evenly among the hungry chickens, "was over here talking to one of the mechanics, George Weiss. He took him down behind the shed there and talked to him in German. They didn't know I heard them, but I did. There isn't much that goes on around Riverside that I don't hear something of. Erickson said talk-

ing German don't mean anything but it does to
me. Don't it to you?"

"Not much." Rebecca Mary helped herself to
another tart. "My word, but these are good, Mrs.
Erickson. No, I don't think it means anything for
Mr. Befort to talk German. He was brought up
practically in Germany." And she told Mrs. Erickson of the Luxembourg town which was just across
the river from Rhenish Prussia. "He hates the Germans," she added, and her white teeth closed over
the crispy flaky tart.

"He didn't sound as if he hated the Germans the
way he was talking German. Maybe you're right,
Miss Wyman, you see more of him than I do, but
seems to me if I was trying to keep what I was doing
from the Germans I wouldn't have no Germans working with me. Major Martingale oughta know his
business, but I dunno——" She shook her head dole-
fully. "And more than once, Miss Wyman," she went
on in almost a whisper, "I've seen Mr. Befort coming
up from the river at sunrise. What's he doing down
there I'd like to know? Why ain't he in bed and
asleep like the rest of folks? Swimming may be excuse enough for you but it ain't for me. I don't
say he ain't what he says he is but I must say that
under the circumstances it's mighty queer. I said

213

to George Weiss myself, said I, 'You got a name that
sounds like sauerkraut to me,' said I. 'What side
was you on in the late war?' I said. And he looked
at me and laughed and said, 'Now Mrs. Erickson,'
said he, 'you know very well that I was one of Uncle
Sam's boys. It wasn't my fault if I didn't get to
France. Maybe my name does have a German sound
but the father what gave it to me didn't stay in
Germany. He brought it to America, and his boys
are a hundred per cent American,' he said. But,
land, you dunno whether to believe him or not. A
man'll say 'most anything he wants to." And she
drew a second sigh from the sole of her thick shoe.

Rebecca Mary should have gasped, but she didn't.
She giggled. "You don't look on the cheerful side
of things, do you, Mrs. Erickson?"

"Well, it ain't so easy to be cheerful when you
know the world as it really is. I've had some experience with these I. W. W. Bolsheviks, Miss Wyman. Not here at Riverside. Land, no! Erickson
keeps too good a watch on things, and our men have
been working here long enough to know which side
of their bread's buttered. But I got a brother up
in North Dakota and last summer his crops was set
on fire and a new thrashing machine ruined by putting nails and other truck into it. I dunno who I

214

do trust, Miss Wyman, but it ain't a man who talks enemy language and acts what I can't understand. I don't blame the Major for being afraid of I. W. W.'s and anarchists, but what I can't see is the way he trusts some folks. My brother said the Germans was back of all the trouble in North Dakota, and he's a truthful man if there is one. Do you know anything about this great work we're doing here, Miss Wyman?"

"Not a thing." Rebecca Mary looked a trifle puzzled. She was a trifle dazed, also, at the flood of words which had poured from Mrs. Erickson's lips.

"No more do I. And Erickson don't know anything or I'd know. More 'n once I've slipped down beside that shop hoping to pick up a word, but they don't use language I can understand, and what they're working on don't look like nothing to me through the window. I don't dare go very close for if the old Major 'd see me he'd be sure to give me a piece of his mind. He's got a harsh tongue when things don't go his way. I declare, Miss Wyman, when I got so much to worry me I almost wish Mr. Cabot hadn't been so free with Riverside. I hope he don't find himself wishing that, too." But she smacked her lips and there was a greedy look in her eyes which flatly contradicted her words.

Rebecca Mary jumped to her feet and brushed the crumbs of crispy flaky tart from her fingers. "It's easy to make mountains out of mole hills, Mrs. Erickson," she said quickly. "But it's rather a waste of time. Major Martingale knows what he is doing. He isn't blind nor deaf. Come, Joan. Haven't you finished yet? We'll be late for our own dinner if you don't hurry."

"I've just finished." Joan held up the empty pan and spoon. "It's such fun, Miss Wyman. Isn't it kind of Mrs. Erickson to let me feed them? But I do think she should teach them better manners. That big white rooster wants to eat it all. If I hadn't driven him away the weeny little ones wouldn't have had a bite."

Mrs. Erickson snorted. "The big white rooster is just like some folks," she told Joan. "And if you can teach him table manners, Miss Joan, you're welcome to the job. I've got enough on my hands without showing roosters how to be polite."

"Isn't she a funny woman, Miss Wyman?" Joan asked when they had closed the farmhouse gate behind them. "She is always asking me about daddy. Every day she asks me if he is an American citizen or if he isn't. And when I asked daddy he said

216

he couldn't be an American citizen because he isn't
through with being another kind of a citizen yet."

"He's a Luxembourger, you know, Joan. Why
didn't you tell Mrs. Erickson that?"

"I did, and she just sniffed and said she never
heard of such a country. She sniffs awfully funny,
Miss Wyman, but she's kind, too. She gave me a
doughnut and a piece of cheese as well as a gooseberry tart. She said they'd probably make me sick
but I could eat them if I wanted to. And I wanted
to, and I wasn't sick. She makes awfully good
doughnuts. I think she must be a good cook. The
chickens liked their dinner awfully much."

"Positive proof that Mrs. Erickson is the perfect
cook. None but the best would do for a flock of
hungry chickens. Joan, I'll race you to the house.
Wait a minute. Now, one—two—three—Go!"

And they were off, down the driveway, by the lilac
bushes to the old oak where Peter and Wallie, on
their way from the shop, stretched a barrier across
the walk.

"You must be in a hurry," grinned Peter. "Hold
on and we'll ride with you, but you must have some
regard to the speed limit."

"Tired?" They did look hot and tired. "It must
be horrid to spend a perfectly gorgeous day like

217

this in a stuffy shop with a gasoline engine that says nothing but puff-puff. Aren't you almost through?"

"We'll never be through," moaned Wallie. "I expect the Major will keep us here on the job until we are gray and tottering. You'll be a dear little old lady then, Miss Wyman."

"Silly!" Rebecca Mary tilted her nose. "But, honest, won't you be through soon? Granny and I have been perfect saints. We haven't made any fuss at all, but we can't stay here forever. Of course, I don't know anything about your great experiment——"

"It is great, all right!" interrupted Peter. "The more we work at it the more sure I am of that. I don't wonder old Germany moved heaven and earth to get hold of it."

When Peter spoke of Germany Rebecca Mary remembered Mrs. Erickson's gloomy fears and she asked impulsively; "Has Germany given up trying to get your wonderful secret?"

The two men stared at her in surprise.

"Don't you know that's why the Major brought the whole works down here?" Peter asked. "In Waloo the Huns made trouble more than once, through the mechanics, you know, regular bolshevik work. You'd never believe how sly they were. That's why Joshua Cabot turned this place over to the Major, and why the rule was made to bar people, and why you are here to shed light on our dark way. The Major isn't taking any chances of having anything stolen from him nor of any dirty sabotage, either, you may believe me. Every man here had to pass a pretty rigid examination that went back to his father and his grandfather."

"Every man?" Rebecca Mary could not help but put a little dash of significance into those two words.

"Every one," Peter told her stoutly. "It is only the women who got in without. When I drove you in here I hadn't any idea how necessary secrecy was. You should have heard the wigging the Major gave me. Perhaps you have been bored but you've been a life-preserver just the same, hasn't she, Wallie?"

"Sure thing!" Wallie gave a strong and hearty indorsement to Peter's statement that Rebecca Mary had been a life-preserver. "I wish we could tell you more about this work, Miss Wyman, you'd be interested, but we're on oath, you know. You'll just have to trust us and wait."

"M-m," murmured Rebecca Mary. It is so much easier to ask for trust and patience than it is to furnish it. "You are sure you can trust your men?"

"Why not?" Peter's voice was sharp and quick. "Why not, Rebecca Mary? What do you mean?"

Rebecca Mary laughed uneasily. "I don't suppose it is anything but——" And she told them what Mrs. Erickson had told her, that Frederick Befort and George Weiss had been heard talking German behind the Erickson woodshed, and Mrs. Erickson feared the worst.

"Just like a woman," jeered Peter. "You take my word for it, Rebecca Mary. I guess I know as much about it as old Mother Erickson. Befort is all right. So is George Weiss. I suppose if I were to go back of the chicken run and murmur 'hickory dickory dock' Mrs. Erickson would swear I was a red Russian. You just keep your hair on, Rebecca Mary, and listen to me. Some day you'll know that I'm right, won't she, Wallie?"

"Sure thing," Wallie said again. "We didn't run any chance of a leak, Miss Wyman. Believe me, we have picked men."

Rebecca Mary looked from Wallie to Peter. They nodded to her as if to emphasize what they had told her. Surely they must know more than Mrs. Erickson, who had only been able to peek through the shop window. Mrs. Erickson had told her that she always looked on the dark side of things and naturally she had hunted for a dark side to the great experiment. It was foolish for Rebecca Mary to look at the dark side when Peter and Wallie were insisting that there was such a bright and sunny side.

"Mrs. Erickson makes awful good gooseberry tarts and doughnuts," Peter said gently. "But she hasn't much of a record as a detective."

"I didn't really think she had. I'm not a complete idiot," Rebecca Mary exclaimed with considerable scorn. "But I thought it was only right to tell you what I heard. Of course, I know that Major Martingale didn't take any chances. Germany couldn't get a clue now to what you are doing."

"Huh," grunted Peter. "I wouldn't go quite as far as that. I think Germany will still make a try, don't you, Wallie?"

"I do, but don't let's talk about Germany as if the war was still on; let's guess what Ben is going to give us for dinner. I'm so hungry I could eat you, Miss Wyman. You'd better not come near me garnished with any bunch of mint."

"Silly!" Rebecca Mary's nose was elevated disdainfully. "Well, you can't say I have any secrets from you. And Ben is going to give you roast beef for your dinner, Mr. Marshall. I heard him tell Joan."

"Trust the kid to find out. I rather thought we might have lamb." And Wallie grinned impudently.

CHAPTER XVI

THE days flew by as days will fly whether they are bright with diamonds or veiled in gray. Granny became rested, Joan was spoiled, and even Rebecca Mary began to feel the effect of too much attention. There had been a time when Rebecca Mary had thought that it would be perfect bliss to have just one man devoted to her, but now that she had four she found that she never had a minute to herself. Whether she wanted to or not she had to play tennis with Wallie Marshall, walk with George Barton, ride the farmhorses with Peter Simmons, recite French verbs to Frederick Befort or play accompaniments for Major Martingale, who still liked to hear the young people sing the old war songs. And you know how it is yourself if you have just had a generous portion of plum pudding you don't care to see another plum pudding no matter how holly wreathed it is. In spite of all the admiration and attention which were falling on Rebecca Mary like an April shower she was not satisfied; she was conscious of a vague longing for something, she didn't know what, for she did not analyze the faint discontent which annoyed her. She only knew that she wanted something which she did not have and she told herself that she was an ungrateful beast to ask more of her talisman when already the clover leaf had given her so much.

It was the same way with Granny, who had looked on Riverside when she arrived as a haven of rest, but she soon was as surfeited with rest as Rebecca Mary was with admiration. Granny had so little to occupy her mind that she just had to think of old Peter Simmons, to wonder uneasily what he was doing, to ask herself if he were thinking of her instead of his factory, if he had received her letter, and a thousand other things all of which had old Peter Simmons for their subject. Twice Major Martingale found her with her hand on the door of the room which he used as an office and which held the only telephone at Riverside and to which he alone had the key.

"Do you wish to leave any message with me?" he asked each time.

"If I said what I wanted to say I expect the message would be left with you," Granny said sadly. "You never would send it on. How much longer will it be before we may leave, Major Martingale?"

"You know as much about it as I do." Major Martingale was discouraged just then and was sadly in need of a word of encouragement.

But Granny hadn't enough encouragement for herself; she couldn't spare a word for any man. "The twenty-second is a week from yesterday," she said significantly. "I told you, you know, that we wouldn't stay a minute after the twentieth," she added in case he had missed the significance.

"I hope none of us will have to stay later than the twentieth, but you should have thought of that before you came."

"Came!" Granny was indignant. "I didn't come!"

"Well, I didn't bring you!" He was too exasperated to remember the courtesy which is ever due a lady.

"A perfect bear, my dear," Granny told Rebecca Mary five minutes later. "If he has his way we'll be here for Thanksgiving," she prophesied gloomily.

Rebecca Mary sat up on the *chaise longue* where she had hidden herself for a quiet half hour and stared at her. "Thanksgiving! We can't stay that long. Why, school begins the first of September!" The beginning of school was an event so large in the life of Rebecca Mary that everything should give away to it. Everything always had.

"Major Martingale wouldn't care for that. It isn't our wishes nor our convenience he is thinking of. If we could do anything to help him I shouldn't say a word. If we even knew anything about this wonderful experiment it would be different, but we might as well be in New York or Bombay for all we know of what is going on in that shop. We couldn't tell anything intelligent enough for even a German to understand. I'm beginning to feel that the whole thing is nonsense, Rebecca Mary, and so I don't think that we have to stay. And I'm worried for fear Edith won't order things the way I want them for my golden wedding. I never meant to stay away so long. I'm sorry we ever started for Seven Pines. But we can go back. We'll run away from here."

"But how can we run away from Riverside?" It didn't sound as easy to Rebecca Mary as it had to Granny.

"I'll find a way." Granny was not to be daunted. "I'll have to. I'm tired being a prisoner."

"So am I." Joan dropped her doll and came to tell them that she, too, was ready to leave Riverside. "I'd like to go somewhere else."

"I'm sorry now," went on Granny, "that I didn't

226

stay at home and let old Peter Simmons ask his tormenting question and take the consequences."

"I'm not!" Indeed, Rebecca Mary wasn't. She had made far too many payments on her memory insurance policy ever to regret the past few weeks. "You see, we've helped here," she explained when Granny and Joan had cried, "You're not!" "The boys say we've been an inspiration to them, that they have worked a lot better because we were here to cheer them up."

"They would have worked a lot faster if we hadn't been here." There was a dry tone to Granny's soft voice which sent the ready color into Rebecca Mary's cheeks. "I've no doubt Joan and I have furnished lots of inspiration. It is pleasant to think so, isn't it, Joan?"

Joan looked doubtful. "Is it the same as being a nuisance? Mrs. Erickson said we were all nuisances, but I was the biggest. But she never said we were inspirations."

"Let her complain to Major Martingale. Is that only two o'clock?" as the old clock called to them from the hall. "How many hours are there left until bedtime?" There was no doubt that Granny was losing patience.

It was a warm sultry day, the sort of a July day

which tries the disposition in normal conditions, and by evening every one was more or less on edge. It showed in the increased politeness with which they spoke and in the silence which fell over them as they sat on the terrace under the stars and tried to think that there was a breeze blowing up from the river. Joan had gone to bed most reluctantly, and her father was sitting beside Rebecca Mary on the broad balustrade. Peter sat on the other side so that they made a sandwich of her. And in front of her lounged Wallie in a steamer chair reciting nonsense rhymes to which she scarcely listened, and not a yard from Wallie was George Barton singing sentimental verses under his breath as he touched the strings of a ukelele.

Not so many days had passed since Rebecca Mary would have thought that it would be heaven for a girl to sit on the terrace balustrade of a beautiful old country place with a Luxembourg count on one side of her and a *croix de guerre* man on the other while two very likable young men were in front of her, but now she was only vaguely conscious that they were not what she wanted at all. She didn't want any more plum pudding. She wished irritably that they wouldn't sit so close to her. She wanted all the air she could get. And her wandering

228

thoughts led her back to where she would be if she were not at Riverside and that brought her to Cousin Susan and the mysterious talisman and to—Richard Cabot. When her thoughts reached Richard they loitered there with a strange little feeling of satisfaction. She knew that Richard would never have let her remain so uncomfortable on a hot July night. Richard would have taken her for a swift ride in his big car to some cool place where ice tinkled in tall glasses. Rebecca Mary was not exactly fair for it was not the fault of Peter nor Wallie nor George nor even Frederick Befort that she was not flying over the country road with them. But Rebecca Mary did not want to be fair. She just wished that Richard were there—she wished——

She startled Peter and Frederick Befort and offended Wallie and George by jumping to her feet in the middle of Wallie's funniest poem and the most sentimental of George's songs. But before she could utter a word of explanation or apology there came the sound of voices and another sound, sharp and clear like a trumpet. It woke Granny, who was half asleep in her chair.

"God bless my soul!" she exclaimed, and she sat up with a bewildered, almost a frightened, expression on her face. "No one blows his nose like that but old Peter Simmons. He must have come for me. Run, Peter!" She was in a panic. "And tell him to stay in the road. Major Martingale will lock him up if he comes in."

CHAPTER XVII

BEFORE the appearance of old Peter Simmons proved the truth of what had sent Granny into a panic, that the sonorous trumpet was a part of him, Granny had disappeared.

"Where's your grandmother?" old Peter demanded of young Peter at once, but young Peter couldn't tell him.

And when Rebecca Mary went in search of Granny she had to come back alone for her knock on Granny's door brought no answer. There was not a sound from Granny's room.

"Perhaps she is asleep," Rebecca Mary suggested, but she stammered for she was quite sure Granny was not asleep. Why, it was not five minutes since she had been on the terrace.

Old Peter Simmons looked at her from under the grizzled eyebrows which he drew together in a frown so deep that Rebecca Mary almost thought he was going to dash up the stairs and make Granny open the door.

"H-m," he said slowly, "I hope she is asleep. She

has had a hard time the last few years; all women
have. I'm glad she had sense enough to come here
away from people and things and get a little rest.
We must humor her." He looked at wide-eyed Rebecca Mary for a second and then turned to young
Peter. "If your grandmother has gone to bed we
might as well get to work at once. I want to see
just what you men have done. We'll go right out
to the shop. Martingale is already there. Take
good care of my wife!" He stopped in front of Rebecca Mary and spoke in the tone of a man who
was obeyed.

"Yes, sir, I shall," stuttered bewildered Rebecca
Mary as she stared from him to young Peter and
back again to him. Young Peter Simmons had
exactly the same forehead, the same bright blue
eyes, the same, oh, the very same square jaw. Rebecca Mary was positive as she looked from him to
his grandfather that when young Peter had been
married fifty years less a few days he would look
exactly like old Peter Simmons, and probably be
exactly like old Peter Simmons, too. Rebecca Mary
caught a startled, a frightened, breath. She was glad
to remember that there had been a twinkle in old
Peter Simmons' eye when he had asked for Granny.

She went slowly up the stairs and Joan, like a small ghost in her white nightie, met her in the hall.

"Who is it?" she asked eagerly. "Is it Santa Claus or Uncle Sam? Granny won't tell me. I asked her through the keyhole, but she never said a word. I looked out of the window and I could see a man as tall as Uncle Sam but he didn't wear Uncle Sam's pretty striped clothes. He was as big around as Santa Claus but he didn't have Santa Claus' bushy whiskers. I should think, Miss Wyman, dear, you would tell me who he is?" she finished fretfully.

"I shan't tell you anything unless you are in bed before I count ten," Rebecca Mary said sternly.

But when Joan was in bed before Rebecca Mary had counted six she looked so small and helpless that Rebecca Mary was ashamed of her impatience and told her quickly that it was not Uncle Sam nor yet Santa Claus who had arrived with such a flourish of trumpets, but old Mr. Simmons, Granny's husband and young Peter's grandfather.

"Shut your eyes, Joan, and go to sleep or it will be morning before you know it."

"Oh!" Joan had seldom been more disappointed. "I don't think that's very interesting, do you? Perhaps it is to Granny," she added with tardy politeness, "but it isn't to me. I'll shut my eyes, Miss

Wyman, but I can't seem to shut my mind to-night, and so I can't go to sleep. I have to think of Uncle Sam and Santa Claus and the big Mr. Simmons. It won't be my fault if it is morning before I know it!" she wailed.

Altogether it took some time as well as two songs before Joan could shut her mind as well as her eyes. Rebecca Mary straightened the counterpane and looked at the flushed little face on the pillow. When she was asleep Joan looked like an angel. Rebecca Mary could scarcely believe that she would ever be as irritating as a mosquito as she patted the black head before she went to her own room.

She crossed to the window and looked down on the garden. A dull puff-puff, the foolish chatter of a gasoline engine, was the only sound which broke the fragrant silence, and Rebecca Mary knew that it came from the shop where old Peter Simmons was being shown what had been done. Now that she had time to think of it, Rebecca Mary could not understand how old Peter Simmons could come trumpeting into Riverside when no one was allowed to enter Riverside. It was shut off from the world and protected by a guard. But old Peter Simmons had managed to pass the guard, and he had come as a general in command. Was that because he was the

head of a large manufacturing plant. or was it because—because—— It couldn't be possible that
old Peter Simmons was the Big Boss of whom the
men spoke with such respect! But if he wasn't the
Big Boss why had the men treated him so defer-
entially and taken him at once to the forbidden
shop? And he had not been at all surprised to
hear that Granny was at Riverside. He had asked
for her at once. Rebecca Mary had to giggle as
she stood there in the fragrant silence and thought
what it meant if old Peter Simmons really was the
Big Boss of the Riverside experiment.

She was interrupted in the very middle of another
giggle for the door into Granny's room opened suddenly and there stood Granny, a much perplexed
but determined Granny. She wore her hat and
motor coat and carried a bag in one hand and an
umbrella in the other. Rebecca Mary wondered
where she had found the umbrella and why she carried it as she stared at her.

"Aren't you ready, Rebecca Mary?" asked
Granny in a stage whisper.

"Ready for what?" Rebecca Mary had to laugh
even though Granny did wear such a perplexed face
for she had to remember that other night when
Granny had come to her in her hat and motor coat.

Granny frowned. "I told you this morning that we would not stay here any longer. And now that old Peter Simmons has come I simply must leave at once. You have no idea, Rebecca Mary, what a tease that man can be. He never would let me forget that I started for Seven Pines and landed a prisoner at Riverside. If you had been teased for almost fifty years by a man like old Peter Simmons you'd understand how I feel. And he would be sure to ask me what I wanted for my golden wedding present. I've told you how I feel about that question. If I should hear it again I should scream. What is old Peter Simmons here for anyway? I didn't ask him to come for me. I never told him I was here. There must have been a leak, just what Major Martingale was afraid of."

But when Rebecca Mary told Granny her suspicions Granny looked at her in horrified surprise before she nodded her gray head. "I believe you are right," she said slowly. "That explains a lot of things I haven't been able to understand. No wonder young Peter was so sure he could get a letter to his grandfather. But that makes it just impossible for me to stay another minute, Rebecca Mary. Imagine what old Peter will say when he hears that I ran away from him only to run right to him. I haven't the nerves I used to have. The situation is too ridiculous. Come, we'll just slip away."

"I'm afraid they will hear me take the car out." Rebecca Mary did not think it would be as easy to slip away as Granny evidently did.

"We won't take the car. We each have two feet. We can climb the fence and once in the road some one is sure to pick us up. I declare I don't see why we didn't go before. If I had known that old Peter Simmons was the Big Boss I shouldn't have stayed a minute. We'll go—anywhere!" Granny flung out her hands, the umbrella and the bag, too, as if she didn't care a picayune where they went so long as they left Riverside. "If we stay here old Peter Simmons will be sure to talk to me. He's so resourceful and determined, and he does have such a way with him. I don't know why I feel like this, Rebecca Mary!" Her revolt was such a surprise to her that she had to speak of it whenever the golden wedding was mentioned. "I suppose this is just the last straw. I've been patient with old Peter Simmons for almost fifty years, but I can't be patient over my golden wedding present. And I can't be teased, so we must run away again."

"Poor little Granny!" Rebecca Mary slipped an

arm around her and hugged her. Even if she wasn't perfectly contented at Riverside, Rebecca Mary wasn't sure that she wanted to run away again. She had heard that a bird in the hand is worth a lot more than one in the bush. If she ran away with Granny she would leave behind her young Peter and Wallie and George and—and Count Ernach de Befort. She might never see one of them again.

Then she straightened her spine and her eyes flashed. If she didn't see them again it would be because they didn't care to see her. They could find her if they really wished to find her. They had been wonderful to her, and it had been splendid to be a popular girl, but perhaps they had given her so much devotion and so much attention just because she was the only girl at Riverside. She had spent a great many minutes wondering which of them she liked the best. It might be as interesting to learn which of them liked her the best, to prove if there was anything in the admiration they had expressed so freely. Which would find her first? Yes, she would run away with Granny and put them to the test, she decided just as Granny caught her arm between her fingers and her umbrella and shook her.

238

"Come, come, Rebecca Mary! Wake up. We must slip away before the men come back from the shop."

"Joan!" exclaimed Rebecca Mary, hesitating, although she had made up her mind.

"We'll leave Joan with her father. That is where a child should be, with her parents. Come, Rebecca Mary, or I'll go alone." And she crossed the room alone.

Rebecca Mary did not feel exactly comfortable to leave Joan with her father although she knew that Granny was right when she said a child belonged with her parents, but she ran after Granny and took the bag from her. She couldn't let Granny run away alone.

The lights were out in the hall, and they felt their way down the stairs. There was something fearsome in the slow descent for Granny's hand gripped her hard, and Granny's breath came in short quick gasps. There was no doubt in Rebecca Mary's mind that Granny really did not want to be teased by old Peter Simmons.

The front door stood wide open so that the moonlight made a bright splash between the dark walls. Rebecca Mary and Granny reached the threshold in safety. It only remained to dash across the lawn, climb the fence and turn up their noses at the authority of fat Major Martingale who had said no one could leave Riverside. The shrubbery would conceal them for more than half the way. Granny's hand relaxed, and she stopped breathing like a spent porpoise.

"I do believe we'll make it," she whispered excitedly.

And then she gave a little scream, for out of the shadow made by a white lilac emerged a short fat figure, and a curt voice asked them where they were going.

"Oh, Major Martingale!" Granny's voice quavered. "I thought you were at the shop with the other men. Whoever would have expected to meet you here!"

"Evidently you didn't." The Major was all grim suspicion. "May I ask where you are going?"

Granny pinched Rebecca Mary's arm. "It was so warm upstairs that we came down for a breath of air," she explained with a little sniff of defiance, as though she dared him to object to their desire for air.

"I'm glad you put on your hats and brought your baggage," remarked the Major coldly, and he glanced significantly at the umbrella and the bag.

240

"Night air is so deceptive, you can't tell when you will need an umbrella." He looked at the cloudless sky. "Or extra clothing." He wiped the perspiration from his hot forehead.

"Yes, isn't it!" Granny emulated Moses and was as meek as meek, butter would not have melted in her mouth just then. "Come, Rebecca Mary. Good-night, Major Martingale." And with Rebecca Mary's hand in hers she turned to the terrace as if she really had come down all hatted and coated for a walk in the moonlight.

"If it is so warm upstairs I shan't go to bed yet," Major Martingale fell in at her other hand. "I'll walk with you."

CHAPTER XVIII

GRANNY woke in the morning with a headache. Rebecca Mary found her with heavy eyes and flushed cheeks when she went in to see if she would get up for breakfast.

"I have such a headache," Granny moaned piteously.

"Poor dear!" Rebecca Mary put her fresh cool hand against Granny's hot old face. "Then you should stay in bed. You mustn't get up for breakfast."

"I shan't." Granny was a model of obedience. "I couldn't," she said with another moan. "I shan't be any good all day. I always have to stay in bed when I have one of these attacks, and I just want to be left alone. I don't want to see any one! You can tell old Peter Simmons that it was worrying over my golden wedding present that gave me this headache. That should make him ashamed of himself. No, I don't want a thing but to be left alone."

But Rebecca Mary shook up her pillows and

smoothed her bed and pulled down the shades and kissed her hot forehead, and said it was a horrid shame that she was ill, and she hoped that Granny would be better soon, and she certainly should tell old Peter Simmons what Granny had said. Then she tiptoed out and shut the door very softly behind her.

Old Peter Simmons was very sorry to hear that Granny was ill, and he thought she was very sensible to stay in bed until she was better; he knew those headaches and there was nothing for them but quiet and rest, but as for the golden wedding present——

"That's nonsense, perfect nonsense!" he declared stoutly. "Can't she trust me?"

Rebecca Mary slowly shook her head. "I think she feels that she has trusted you and now she isn't sure she can trust herself," she ventured demurely. It was rather fun for Rebecca Mary to stand before the great Peter Simmons and find fault with him.

"And my past is against me." Old Peter Simmons admitted it ruefully. "I don't know why it is so confoundedly hard to remember some things. You women! Can't you learn that an anniversary or a holiday is just a day, just one of the three hundred and sixty-five which make up a year?"

"Anniversaries and holidays are the decorations

243

of the year," Rebecca Mary told him quickly. He should have known that without being told. No one had ever had to tell her.

Old Peter Simmons looked at her from under his shaggy eyebrows. "You are all alike, you women," he grumbled. "And I guess men are pretty much alike, too. Decoration doesn't mean as much to us. But my wife might remember that I've had a good deal on my mind the last few years. She has, too," he admitted honestly. "Peter will never know how many nights his grandmother lay awake worrying about him. She did too much, all that Red Cross work during the war and all the refugee work after the war. And now she's worrying over this golden wedding of hers." He spoke as if the golden wedding belonged exclusively to Granny. "She should be home where she could look after it herself. She shouldn't be here."

"She can't help that!" Rebecca Mary was indignant that old Peter Simmons should blame Granny for what wasn't her fault. "She didn't want to stay."

"You made the rule yourself," stammered Major Martingale, who was waiting fussily to carry old Peter Simmons away. Major Martingale was indignant, also. "When we had so much trouble with

the labor agitators you said no one was to leave
Riverside. Absolutely no one, you said!" He
bristled like an angry turkey cock.

"Sure, I made the rule," admitted old Peter Simmons. "I made it for you and the boys and the
mechanics. But I didn't make it for my wife and
her friends."

"How did I know you hadn't sent her?" began the
Major bitterly, but old Peter Simmons wouldn't
let him finish.

"Why should I send a woman, two women, to a
place I had chosen for an important experiment
which I wanted to work out in secret? That's nonsense, Major! At the same time I believe that it
has done Mrs. Simmons good to be here. I'm glad
you did keep her. There hasn't been anything for
her to do so she has been able to get some rest.
It hasn't been bad for you, either, young lady."
And he nodded his grizzled head approvingly as he
looked at rosy cheeked Rebecca Mary.

"Women," muttered the Major in a dark dank
way, "are always interfering. They do their best
to ruin things for a man."

"Oh!" Rebecca Mary looked at old Peter Simmons for help.

He gave it to her at once. "My experience,
245

Major Martingale," he said slowly, "is that women help men more than they hinder them. I've had fifty years to prove a decision I made on my wedding day, that a woman perfects a man's life, and I know that I'm correct. Yes, I'll be right out," as the Major moved hastily and suggestively toward the door. "Don't wait for me."

"If you feel that way," Rebecca Mary said impulsively, "why do you tease Granny?" She was rather scared when she had put the question, but she looked at him as if she were not scared at all.

Old Peter Simmons seemed nonplussed for a moment. "On my soul, I don't know. Mrs. Simmons used to like me to tease her, and so I kept on. But I'm afraid she doesn't care for it as much as she did," he admitted ruefully.

"Indeed, she doesn't!" Rebecca Mary wondered why on earth he kept on teasing Granny when he knew Granny didn't like to be teased. Rebecca Mary was beginning to feel sorry for old Peter Simmons, although she did think that even the head of a big manufacturing plant should have room in his mind for anniversaries and holidays. His mind shouldn't be filled entirely with contracts.

"Does she honestly expect me to remember that golden wedding present?" The twinkle was more

pronounced than ever in old Peter Simmons' blue
eyes. "Can't you give me a clue?" he begged with
a chuckle, but Rebecca Mary couldn't. She hadn't
any idea herself what it was that Granny Simmons
and her husband had talked about so many times.
Granny Simmons had never told her.

So old Peter Simmons had to go away muttering
that women were the dickens, the very dickens.
That was exactly what they were. How was he to
know what one of them wanted for a golden wedding
present? And even if his wife had told him what
she wanted, if they had talked it over hundreds of
times together, how could he be sure that she would
want it on the golden wedding day? Women
changed their minds once a minute. A man was
never sure of them. But his eyes twinkled as he
grumbled, and Rebecca Mary's eyes twinkled, too.
There was no doubt that old Peter Simmons was the
greatest kind of a tease. Granny had described him
perfectly.

They were in the big parlor where the old por-
trait of Richard Cabot's great-grandmother hung.
Rebecca Mary never thought of that portrait as
Joshua Cabot's great-grandmother, but always as
Richard's great-grandmother. And when old Peter

Simmons went grumbling and twinkling away, Rebecca Mary looked up at the portrait.

"I wonder if your husband gave you what you wanted on holidays and anniversaries?" she asked impulsively. "And do you think your great-grandson will remember his golden wedding without being reminded?"

"I don't know what it is, but I'm sure this great-grandson will make a desperate effort to remember anything you want him to remember," exclaimed a voice behind her.

Like a red and yellow wooden top, Rebecca Mary swung around and saw—would wonders ever cease? —Richard Cabot, himself. It was not the Richard Cabot she had seen in Waloo for that Richard had always looked as if he had just stepped from a brand new bandbox and this Richard didn't look as if he had ever seen a bandbox. His hair was too rumpled and his clothes too crumpled. Rebecca Mary stared at him, her eyes and mouth big round O's of astonishment. Her heart suddenly climbed into her throat and promised to choke her as he crossed the room with quick eager steps.

"Aren't you going to say that you are glad to see me?" He took the hand she was far too surprised to offer him.

"Where did you come from?" She didn't seem able to find her every-day voice and had to use her Sunday one, which shook a little. "Are you a prisoner, too?" Rebecca Mary hoped that he was. Although there were four men at Riverside all devoted to her, you see she was not satisfied. She wanted a fifth, even if this fifth man did make her heart beat so uncomfortably. "There is a very jolly crowd of prisoners here," she added encouragingly. "I'm sure you will like them."

Richard looked from her sunburnt fingers to her face, which was a most adorable pink, and knew that he had not been mistaken—she was just what he had thought she was.

"If I had known you were here I should have come long ago," he said quite as if he could come and go as he pleased. Evidently he had not met stern Major Martingale. "How could you run away without leaving a word for me?" he went on reproachfully. "I tried to make old Pierson tell me where you were, but all she would say was that Granny had taken you on a motor trip. I thought that meant Seven Pines and called up the house only to be told by Mrs. Swenson that for the first time in seven years old Mrs. Simmons had disappointed her. She had promised to come to Otillie's

249

wedding and the wedding was on and Mrs. Simmons hadn't come. Mrs. Swenson didn't know whether to be mad or worried. And I was in the same boat. I wrote to Mifflin, and when I didn't hear a word from you I thought that perhaps you had decided that you didn't like bankers. I sure was sore!" He laughed softly as if now, with Rebecca Mary's hand still in his, it was rather amusing to remember how sore he had been.

Guilty consciousness was plainly written on Rebecca Mary's pink and white forehead. "It wasn't my fault." She made the best defense she could. "I didn't have a minute in which to send any one word. And since we have been here we couldn't send words. You must remember that I have been a prisoner." And she laughed as if it were the greatest fun in the world to be a prisoner.

"A prisoner in my great-grandmother's old home," smiled Richard, who had not been half as surprised to see her as Rebecca Mary had expected him to be. Indeed, he had not seemed surprised at all. "How do you like my great-grandmother?" he asked in a whisper as if he did not wish his great-grandmother to hear Rebecca Mary's answer.

"We're the greatest friends," she whispered back. "And I like your great-grandfather's old house enormously, but I don't quite like to be a prisoner."

"You'll be given your freedom soon," promised Richard, quite as if he knew all about her case. "Things are moving right along out there." He nodded in the direction of the shop. "I shouldn't be surprised if you were released very soon now."

"Are you interested in this mysterious experiment, too? Granny and I are dying to know about it for all that we are sure of is that an aviator, a chemical engineer and an electrical engineer and a United States Army officer and a Luxembourg count are working on it with a lot of Waloo mechanics. It is a very confusing combination. Major Martingale insists that it is, oh, frightfully important and that Germany is reaching out grabbing hands for it. He scowls like a pirate if we ask any questions at all. At first we thought it must have something to do with aeroplanes, on account of Peter, you know, and then we thought of a wireless something, but when the Luxembourg count was tangled up with it we stopped trying to imagine what it was. We hear the weirdest noises and smell the weirdest smells but they don't tell us anything." She smiled expectantly and waited for him to tell her all about the great experiment, but when he never told her a word but just smiled at her she

251

crinkled her nose and went on more slowly: "And now if a banker is added to the staff we shall be more hopelessly at sea than ever."

His smile grew into a laugh. "The banker hasn't very much to do with it, but Major Martingale is right. The thing is tremendously important. And Germany does want to grab it. It would do a lot to reinstate her commercially and she is still making every effort to get control of it. That's why Major Martingale has been so cautious. He didn't want to run any risk of a leak. Did you know that old Mr. Simmons is the Big Boss?" Then Rebecca Mary had guessed right. She was sure she had, but she liked to hear Richard tell her that she had.

"He brought me down with him last night and old Martingale caught me as soon as we passed the guard and carried me off to the shop. That is why I didn't see you last night and why now I'm so suggestive of 'the morning after.' But you haven't said yet that you were glad to see me," he said suddenly, and he took Rebecca Mary's other hand. "It has seemed a thundering long time since I saw you. Has it seemed long to you?" He bent his tall head so that he could look into her eyes.

But before Rebecca Mary could tell him whether

the days since she had seen him had dragged or whether they had exceeded the speed limit Major Martingale's harsh voice was heard in the hall.

"Cabot!" he bellowed. "Where are you?"

CHAPTER XIX

REBECCA MARY'S nose was out of joint. The great experiment proved so absorbing that at noon Ben carried sandwiches and milk to the shop, and Frederick Befort was the only man who joined Rebecca Mary and Joan at the big table in the dining room. Frederick Befort seemed in a strange mood. At one moment he would be wildly excited and tell some extravagant story which made the two girls laugh heartily, and the next minute he would frown at his plate or jump up and go to the window which overlooked the path which led to the shop.

"Those may be Luxembourg manners," Rebecca Mary thought disapprovingly. "But why isn't he at the shop with the others?"

"If Granny Simmons were here she'd say you had the fidgets," remarked Joan precociously. "She always tells me that I have the fidgets when I can't sit still."

"It is a day to make a man have the fidgets," and her father stopped on his way back from the

254

window to pat her cheek. "You will never know, *mignonne*, what this day means to your father."

"You could tell me?" hinted Joan.

But he only laughed and patted her cheek again before he went back to his place. Rebecca Mary looked at him curiously. What a strange man he was, not a bit like an American, like young Peter or—or Richard. She wasn't sure she understood him, he was so strange. But she really didn't bother very much about Frederick Befort then for she, too, was in a strange mood. She wanted to be by herself and think. She scarcely knew of what she wanted to think but she was conscious of a little glow of content. Perhaps if she went down by the river bank she could discover why she felt so contented and happy when she had been so restless and unreasonable. She was glad to hear Frederick Befort promise to play ball with Joan although she wondered again why he did not go to the shop, but that was his business, not hers.

She ran upstairs to find Granny asleep and with a sigh of relief she crossed the terrace on her way to the river bank. But Joan called to her from the tennis court and ran toward her. Rebecca Mary might have ignored the childish hail once, but she couldn't do it now, and she walked slowly toward the court.

"Look what my father made for me!" Joan demanded breathlessly. She always spoke of her father with an emphasis as if her father was made of "sugar and spice and everything nice" while other fathers were compounded of dust and water without a grain of seasoning. She held up what was meant to be a ball, but it was made from an old glove stuffed with—papers. Rebecca Mary could feel them crackle. The glove fingers were wound around the palm to hold the papers firm. It really wasn't much of a ball to any one but Joan, who capered proudly and almost snatched it from Rebecca Mary as if she could not quite trust even her with it. "My father made it for me," she repeated joyously.

Her father laughed. "Miss Wyman does not think that was any great feat, *ma petite*," he teased. "She does not think it is a very good ball."

Miss Wyman was a true descendant of George Washington, and she horrified Joan by confessing that Frederick Befort was right, and she had seen better balls than the one he had made out of an old glove and some scraps of paper.

"What do you really think yourself?" She

caught a tennis ball from the court, where it lay neglected, and showed him what a ball could be.

"But that's a ball from a store!" Joan saw the difference in a flash. "And my father never made a ball before. He said so. This is the first one he ever made, and he made it for me."

"No one else would accept it." He pinched her cheek. "Now, Joan, you must play by yourself. I must go to the shop, but I tell you again you cannot throw this ball I made over the hedge. It is not like a store ball."

"If you wait I'll show you!" Joan was only too eager to show what she could do, but he turned impatiently away.

"This may be the greatest day of my life, Miss Wyman." He stopped in front of her. "Will you be so very kind as to wish me luck?" He took the hand which hung at her side and pressed it.

She looked at him in surprise, and she was more surprised when she saw the flush on his usually pale face. She wondered why this should be such a great day, but as he did not tell her she did not ask but prettily offered her best wishes. He pressed her hand again and went toward the shop with long eager steps. Rebecca Mary looked after him curiously. She shook her head. No, she didn't understand him at all, not even a little bit. And because a closed box is always more fascinating than an open one she would have continued to think of Frederick Befort if Joan would have let her. But Joan was pulling her sleeve.

"I'll show you, then, Miss Wyman. Shall I? Shall I show you that I can throw my ball over the hedge?" She was on tiptoe to show Miss Wyman.

Rebecca Mary looked at the only hedge near them, the arbor vitæ which kept Riverside from spilling into the road, and shook her head. "You'll lose it if you do. You can't go after it, you know." She reminded Joan that she was a prisoner.

"The guard will bring it to me if I ask him." Joan was not a bit afraid that she would lose her ball even if Rebecca Mary did shake her head and doubt whether the guard would leave his post by the gate to hunt among the bushes which edged the road for a ball. She raised her arm to send the ball flying over the hedge, but Rebecca Mary caught her hand.

"I fear your father is not a very good ball maker, Joan. See, the fingers have come unfastened. The stuffing is falling out." She took the glove from Joan and tried to push the papers back into it.

"The stuffing is my father's papers. He took

258

them from his pocket," Joan told her proudly. "Can you put them back?"

"I'd better sew them in or they will be all over the place. Why——" she broke off to stare at one of the scraps of papers which had fallen into her hand. There were figures on it and a tiny drawing and a few German words. How strange! She pulled a larger piece from the glove and after she had smoothed it she found more German words.

Like an express train dashing through a country station many things dashed through Rebecca Mary's brain as she stood and looked at the bits of paper. She remembered what Major Martingale had said about the great experiment, how important it was and how Germany was trying to get control of it to regain her old position in the commercial world. She remembered that Frederick Befort had been named for one kaiser and had been a friend of another kaiser, who had decorated him. She remembered many things Joan had said about Germany and that the kaiser had called her *"ein gutes Kind, Johanna,"* and Joan's whisper that her father did not wish her to speak of Germany now, he wanted her to forget Germany. She remembered also that Frederick Befort had said he was from Luxembourg where the Germans had had great influence and power, that he had gone to school in Germany. And Mrs. Erickson had heard him talking German to one of the mechanics behind the woodshed!

Rebecca Mary had heard many a spy story during the war, and she shivered as she looked at the bits of paper in her hand. Oh, it couldn't be possible that Frederick Befort had come to the Simmons factory, that he had come to Riverside to obtain possession of the secret of this great experiment which was to do so much for the world. He couldn't be one of the German secret agents which the newspapers had had so much to say about during the war. It wasn't possible, and yet when she had added one to one and then to two and three she could obtain but one answer.

The work at Riverside was practically finished. Richard had told her so that morning. Frederick Befort would have all the information he wanted by now, and, of course, he would wish to get it to Germany as soon as possible. That was why he had torn his papers and stuffed them into an old glove which Joan was to throw over the hedge. If the guard saw it he would think it was only a child's plaything. A confederate was hiding in the bushes and would catch the ball when it was tossed out. The whole plan had been skillfully thought out and was now as plain as print to Rebecca Mary's horrified mind.

Joan pulled her sleeve impatiently. "Can't you fix it? Let me take it and throw it over the hedge as my father told me." She tried to take the ball from Rebecca Mary.

"No, no! Leave it alone, Joan, or you'll have the papers all over the grass." She had to think like chain lightning. "I'll run in and sew it up. Don't tell your father," she cautioned chokingly. "He wouldn't like it if he knew that his ball came to pieces so soon."

With the ball in her hand, and Joan trotting along beside her, she went back to the house wondering what on earth she should do and how she could get rid of Joan for a few minutes. Joan found the way herself when she saw the farmhouse kitten asleep on the steps.

"It has run away. I'd better take it right back or Mrs. Erickson will be cross with me again. She said I was always taking her things and forgetting to bring them back."

"Yes, run over with the kitten." Rebecca Mary knew if Joan once ran over she would stay for some time, long enough perhaps to forget about the ball, for there were wonderful things to interest a child at the farmhouse.

Rebecca Mary shut the door of her room and turned the key before she pulled the rest of the papers from the old glove. Oh, there was no doubt about it! The papers were covered with drawings and German words. Rebecca Mary groaned. What should she do? She put her hands over her eyes to shut out the sight of those German words, but she could not shut the thought of them from her brain. She felt nauseated. To think that a man would use his little daughter as Frederick Befort had planned to use Joan. It was despicable. She never wanted to see Frederick Befort again, and she had liked him so much. Why, only this noon—— She began to understand now his extravagant gayety at luncheon, he had thought his work was done, and he had stayed with them to find a way for Joan to give the information he had collected to his confederates. No one would suspect Joan. And she had wished him luck! She groaned again. It was all so very plain to her that she turned and hid her face against the back of the chair.

After a long, long time, five minutes perhaps, she rose suddenly and with her lips pressed tight together went to the desk and found an envelop in which she put the scraps of paper. She looked about for a place to hide the package for it was too bulky to carry in her pocket.

Where would be a good place? She opened the closet door. Across one end were several drawers and above them were two shelves. On the top shelf was a bandbox. Rebecca Mary climbed up to the bandbox and looked into it. She took out a hat and turning it over, tucked her package inside the lining. Then she replaced the hat and put the box on the shelf. She stood in the doorway and gazed anxiously at the box. It looked as innocent as a box could look. No one ever would imagine that it held a secret. Rebecca Mary sighed as she shut the closet door.

Then she took several sheets of Sallie Cabot's best note paper and drew meaningless lines on them and wrote what might be taken at a careless glance for German words, and tore the paper into scraps with which she stuffed the old glove. She would let Joan toss it over the hedge so Joan could tell her father. If Frederick Befort thought his plans had reached his confederate he would do nothing more. He couldn't get away himself, and Rebecca Mary would have a little time in which to think what she should do. She must tell someone, not Major Martingale, he would be merciless, but Peter, or, no—Richard! Richard would be the man for her to tell. But, oh, how she did hate to tell any one. Suppose she should speak to Frederick Befort himself, persuade him to promise to forget everything that had happened at Riverside, to remain true to the oath he had given Major Martingale? If she could do that —if she only could.

She had liked Frederick Befort. He was so different from any man she had ever met. He had fascinated her with his talk of courts and grand duchesses and emperors, she thought now a little bitterly. There was an air of mystery about him which would pique a girl's interest, but if the mystery meant that he was a German secret agent she wouldn't be interested another minute. She would only be horrified and disgusted. Oh, what should she do? Never had a teacher in the third grade of the Lincoln school been given such a problem to solve. If only she could wake up and find that it was a dream she would be so happy to forget it all. She shouldn't want to remember this when she was sixty, she told herself drearily.

But it wasn't a dream. The old glove on the

desk told her it wasn't, and she took it in her hand. "Well, Count Ernach de Befort," she said under her breath, "I have spoiled your scheme for the present. If Joan throws this to your confederate he will be puzzled what to make of it."

Even as she spoke Joan pounded on the door.

"Are you there, Miss Wyman? Have you mended the ball my father made me? Can't you be quicker? I want to throw it over the hedge before my father comes to dinner."

And she did throw it over the hedge as she stood on the tennis court. It was a good throw for a little girl, and Joan was jubilant as she ran across the court and climbed up on the stone wall, behind the arbor vitæ to see where the ball had fallen. Rebecca Mary ran too, although her legs did feel too weak to carry her, and her heart was beating so fast. She caught the toes of her white oxfords in a cranny of the wall and lifted herself so that she might look. But although they both looked and looked there was no ball to be seen on that stretch of the road. Down by the gate the guard was leaning against the fence, but the guard was not a ball, and they were looking for a ball.

"It's gone!" Joan was surprised. "Some one

must have taken it. Who do you think it was, Miss Wyman, a fairy or an ogre?"

"An ogre!" Rebecca Mary said fiercely. She felt so fierce that she was faint. "A horrid black ogre. Oh, Joan! Why did you throw it?" she wailed.

CHAPTER XX

REBECCA MARY'S feet were as heavy as lead as she went back to the house, and her heart was far heavier than her feet. Oh, Cousin Susan, Cousin Susan, what a tangle you caught Rebecca Mary in when you persuaded her to take out a memory insurance policy!

It was later than she had thought, but the men had not come up from the shop. Ben told her that they weren't coming, that he had just taken them something to eat. He supposed that they would work all night again.

Rebecca Mary looked at him blankly. She had thought that all she would have to do would be to return to the house and call Richard aside and slip her responsibility from her slim shoulders to his broad back. She was so disappointed that she felt almost sick. What should she do?

"Is Mr. Befort at the shop?" she asked Ben, trying her best to keep her voice steady and her chin from trembling.

"Yas'm, he's there with all the rest of 'em.

They's gwine to make a night ob it fo' suah. Will you gwine have yo' dinner now, Miss Wyman? It's ready an' it won't be no better fer waitin'."

Rebecca Mary was so relieved to hear that Frederick Befort was at the shop that her chin stopped trembling. If Frederick Befort was with the other men, with Richard and young Peter and old Peter, he wasn't trying to get in touch with his confederates, and she could draw a long breath. It didn't seem as if she had had a good breath since she had seen the scraps of paper fall from the old glove.

"Just a minute, Ben, until I run up and see if Mrs. Simmons feels well enough to come down."

"She don't," grumbled Ben. "Ah asted her an' she said Ah was ter brung her up a tray. Folks seems to think Ah hain't got nothin' else ter do but carry dinner here an' there an' yonder. Three in one night is more than one nigger's job."

"I know." Rebecca Mary was as sympathetic as she could be with her mind full of something so much more important than dinner. "But perhaps it won't happen again. You might serve Mrs. Simmons first. She didn't eat any luncheon, and she must be hungry."

As Rebecca Mary's leaden feet carried her up the stairs she wondered if she should tell Granny and show her the proof of her story which was in the bandbox in her closet. But as soon as she saw Granny in a thin lavender negligee on the *chaise longue* she decided that she wouldn't tell her. Granny couldn't do anything, and she had enough to bother about. Indeed, Granny did look pale and tired from spending her day with the headache. She held out a welcoming hand when Rebecca Mary came in.

"Where have you been all afternoon? I thought you were lost."

"Have you missed me?" Rebecca Mary stooped to kiss the pale cheek. "You were so sound asleep when I looked in that I thought you wouldn't be awake for hours. I'm a brute that I didn't come in again."

"I really haven't been awake very long," Granny admitted when she heard how repentant Rebecca Mary was. "I do wish I were home, Rebecca Mary. It was so silly to run away as we did. I might have known something would happen. I'd give anything if we could be back in Waloo before old Peter Simmons. I shan't mind his teasing so much at home. I shan't feel quite so foolish there. A woman can't stand up to her husband as well as she should if

269

she feels foolish. I don't suppose there is any way we could slip out?" she asked wistfully.

No, Rebecca Mary didn't think there was any way, and even if there had been she couldn't take it until she had told her story to Richard and showed him the scraps of paper. But she would not tell Granny that; she could only kiss Granny again and pet her and tell her that Richard had said that they would be free soon to go where they pleased.

She told Granny also what old Peter Simmons had said, that he had proved the decision he had made on his wedding day, that his wife had perfected his life. She made a very pretty speech of it, and it pleased Granny enormously.

"He always did have a nimble tongue," she murmured. "And he really does have a lot of patience with me. Here is Ben with my dinner. I hope you brought a lot, Ben. You know I didn't have any luncheon."

"Yas'm. Ah hopes you gwine ter like the lower half of this spring chicken, Mrs. Simmons? When Ah took the dinner out ter the shop Mr. Simmons, he sez what you gwine give Mrs. Simmons fer her dinner? An' when Ah done tell him spring chicken he sez ter brung you de lower half 'cause you gwine ter like de dark meat better 'n you do de white."

"He did?" Granny was surprised. "Well! well! So he does know what I like. Rebecca Mary, why do you suppose he always asks me? Perhaps he has remembered other things, too. Didn't I tell you he was a great tease? Run down to your own dinner, child. I shall do very well. And you and Joan must be hungry."

Rebecca Mary had never felt less hungry in her life but she obediently ran down. She thought she wouldn't eat a mouthful until she saw the array of good things which Ben had prepared when she suddenly discovered that she was hungry. Nothing would be gained by starving herself, she thought, as she patted Joan's shoulder.

"We shall serve ourselves," she told Ben. "And will you please go over to the shop and ask Mr. Cabot if I may speak to him at once?"

"Ah dunno as Ah dares. Old Mr. Simmons said he didn't want ter see any one 'thin gunshot ob dat shop ter night. Maybe Ah could stand away an' holler," he suggested helpfully.

"Never mind then." Rebecca Mary spoke as carelessly as she could. "Perhaps he'll be up before long."

"If you ast me Ah'd say they won't be along 'fo' sunrise. Ah'm to take 'em another meal at mid-

271

night. That 'speriment suah makes 'em hungry."

"You can tell Mr. Cabot then that I should like to speak to him at once." Midnight was better than nothing, than morning.

"Yas'm. Maybe Ah can. Ah can try."

"Do you want to tell we why you want to talk to Mr. Cabot?" asked Joan curiously. "You haven't talked to me very much since we came to dinner."

"I think I must be tired. Suppose you talk to me? What did Mrs. Erickson say when you took the kitten back?" It was a safe question for Mrs. Erickson was sure to say considerable. Joan repeated Mrs. Erickson's words and added enough of her own to last through dinner. She caught Rebecca Mary's hand as they rose from the table.

"Shall we go and play ball, Miss Wyman? I have a new tennis ball I borrowed from Mr. Marshall."

Ball! Rebecca Mary never wanted to see another ball in her life. There had been one ball too many in it as it was. She forced herself to smile at Joan. "I must go up to Granny, honey," she said slowly. "She has been alone all day. You will have to play by yourself. If Mr. Cabot comes

up from the shop, or Mr. Peter, or even old Mr.
Simmons, will you call me, please?"

She stood in the doorway and looked across the
lawn in the direction of the shop. The chatter of
the gasoline engine came to her faintly, puff-puff.
She wondered if she should run across and call to
Richard herself, and she decided that she had better
wait. She must do nothing to make Frederick
Befort suspect that she knew why he was at Riverside.

When at last she went upstairs she found that
Granny was not inclined for conversation.

"If you'll hand me that book, Rebecca Mary, I'll
finish it. There is a silly little heroine in it who
can't make up her mind which of three men she loves."

"Do you think it is always easy for a girl to
know what to do?" Rebecca Mary asked wistfully.
Rebecca Mary was almost overwhelmed at the number of things she had discovered that a girl should
know.

Granny began a rather scornful speech but as
she looked at Rebecca Mary's troubled little face
she changed it for a more sympathetic one.

"No, I don't. I think it's very hard sometimes
for every one, for even an old lady, to know what is
best to do. But if you were in a book, Rebecca

Mary, it would be easy. All you would have to do would be to wait for your knight of the four-leaf clover," she laughed.

"Oh, that!" Rebecca Mary had lost all pleasure in her mysterious talisman; it had brought her all at once such a huge amount of bad luck. "But how am I going to find him?" she asked impatiently. "It's weeks since that day at the Waloo, and I don't know any more than I did then."

"Don't you?" Granny raised quizzical eyebrows.

"Well, not much." Rebecca Mary didn't wish to talk of clover leaves, but it would be easier to follow Granny's lead than to offer one of her own. If she talked of what was really in her thoughts she would frighten Granny into hysterics. "I know that Peter and Mr. Cabot were there that afternoon and Wallie Marshall and George Barton. Even old Major Martingale was there eating hot buttered toast, but I can't make one of them say that he gave me that clover leaf. You don't think it was Major Martingale, do you?" Rebecca Mary would rather never know the truth if fat old Major Martingale had given her the talisman.

Granny chuckled. "Ask him, Rebecca Mary. Run along and ask him. You are sillier than this silly heroine."

Rebecca Mary never passed such an evening in her life. It was long, endlessly long, and dreary and lonely, for Joan went to bed and Granny insisted on following the adventures of her silly heroine. Rebecca Mary thought she would go mad as she stood on the terrace and listened to the chattering gasoline engine or raced up the stairs to see if the bandbox was still on the top shelf of her closet.

At last she couldn't wait another minute. She didn't care what old Peter Simmons had told Ben. She would go within gunshot of the shop and call to—she wasn't sure yet whether she would call for Frederick Befort and beg him to turn over a new leaf and be loyal to the men with whom he was working, or to Richard and tell him the suspicion which was tormenting her. She couldn't go to bed until she had told some one. She called herself names because she hadn't gone to the shop at once.

Ben had forgotten to turn on the lights and the hall stretched before her as dark as Egypt. She felt as if she were making her way through a length of black velvet as she went down the stairs. But as she turned to run out of the side door, which was the shortest way to the shop, she saw a thread of light. It came from the right, from the room

Major Martingale used as an office. The door was always kept locked, but now it was ajar.

Through the wide crack Rebecca Mary could see a light on the desk beside which a man was standing as he fumbled among the Major's papers. He was too tall and not wide enough to be Major Martingale, and even before he turned so that the light fell on his face Rebecca Mary knew who he was.

Quickly, without taking even a second to think, Rebecca Mary pulled the door shut. The key was in the lock, on the outside, and she turned it. Then she leaned against the door frightened to death and ready to cry.

CHAPTER XXI

REBECCA MARY had caught a spy! And, oh, how she wished that she hadn't. When she turned the key she had felt like Joan of Arc but immediately she became the most arrant little coward that ever was. She leaned against the door and trembled in every inch. She didn't know what to do with her spy now that she had caught him.

Of course, there was but one thing to do. She would have to tell old Peter Simmons and give him the key. And now that she had Frederick Befort locked in Major Martingale's office she was sorry. She had liked Frederick Befort. He was so different from any man she ever had met. He had seemed romance to her with his title, his centuries-old château, his rose-embowered country, his stories of boar hunts and kaisers and grand duchesses, and all sorts of people such as Rebecca Mary had never met on her way to and from the Lincoln school.

But Rebecca Mary had learned a lot of the little grand duchy about which she had known so little, and she knew that while there were many men in

Luxembourg who had hated and feared German power there were others who would have welcomed it. Frederick Befort had told her that himself, and she had read it in a book, also. Frederick Befort had been at school in Germany, he had been born and raised almost in Germany; only the width of a river had separated him from Germany. How did they really know whether he actually had come from the Luxembourg side of the River Sure? But whether he was in sympathy with Germany or not he had stolen the secret of the great experiment which Germany wanted. That was the one thing Rebecca Mary was sure of. She had the proof of that.

And if he was a traitor he should suffer only— only—— There was Joan! As she remembered Joan, Rebecca Mary wanted to open the door and plead with Frederick Befort, make him promise to forget all about Germany, to keep faith with old Peter Simmons. If he would do that, if he could make Rebecca Mary trust him again she might—she might—— It would be too horrible for Joan to be labeled the daughter of a spy.

It was so horrible to Rebecca Mary that her hand was on the key when she heard a smothered exclamation and a thud as if a movable body had suddenly come in contact with an immovable body. Rebecca

Mary cowered down beside the door and held her breath until the hall was flooded with light, and she raised her frightened eyes and saw Richard Cabot staring at her.

"What are you doing there?" He could not believe that she was listening. Rebecca Mary was not the sort of a girl who would listen at keyholes.

"H-sh!" She waved a frantic beckoning hand to him. She was so glad that it was Richard who had found her. He was so sensible, so dependable, he was Waloo's youngest bank vice-president and so was a man whom many people trusted. She had never appreciated what it meant to be sure she could trust a man before. A little glow broke through the smothering blackness which had enshrouded her as she thought of how she could trust Richard. Rebecca Mary knew that she was quite incapable of handling this situation, but she knew that Richard could handle it. She could not imagine a situation which Richard could not handle. So when Richard asked her with a compelling mixture of curiosity and determination: "What's in there?" she stammered painfully, but she told him. "A leak!"

"A leak?" he repeated stupidly for he had not heard the words Major Martingale and the others were constantly using and which had impressed

themselves upon Rebecca Mary's brain. He stared
at the hand which clung to the door knob. If there
was a leak, although Richard did not see how that
could be for there were no pipes in the office to leak,
did Rebecca Mary think she could stop it by clinging to the door?

Rebecca Mary put out her other hand and
clutched his arm. She had to feel him as well as
see him. "I know Major Martingale has been
afraid of a leak," she faltered, "and as I was coming down the stairs I saw that this door was open.
You know it always has been kept locked." She
went on more hurriedly after she had started as if
she wished to finish her story as soon as possible.
"And I saw a man at Major Martingale's desk. I
did! It wasn't my imagination. I really saw him
and I shut the door and—and locked it. He hasn't
made a sound so he couldn't have heard me. But—
but I'm frightened!" And indeed she looked frightened.

Richard frowned, but he put his hands over the
fingers on his arm. "Did you see who he was?"
he asked quickly in a hushed voice, almost a whisper.

She didn't answer. She simply couldn't tell him
that she had, that the man who was rifling Major
Martingale's desk was Frederick Befort, Count

Ernach de Befort. Richard pressed her fingers gently.

"Was it Befort?" he asked in that same quick whisper.

Rebecca Mary pulled her fingers from him. "How did you know? Oh, I've told you! I've just the same as told you!" She covered her face with her hands.

Richard reached behind her and turned the key in the lock so that the door could be opened while Rebecca Mary watched him in cold despair. She couldn't understand why he did that. Surely Richard could be trusted. After Richard had unlocked the door he put his arm around Rebecca Mary and drew her out on the terrace.

"But—but——" objected Rebecca Mary, who couldn't understand why he wanted to take her away unless he wished to give Frederick Befort an opportunity to escape.

"Rebecca Mary," Richard said most irrelevantly as he drew her out with him, "you are a goose. A dear little goose," he added as if to explain to Rebecca Mary exactly what kind of a goose she was.

Rebecca Mary pulled herself away impatiently. Why should Richard waste time calling her names when there was a spy in Major Martingale's office?

She stammered as she tried to tell him that there were other things for him to do now than to call her names. With a laugh Richard tightened the arm which was still around her.

"I'm going to tell you something," he said, bending his head so that he could speak directly into her pink ear. "When you locked Befort in the office you locked up the man who invented the thing we are working on. Yes, you did!" as Rebecca Mary pushed him away with a funny little strangled exclamation. "Wait a minute and listen! Yes, I know that we have all been afraid of a leak, but there hasn't been one. No, there hasn't! Listen! You know Befort comes from Luxembourg?" Rebecca Mary nodded a dazed head. She did know that, from the River Sure. "And how hot he is at the way the Germans have treated his country and his grand duchess? He was so mad that he couldn't stay neutral. He joined the French Foreign Legion and fought until he was wounded and discharged. He had invented this—this"—evidently Richard didn't know what to call the great experiment when he was talking to Rebecca Mary—"this thing," he said at last. "He had talked about it to the kaiser before he perfected it, and the kaiser wanted him to promise to give the thing to Germany. Joan and her mother had come to this country. The countess was an American, you know. She died and Befort came over for Joan. He decided he couldn't find a safer place to work out his idea than the United States. He came to Waloo and worked alone for months. Then he discovered that German agents were watching him, and he was afraid they would steal his plans. He was in the bank one day and talked to me. He never spoke of Joan so perhaps it isn't strange that I didn't connect your loan child with him. I arranged for him to meet Mr. Simmons. The thing was just in his line, and he could give Befort protection. Mr. Simmons found him a place in his factory and mechanics to help him and got the government interested for it is a big thing, a mighty big thing. Everybody came down here to finish up the job where there would be no chance of German I. W. W. interference. But you see Befort didn't have to steal the plans. He had them in the brain that invented them."

"Oh!" Rebecca Mary couldn't say another word to save her life. Her face crimsoned. She wished the terrace would open and drop her into Pekin or Shanghai. She didn't care which. How could she have made such a mistake? "But the ball!" she exclaimed suddenly, and she told Richard about the glove which Frederick Befort had turned into a ball and which was stuffed with drawings and notes for something.

"I've no doubt it was. Befort has a lot of ideas, and if he took any papers from his pocket they would be sure to be covered with drawings and figures. As for German words, you know he was practically brought up in Germany?"

"Yes," sighed Rebecca Mary. It was all so clear now that Richard had explained it to her. "No wonder you called me a goose," she said ruefully.

"A dear little goose!" When Richard was quoted he wished to be quoted exactly. His voice was very tender as he corrected Rebecca Mary.

"A goose," repeated Rebecca Mary somewhat crossly. She was in no mood for tenderness, she was too ashamed and mortified. She was almost inclined to blame Richard for the mistake she had made. If he had only told her something—anything. But if he hadn't come stumbling over the hall chair she might have accused Frederick Befort to his face. "Oh," she wailed, "I never want to see Frederick Befort again! What shall I do? I never want to see him again!"

"Don't you?" Richard seemed quite pleased to

hear that she had seen enough of the romantic
Luxembourg count. He had feared that Rebecca
Mary might wish to see a lot more of him. "Well,
you don't have to see him again," he said quickly.
"I'm going to Waloo in the morning, and I'll take
you with me."

"Will you?" Rebecca Mary couldn't believe there
was such a simple solution to her puzzle. "Can
you?" She remembered that one could not go from
Riverside as one pleased.

"Sure I can." Richard spoke quite confidently.
"I'd take you this minute but you've worn yourself
out over this thing and you need sleep."

"I don't feel that I shall sleep until I am back
in Waloo," sighed Rebecca Mary, and her lip quivered.

"Yes, you will. You'll be asleep as soon as your
head touches the pillow now that you have nothing
to bother over. You meet me at—is six-thirty too
early? I have to go up and back before noon so I
must start early."

He couldn't start too early to suit her. "There's
Granny!" Rebecca Mary had almost forgotten
Granny.

If Richard had thought he was going to take an
early morning ride with no one but Rebecca Mary

he hid his disappointment very well when he learned that they were to have company.

"Sure, there's Granny. We'll take her with us."

"And Joan?" doubtfully. Perhaps Richard would think that Joan should be left with her father.

But Richard didn't. "Joan, too. Her father will be too busy for the next twenty-four hours to look after her. He was so excited we had to send him away to-day." So that was why Frederick Befort had not been at the shop. "It has been a great day for him and unless I miss my guess there will be a greater one to-morrow." And so that was why Frederick Befort had asked her to wish him luck. Rebecca Mary blushed again as Richard went on. "Six-thirty, you know. And not a word to any one!" And lowering his voice, he whispered a few directions. He chuckled as if he were going to enjoy carrying Rebecca Mary away from Riverside. There seemed to be more in his mind than he was telling Rebecca Mary.

But Rebecca Mary was not critical nor observing. She was only grateful.

"I'll never forget your heavenly goodness!" she exclaimed as she turned to go in and tell Granny that they were to leave Riverside at six-thirty in the morning, that Granny was to have her wish and reach home before old Peter Simmons. "I'll re-member it to my dying day!"

"Will you, Rebecca Mary?" Richard seemed quite pleased to hear how long he was to be remembered, and he caught her hand and pressed it before he let her go. "Will you?"

CHAPTER XXII

IF Richard was a tower of strength that night he was a veritable magician the next morning, for he extracted the two women and a half from a carefully guarded place as easily as most men would take a friend out for a walk or to a theater or church. Granny had been delighted to accept Richard's kind invitation to run away to Waloo. Her faded blue eyes sparkled when Rebecca Mary gave it to her.

"Of course, I'll go," she said at once. "It's too great a strain to be under the same roof with old Peter Simmons. I'm crazy to see him, Rebecca Mary, but I don't dare. Perhaps if I run away again he'll know that I don't want to be teased. I simply can't discuss a golden wedding present now. We've done it too often. But I don't know what I'll do, Rebecca Mary, if he doesn't remember what we planned. If I weren't so proud I should tell him that it begins with an H. But I can't even do that, Rebecca Mary. It's funny I should feel this way after fifty years, but I do. I can't help it even if I do know how silly it is."

So in the early morning Granny and Rebecca Mary and a very sleepy Joan left the house as stealthily as if they had been robbing Riverside and made their way from one clump of shrubbery to another to the gate. It thrilled Rebecca Mary, whose teeth fairly chattered. It even thrilled old Granny a bit, but it only puzzled Joan, who could not understand why she had been wakened so early nor why she was being taken from Riverside without saying good-by to her father although Granny told her that they had left a note for her father and one for old Peter Simmons. How Rebecca Mary did blush when Count Ernach de Befort was mentioned!

Before they reached the gate Richard came down the driveway in the car which had brought Granny and Rebecca Mary and Joan to Riverside. He stopped to speak to the guard, who was on the other side of the car so that the three prisoners were able to slip by it and hide themselves in the bushes which were most conveniently placed just outside the gate.

"Pooh!" exclaimed Granny as she settled herself in the tonneau with Joan, "if I had known how easy it would be I shouldn't have stayed twenty-four hours. Oh, well, I don't know as I care so long as I shall get home before old Peter Simmons. We have had a rest and a change. I don't often find fault with an experience after it is over. I did want to go to Seven Pines before the golden wedding, but perhaps it is just as well. You haven't anything to complain of, have you, Rebecca Mary? Riverside was more interesting for you than Seven Pines would have been. Wasn't it?"

"Much more interesting!" Rebecca Mary had never seen a foot of Seven Pines and so should not have been so quick to decide that Riverside was more interesting. "I'm glad that Major Martingale made prisoners of us." And then she remembered what had happened the last day she had been a prisoner, and she flushed and stammered. "At least I was glad." She looked at Richard to see if he remembered the secret that they shared, and he nodded and smiled. Rebecca Mary did not like to think of that last night. It made her hot all over, from the top of her head to her very heels, to remember what she had done. She hoped that no one but Richard would ever know.

"We're going home, we're going home," sang Joan to an air of her own composition. "I'm the only one who has what we came for," she announced

290

jubilantly. "I came for my father and I found him right away. But you haven't your young heart, have you, Granny? And dear Miss Wyman hasn't found the payment for her insurance, have you, Miss Wyman?" How disappointed Granny and Rebecca Mary must be!

"Perhaps I didn't find the real young heart I wanted, Joan, but then I knew that an old body isn't just the place for a real young heart," Granny confessed honestly. "But my old heart is a lot younger than it was. It makes an old heart young in just the right way to match an old body to be with young people, you know." She gave the prescription gravely to Joan, and Joan received it as gravely.

"That makes two of us who have what we came for." Joan was even more jubilant. "I'm sorry you haven't, Miss Wyman." Miss Wyman couldn't know how sorry she was.

But Rebecca Mary didn't want sympathy from any one, and she said so at once. "Indeed I did make a payment on my memory insurance policy, Joan. I made a lot of payments. Why, at the rate I've been paying I shan't be able to collect all the payments on that memory insurance policy, not if I live to be a hundred!"

Joan bounced up and down on the seat beside Granny. "Then it's time to go home," she said with funny solemnity. "When you get what you want it is always time to go home."

They stopped at a farmhouse to telephone to Pierson to have breakfast ready for them, and when they reached the house a most delicious breakfast was waiting in the dining room.

"I'm glad you're back, Mrs. Simmons," Pierson said. "Young Mrs. Simmons and I don't agree about the arrangements for your golden wedding."

"Don't you, Pierson?" smiled Granny. "I wonder if you and I will agree about them. If we don't you must remember that the golden wedding is mine. Gracious, but I am glad to be home again where I can look after things myself! I declare, Rebecca Mary, I can't think now why we ever went away. I must have been in a panic."

"Mr. Simmons came about fifteen minutes after you left, ma'am," explained Pierson, who stood beside Granny, eager to tell her what had happened. "He was quite put out, I can tell you, when I told him you had gone on a motor trip. He wanted to know where——"

"You couldn't tell him that, could you, Pierson?" Granny seemed quite pleased to think that Pierson couldn't. "You didn't know where we were. We haven't been near Seven Pines."

"No, ma'am, I know. Mrs. Swenson called me up to ask where you were. But when Mr. Simmons asked me the way he did he got me all flustered and before I knew it I told him you had gone to the Cabot country place. You often go there, you know, Mrs. Simmons, so it wasn't strange I told him you were probably at Riverside."

Granny put down her knife and fork and stared at her. "You never told him that, Pierson?" She hid her face in her napkin, and her shoulders shook. "What did he say? What did Mr. Simmons say, Pierson?"

"He didn't say anything for a minute, ma'am, and then he laughed in a funny sort of a way. 'At Riverside?' he said, ma'am. 'Well, I'll be darned! The devil she is!' That's exactly what he said. But you often go there as Mr. Simmons knows, and yet he seemed surprised as anything to hear you might have gone there now. But I had to tell him something, Mrs. Simmons, when he asked me like he did."

Granny was laughing so that she almost choked. "Pierson," she said when she could control her voice, "I shall raise your wages. I never suspected that you had an imagination. No wonder Mr. Simmons wasn't surprised to find us at Riverside. I dare say Major Martingale told him, too, and young Peter, in spite of their promise to me. Dear, dear! Mr. Simmons always seems to get the best of me." She shook her head ruefully. "I wonder what he said when he found that we had run away from Riverside."

"He probably said 'Well, I'll be darned' again," laughed Richard as he repeated a phrase which was often on old Peter Simmons' lips when he was surprised. "You mustn't be too hard on him, Granny. You know this experiment is frightfully important and—you know him," he finished rather lamely.

"I do," nodded Granny. "If I didn't know him I should never have done a lot of things that I have. You must put off fireworks to make old Peter Simmons see anything besides his business. If men weren't so queer women wouldn't have to be so peculiar," she sighed. "You might remind old Peter Simmons that he was married at noon. It would be just like him to come in at night," she prophesied gloomily.

"Mr. Simmons won't be late," Richard promised somewhat rashly. "I'll see myself that he is here by noon."

"You always were a good dependable boy. I can trust you. It is a great thing, Rebecca Mary, to have a man about whom you can trust." There was something so significant in the way she spoke that Rebecca Mary turned pink until she matched the sweet peas in the center of the table.

She looked so pretty in her self-conscious confusion that Richard had to stop eating omelet and muffins and look at her.

Granny went to telephone to young Mrs. Simmons about the golden wedding, and Joan ran after Pierson to tell her all that they had found at Riverside. Rebecca Mary pushed back her chair and rose, too. She just couldn't sit there and let Richard stare at her as he was doing. It made her feel—she could scarcely tell you how it did make her feel when she remembered the way Richard had comforted her the night before. She could still feel the pressure of his arm about her when he had told her that she was a goose. She slipped out on the porch where Richard found her in the swing beside the rambler rose.

She looked up with a smile. "It doesn't seem as if it could be true that we are free again. I think it was wonderful the way you got us out of Riverside."

He smiled, too. "Can you keep a secret?" he asked impulsively.

"I can!" She turned a curious face toward him. "I'm a perfect wonder at keeping secrets. I love 'em so I just can't give them away. Do tell me one!"

"I hate to be told how wonderful I am when I haven't been wonderful at all," he said honestly. "So I'll confess that Mr. Simmons asked me to bring you and Granny and Joan home."

"He did?" Rebecca Mary couldn't believe it. She visualized the caution with which Granny had slipped from bush to bush, how stealthily she had crept to the gate. And there had been no need of caution. How old Peter Simmons could tease Granny now! By running away from his teasing she had only given him more material with which to tease her. "She'll be furious," she said, not sure but she was a little furious herself.

"She must never know." Richard reminded her that what he had given her was a secret. "Mr. Simmons said if Granny could slip out of Riverside and get home before he did she would think she was getting the better of him and be a lot happier."

"The dear old man," breathed Rebecca Mary,

forming a new opinion of old Peter Simmons instantly. "What next?"

"And he asked me to bring her to Waloo. That's all, but you see you can't pin any cross on me. I was just obeying orders. I thought you would enjoy the joke, but we won't tell Granny. Let her think that she did get ahead of Mr. Simmons."

"I should say so. That dear old Peter Simmons to let Granny retreat with honor! He's not such a bad sort if he does forget his anniversaries and presents and things. Dear me, how long ago it seems since we ran away from here! Otillie Swenson must be an old married woman by now."

"I don't suppose you thought of me once while you were at Riverside," Richard said jealously.

"Well," a perverse imp appeared in Rebecca Mary's cheek just above the corner of her lip, and there was a perverse imp in her voice, also, "I was rather busy you know. I was the only girl there and four, no, five, men, for old Major Martingale had to have a word now and then, five men in the hand didn't leave much time for one in——"

"The heart," suggested Richard quickly and eagerly, and he dropped into the swing beside her. "If you tell me you kept me in your heart, Rebecca

297

Mary, I shan't mind how many men there were in your hand?"

But Rebecca Mary wouldn't tell him that although the question sent her into the strangest flutter she had ever been in in her life, and Richard frowned. He remembered how the men at Riverside had hung about Rebecca Mary.

"You girls are all alike," he said bitterly, and he jumped up from the swing. "I thought that day at the Waloo you would be different——"

"At the Waloo!" interrupted Rebecca Mary. "I should say I was different that day! Why, nothing had ever happened to me then; every day was just like every other day, gray and stupid, but now——" she stopped, appalled at all that had happened since that day at the Waloo, at the few gray stupid days there had been and the many many rosy interesting ones. "Just suppose Cousin Susan had bought kitchen curtains!" she exclaimed with what Richard considered irritating irrelevance.

"Never mind about curtains." Richard wasn't interested in anything connected with the kitchen just then. "They aren't important——"

"Oh, but they were! Frightfully important. Why, there was a moment when my whole future was wrapped up in ten yards of cheap swiss!" She looked almost frightened as she thought of her future in a neat parcel with ten yards of cheap swiss. "You know I was a very selfish self-centered disagreeable person,—yes, I was!—before I went to the Waloo with Cousin Susan that day. But there must have been magic in the tea or—or in the favors," she laughed tremulously as she remembered the favor she had received. "I haven't been the same since," she confessed in a way which told him that she was very glad that she hadn't been the same.

"If you would only be the same for two minutes in succession," begged Richard helplessly. He never felt helpless before a man at the bank, no matter who he was, but he felt absolutely helpless as he stood before Rebecca Mary and looked into her rosy face. There was so much he wanted to tell her, and yet he didn't seem able to form an intelligent sentence. He could only stand there like a silly fool and look at the rosy face in which two gray eyes sparkled so adorably. His own face reddened, and his heart seemed to miss a beat.

"Better change your mind and stay for luncheon, Richard." Granny came out with a cordial invitation. "My, Rebecca Mary, but it does seem good to be at home again!" And she said, as she had said so many times in the past few days; "I don't understand now why I ever ran away. But if you won't stay, Richard, you must be sure and tell Mr. Simmons that he should be here by twelve o'clock at the latest. If he isn't here—if he isn't here——" she stopped aghast at the possibility she had voiced. "If he isn't here I don't know what I shall do," she finished truthfully if weakly.

"HELLO. KITTY!"

CHAPTER XXIII

GRANNY had no opportunity to know what would happen if old Peter Simmons was late for his golden wedding for he came striding in long before the clock struck twelve on the twenty-second of July. Young Mrs. Simmons with Mrs. Hiram Bingham and Mrs. Joshua Cabot were assisting the maids in the pleasant task of arranging the quantities of yellow and white flowers which came pouring in.

Rebecca Mary in a pretty pink gingham, lent a hand wherever she could, but she really wasn't of very much help for her thoughts would stray to Richard and to Count Ernach de Befort. She couldn't keep them on the yellow and white flowers, and every time her thoughts strayed the color in her cheeks grew pinker than the color in her frock. She was, oh, so ashamed and mortified when she remembered that she had locked Count Ernach de Befort in Major Martingale's office and she told herself that she hated Richard Cabot when she remembered that

301

he had found her clinging to the door. She should have been grateful to Richard, but she insisted that she wasn't, not a bit. Richard had diagnosed her case as that of a goose, a dear little goose, but she did not agree with him at all. She told herself that she had been a fool, a perfectly idiotic fool. And she told herself, also, that she hoped she would never see either Richard or Frederick Befort again for she wanted to forget what a perfectly idiotic fool she had been. She wanted to see young Peter and Wallie and Ben. The line of her lips softened when she thought of them. What fun they had had at Riverside! She wondered if they had thought of her at all or if they had been too busy with the great experiment to think of any girl. With her thoughts roving from Waloo to Riverside it was no wonder that Rebecca Mary was not of more assistance and that she put the white flowers where Judy Bingham had planned to place the yellow flowers.

When old Peter Simmons came striding in like a conqueror, Granny was just coming down the stairs, and she looked more like an old saint in her white linen house gown than she did like a woman who had ever run away from her husband's question.

"Where's Mrs. Simmons? Where's my bride?" demanded old Peter Simmons almost before he crossed the threshold, and then he saw her on the stairs. "Hello, Kitty!" He met her at the foot of the stairs with outstretched hands. "You don't look a day older than you did fifty years ago. And you don't act half as old. Aren't you ashamed of the way you've been running about the country?" He gave her a little shake before he kissed her.

"You need stronger glasses, Peter, dear, if you think I don't look older than I did when we were married. Goodness knows I don't feel as old! I should say I didn't! Then I was eighteen on the outside and felt at least seventy on the inside, and now I'm sixty-eight on the outside, and I don't feel more than eighteen on the inside. But I look sixty-eight. Yes, Peter, I do, and you look seventy-one. Perhaps a person can cheat old Time on the inside, but he can't do it on the outside. There are tattle tales here—and here." And her finger touched the wrinkles which separated old Peter Simmons' two grizzled eyebrows and the lines which ran from the corners of his nose to the corners of his mouth. "You didn't have those when you married me, Peter Simmons!"

Old Peter Simmons laughed as if it were a huge joke to have wrinkles on his golden wedding day. "I've a lot now that I didn't have when I married you, old lady. Well, we've had fifty pretty fair years together, haven't we?" He looked down at her fondly. "Want fifty more?"

Granny never hesitated the fraction of a second. "Mercy, no!" she declared quickly. "That would be far too much of a good thing, a regular gilding of a beautiful lily. Just a few more years, Peter, dear, and we'll be through. We've earned our rest."

"Rest!" roared old Peter. "What does a flighty young thing like you want of a rest? I heard of your scandalous doings, Mrs. Simmons, running off in the middle of the night, being locked up by the government. I came very near letting you celebrate your golden wedding by yourself." He pinched her cheek. "But Dick Cabot told me a man couldn't do that." He roared again as he remembered the worried face Richard had worn when he told him that he must, he simply must, be on time for his own golden wedding; he couldn't leave Granny to go through that alone. "So I came back."

"You didn't come empty handed?" demanded Granny quickly. "Don't tell me you came empty handed, Peter Simmons?"

"No, I didn't do that. I didn't dare. I was afraid you would run away again, and I need you in this big old house. The only way to keep some wives is to give 'em trinkets." He bent to kiss Granny again before he put his hand in his pocket. "I hadn't any idea what you wanted." His eyes twinkled. "You wouldn't tell me——"

Granny watched him eagerly, anxiously. "I did tell you," she interrupted. "We've talked it over together a hundred times since our silver wedding. You know we have. You didn't forget, Peter?" Her voice told him that she could forgive almost anything but his failure to remember what they had planned first on their silver wedding day.

"Twenty-five years is a long time for a man to remember a little thing like a golden wedding present," went on old Peter Simmons in a teasing voice, and he winked at Rebecca Mary over his wife's head. "I haven't lost it, have I?" He was feeling in all of his pockets. "I was sure—Dick saw that I had—— No, here it is!" And from one of the many pockets he took a long envelop.

Granny gave a little scream which made the decorators draw closer. They were all interested in Granny's golden wedding present for Granny had made the gift seem so important.

"And here's mine," she said, and she took a long envelop from the pocket of her skirt. It was tied with yellow ribbon while old Peter Simmons' long

305

envelop had a practical rubber band around it.
Granny fairly thrust her envelop into her husband's
hands and snatched his from him in a way which
was quite inexcusable in any one, in even a bride
of fifty years. "Peter, you never——you did! If
this isn't the greatest! You old darling!" And she
laughed until the tears ran down her cheeks.

Old Peter looked at what was in his envelop, and
he laughed, too, until the tears stood in his eyes.
"You didn't trust me, old lady!" He shook his head
at Granny. "You thought I had forgotten!"

"I did!" Granny frankly admitted her thought.
"You just the same as told me you had forgotten
when you kept asking that foolish question—'What
do you want?' I didn't trust you, and I made up
my mind that I shouldn't be disappointed even if I
had to carry out alone the plan we made together
so I went down to Judge Graham yesterday and had
him fix things up. I was so afraid that you'd give
me a diamond necklace or a string of pearls." She
sighed happily because he hadn't given her either
diamonds or pearls.

He stopped in the middle of another laugh, and
looked at her with a funny expression as if he wasn't
sure, not at all sure. "H-m," was all he said.

"H-m," replied Granny. "Why did you pester me so if you remembered?"

Old Peter finished his interrupted laugh and had another one before he pulled her gray hair as he undoubtedly had pulled her brown hair in the days when she was eighteen on the outside and felt seventy on the inside. "Because I like to tease you, old lady. You go up in the air quicker than any one I ever knew, and I like to see you rise. It's meat and drink to me. You always come down gracefully. I must say that for you," he added admiringly.

"Not this time," she told him honestly. "I didn't land gracefully this time, Peter. You got the better of me all around. But whoever would have imagined that when I ran away from you I should run right into you?"

"It was Fate," old Peter told her emphatically. "And it means that you can't get away from me, no matter where you run."

Granny kissed his brown wrinkled cheek. "Yes," she said soberly. "I guess that's what it means. And I'm glad of it!" she went on firmly. "I could go farther and fare worse even if you are the biggest tease on earth, Peter Simmons!"

Young Mrs. Simmons and Judy Bingham and Sallie Cabot could bear the suspense no longer.

They had heard so much about the golden wedding present which Granny wished to receive that they just had to see it.

"What did father give you, Mother Simmons?" Young Mrs. Simmons was an impatient spokeswoman. "What did she give you, Father Simmons?"

"Yes, what did you give her?" Sallie Cabot drew Rebecca Mary into the ring around Granny and old Peter Simmons.

Joan did not wait to be drawn, she ran in herself for she, too, was eager to see what Granny had wanted so much that she had run away from old Mr. Simmons so that he would be sure to give it to her. It was a funny way to obtain a present. Joan did not understand the method. Perhaps she would if she could see the gift.

Granny was laughing so that she could scarcely tell them what it was. So was old Peter Simmons.

"You see, dears," began Granny, breaking a laugh in two and wiping the tears from her eyes, "we felt older twenty-five years ago than we do now, didn't we, Peter? And we wanted to do something for the world that had been so good to us. We had had twenty-five as perfect years as a man and woman could have together, and we wanted to show that we appreciated them. Peter thought of a trade school,

308

and I thought of a children's home because women naturally think of children, you know, and then we had an inspiration. I don't remember which thought of it first, do you, Peter?"

"I expect you did," old Peter suggested handsomely.

"Well, perhaps I did, but it doesn't matter, for when two people live together for twenty-five years they grow to think the same things. Yes, they do, Rebecca Mary, as you'll see some day. I often catch myself thinking of contracts. But this time we thought of a home for old couples. We were so sorry for the old couples who couldn't grow older together that we decided that we'd give them a home when we had been married fifty years and were an old couple ourselves. A home for friendless old couples. We shouldn't wait until we were dead and some one would look after it for us. We'd do it ourselves and get to know some of the old couples. That was why we bought Seven Pines, wasn't it, Peter? And that was why I wanted to take you to Seven Pines, Rebecca Mary. I wanted to go there to stay for a few days before my golden wedding. We've talked and planned a lot about it, and I was a silly old fool to let Peter tease me with his question. I should have known you, Peter, but perhaps

309

it was because it meant so much to me that I was frightened to death for fear you had forgotten or changed your mind. But you hadn't for—— See!" She held up the envelop old Peter had given her, and her face was radiant as she told them what was in it. "Here is the deed all ready for me to sign for the Katherine Simmons Home for Old Couples."

"And here," old Peter Simmons held up the envelop which had been given to him, "here is the deed for the Peter Simmons Home for Old Couples all ready for me to sign. We'll have to compromise on the name, Kitty, and merge it into the Simmons Home."

"Is that all the present is?" Joan had never been more disappointed in her life. She could not join in the chorus of admiring approval. But she could understand why Granny cried. She would want to cry if old Peter Simmons gave her an old home for old people. There was only one thing which would make it right to Joan, and she pulled Granny's sleeve. "Will you give the old couples young hearts, Granny?" she whispered eagerly.

"We'll try," Granny whispered back. "That's exactly what we are going to try to do, Joan, to make tired old hearts younger. The world would be so much happier if there were not so many old hearts in it. You keep yours young, Joan, as long as you live," she advised quite confidentially. "Bless my soul!" she exclaimed as she heard a machine puff up the driveway. "Is that young Peter with our jailor? I've been so taken up with our golden wedding presents, Peter, dear, that I never asked how your experiment worked. Was it a success?"

"It was a big success." Old Peter Simmons looked as if he was more than satisfied with the way the great experiment had worked. "We've given it every sort of try out and it can't go wrong. If we hadn't made sure of that I couldn't have come to your golden wedding, Kitty. I should have had to send my regrets." He winked at Rebecca Mary and tickled Joan under her chin. "Some day, Miss Wyman," he told her more soberly, "you will be proud to remember that you were a prisoner at Riverside when Befort's big idea was worked out."

"What will it do?" Joan wanted to know at once. "What can you do with my father's idea, Mr. Simmons?"

Mr. Simmons tickled her under her chin again. "That would be telling," he whispered with a great show of secrecy. "And then you wouldn't be curious any longer. There is only one way to keep people interested and that is to keep them guessing," he

311

went on with a twinkle. "If you knew what to-morrow was going to bring you wouldn't care whether you had a to-morrow or not. You'd never want to go to bed to-night."

"I'm not going to bed to-night, anyway not until the old people do. Granny said I needn't, that I could stay up until the last minute of the golden wedding!" Joan drew herself up with proud importance. "But I'll tell my father what you said about the way to keep people interested, and I'll tell Miss Wyman, too," as if she thought old Peter Simmons wanted his recipe circulated as rapidly as possible.

Old Peter Simmons chuckled. "You may tell your father if you want to, but I rather think that Miss Wyman knows. The knowledge is born in some girls. That's what makes them such a puzzle to us men. How about it, Miss Wyman?" he said teasingly to Rebecca Mary. "You don't need to be told, do you?"

CHAPTER XXIV

GRANNY'S golden wedding celebration was a very informal affair although many important people came to offer their congratulations and to ask Granny where on earth she had been and to tell her how much she had been missed. Although she had been married at noon Granny had chosen to have her party in the evening, and July the twenty-second offered her a wonderful evening, cool and pleasant as a July evening can be occasionally.

Old Peter Simmons was continually leaving his place beside Granny to draw Rebecca Mary into a corner and ask her if she thought that Granny really was satisfied to have a home for old couples for her golden wedding present or if Rebecca Mary thought Granny would rather have had something more personal.

"I always have given her something personal," he explained, "ever since the Christmas when she gave me a carpet sweeper. For years before that I'd showered her with rugs and library tables and a brass bed and other household furniture. She said then she guessed the house was mine as much as it was hers and it was only fair for me to take my share of the stuff. And she was right. But that made me suspicious ever after. And now—of course, she planned this aged home herself, but women do change and you heard what she said. Do you think she would rather have had a string of pearls?" Granny had given old Peter Simmons something to think of when she had said she was so afraid that he was going to give her pearls or diamonds for a golden wedding present.

"What is that about pearls?" And there was Granny herself. She had followed them to ask old Peter Simmons why he couldn't stand beside her and say thank you when people told him how lucky he had been to have had her to live with for fifty years instead of rushing off into corners with Rebecca Mary. "Indeed, I do want that Simmons Home for Old Couples," she declared when old Peter Simmons had stammered "Why." I should have been broken-hearted if you had brought me anything but that deed. Pearls!" she sniffed scornfully. "What would I do with a string of pearls? I should only put it away for young Peter's wife."

"But young Peter hasn't any wife!" objected Joan, who, of course, was at Rebecca Mary's elbow.

314

"He will have some day," laughed young Peter, who had been drawn to the little group in the corner. "Won't he, Rebecca Mary?"

Rebecca Mary was furious because she colored when Peter asked her if he wouldn't have a wife some day, and she was more furious when she stammered in her answer. Why should she always be so horribly self-conscious? If she had known how charming she was as she colored and stammered she wouldn't have been so angry.

"Most men have," was all she said.

"Not all men," insisted Joan. "There's my father. He hasn't any wife."

"He has had one, and one is enough for any man," Peter told her.

"I don't think it's enough for my father. He always wants two of everything, roast beef and ice cream and handkerchiefs and pencils and—and everything," she declared, and Peter pulled her hair and asked her how she dared to compare a wife to roast beef before he went away to dance with Doris.

Rebecca Mary looked across the room at the man who wanted two of everything. He was standing by the window, and he wore the absent-minded detached expression which Rebecca Mary and Granny had seen him wear at Riverside. Only a part of Frederick Befort was at that moment at Granny's golden wedding party. But as Rebecca Mary looked at him he raised his head and their eyes met. Rebecca Mary blushed again. Oh, dear, wouldn't she ever overcome that silly conscious habit? But she just had to blush as she remembered that she had thought he was a spy. The absent-minded expression slipped from Frederick Befort's face as all of him came to the party, and he started toward Rebecca Mary. She turned away quickly. She couldn't speak to him. She was glad to have Sallie Cabot stop beside her, although Sallie Cabot's words were far from quieting.

"What have you done to my Cousin Richard?" Sallie demanded with a laugh. "I used to say he was like a piano, grand, upright and square, but lately he has quite a ukelele look. What have you done to him?"

Rebecca Mary blushed a third time as she involuntarily looked at Richard as he stood talking to two most important men. She couldn't detect any ukelele look, she thought indignantly. He looked as he had always looked, perfectly splendid, to her. What did Mrs. Cabot mean? But Mrs. Cabot drifted away, she did not wait to explain, and Rebecca Mary was left alone with her question.

She felt rather forlorn and neglected for it was a long time since she had been left alone. There had been a young man to ask her to do this and another young man to ask her to do that. But now young Peter was dancing with Doris and Wallie was talking to Martha Farnsworth and George was in a corner with Helen Lester. So they had been devoted to her at Riverside just because she was the only girl there. She had known that all the time, she told herself, but it did hurt a bit to have it proved so conclusively. But there was one thing she did have, she thought stoutly, and that was the memory of the good time she had had at Riverside. That couldn't be taken from her—ever! And as if the memory of a good time had soothed the little feeling of neglect which had hurt her she slipped out of her corner and made herself very pleasant to the people she found neglected in other corners. Many eyes followed Rebecca Mary as she moved here and there, for she wore a new crisp organdie frock with pink ribbons exactly where pink ribbons should be and tiny blue forget-me-nots tied in with the pink rosebuds. It was a very charming frock and Rebecca Mary was very charming in it. Young Peter told her so as soon as his dance with Doris was finished.

"Rebecca Mary," he said sternly, "I hope you are as good as you are good looking."

Rebecca Mary laughed and then she sighed. "I'm not," she said with a little quiver of her lower lip. "At least, I'm not good, Peter. I'm envious and jealous and all sorts of horrid things."

"Glad of it." Peter did not seem at all shocked to hear how horrid she was behind her good looks. "If you weren't a few of those things you wouldn't be down here with me. You would be up in the blue sky tuning your harp. I like a girl, especially a pretty girl, to be human."

"I guess I'm awfully human." And Rebecca Mary sighed again.

"Who is calling you names?" And Wallie and George stopped to ask her what she had meant by running away from Riverside and leaving them without a girl to play with. They never could tell her how they had missed her—every hour.

"Pooh," laughed Rebecca Mary. "You were too busy with your great experiment to miss me for a minute."

They pretended to be cut to the quick by her doubt of their veracity, and Rebecca Mary was once again the center of a merry chattering group. It was such fun to laugh and joke with them again.

318

She hoped they had missed her. And then she caught her breath with a frightened little gasp for Frederick Befort was coming toward her again, and this time he did not look as if he could be evaded.

"May I speak to you?" he asked Rebecca Mary with a serious directness which made Peter and Wallie and George murmur a few words and drift away, although Rebecca Mary did try to clutch Peter's sleeve.

Rebecca Mary did not wish to be alone with Frederick Befort for a minute. She was so afraid that he knew that she had locked him in Major Martingale's office at Riverside, that she had taken him for a spy. She had avoided him all day, and she would have avoided him now if it had been possible. She was very uncomfortable as she went with him to the porch and dropped down among the pillows of the swinging seat. Her heart was beating so loud that she was sure he would hear it.

Frederick Befort stood in front of her and looked down at her. He did not say a word. Rebecca Mary shivered among the cushions and tried to say something.

"It is a lovely golden wedding, isn't it?" she said, and she could have slapped herself when she heard her voice shake.

Frederick Befort drew himself up, clicking his heels together in the way which had roused Rebecca Mary's suspicions, and looked straight into her eyes.

"Miss Wyman," he said very formally, "I beg that you will honor me by becoming my wife?"

"Wh-a-t?" Rebecca Mary slipped from among the cushions and stood staring at him with wide-open-startled eyes. She had expected him to berate her for taking him for a spy and he had asked her to marry him. She had never been more astonished in her life. She dropped weakly back among the cushions.

"You touched my heart at once by your kindness to my little Joan," Frederick Befort went on swiftly, and his voice was like a caress as he took her hand and raised it to his lips. "Whenever I think of Mrs. Muldoon I am in such a rage that it is well that she is not near me. What would have happened to my little girl if it had not been for your heavenly sweetness and generosity!" He shivered as he thought of what might have happened to Joan.

Rebecca Mary shivered, too. "Oh," she gasped faintly. She couldn't say another word. She could only stare at him with big unbelieving eyes.

"And always you were kind to every one," Frederick Befort went on in that soft low voice which was so like a caress. "Kindness means much to me now. I have seen so much—unkindness. To-morrow I go to Washington with Mr. Simmons and Major Martingale to make a report on our work at Riverside, and then I must go home. I did not think I ever would go back. I thought I was through with empires and kings. I wanted to live where a man could be himself and not just one of a pattern. But I have a duty over there, I must go back. May I come for you first, and will you go with me and Joan to my poor changed Luxembourg? Will you?" His grave eyes searched her face.

Rebecca Mary kept her eyes on the fingers which fumbled so nervously with an end of pink ribbon. It couldn't be true that this man, who had once been to her like the prince in the fairy tale, really had asked her to marry him. She must be dreaming. Countess Ernach de Befort! That didn't sound a bit like Rebecca Mary Wyman. She couldn't make it sound like Rebecca Mary Wyman. And then she remembered that he never once had said a word which is usually mentioned in a proposal of marriage. With a relief so great that it almost choked her, Rebecca Mary understood that Frederick Befort had asked her to marry him because she had been, as he had said, heavenly kind to Joan, and not because he loved her so that he could not live without her. Rebecca Mary believed firmly that love is the only reason for marriage. And she did not love Count Ernach de Befort. There had been a time when he had fascinated her, when she had dreamed that perhaps he might some day ask her to marry him, but that time was past, and anyway fascination was not love. She tried to think how she could tell him that it wasn't without hurting his—his pride, for she felt that she had done him an almost irreparable injury in questioning his honor. Oh, she never could be grateful enough to Richard Cabot if he hadn't told Frederick Befort that she had questioned his honor. Perhaps it was the thought of Richard which gave her courage to raise her eyes to the grave face above her.

"I'm—I'm so sorry," she stammered, and she put her little hand on his sleeve. "But you don't really want me. It's just for Joan. You don't care for me and—I don't care for you. You know you don't really care?"

Frederick Befort drew his heels together again and bowed ceremoniously over the small white hand he had taken from his sleeve. "I, too, am sorry," and his voice sounded sorry, so sorry that just for a second Rebecca Mary thought she might have been

"I LOVE YOU, REBECCA MARY"

mistaken. "But if I cannot have your love I hope always to have your friendship?"

"You shall!" she promised quickly, glad that she could give him something that he wanted. "You shall always have my friendship—you and Joan."

He raised her hand to his lips again and went away, taking with him the only chance Rebecca Mary ever would have to be a countess.

Richard passed him as he came looking for Rebecca Mary, and he stopped to regard him with suspicion. "What did he want? Did he ask you to marry him, Rebecca Mary?" he demanded so anxiously that Rebecca Mary could not resent the question.

"He was just telling me how grateful he was for what I did for Joan." Rebecca Mary quite truthfully translated what Frederick Befort had said to her, and which she had been clever enough to understand. "I couldn't marry him," she went on quickly. "We belong to different countries and—and everything. Once I thought I should like to," she confessed with an adorable blush. "It would have been so romantic to be a countess. He has taught me a lot about—about Luxembourg and things, but he doesn't want me to marry him. He is just grateful for what I did for Joan, you know."

323

The jealousy died out of Richard's face and in its place was an eager expectation. "Well, I love you, Rebecca Mary," he said quickly. "I care for you a lot. Could you—do you care for me?" He took her hands and lifted her to her feet so that she stood before him.

And Rebecca Mary confessed that she did, that she cared a lot for him, she had ever since that day at the bank.

"You were always so—so good to me," she murmured as if she just had to have a reason.

"Good to you!" Richard choked as he took her in his arms and kissed her. "Good to you, sweetheart! How could a man be anything but good to you? I want to be good to you all the rest of your life!"

Through the open window they could hear Granny's voice; evidently she was giving a toast for she said—"To all those who keep their hearts young for they shall live forever!"

"That means me," Joan said shrilly. "For I have a young heart, and I'm going to keep it young forever."

"That means us, too," Richard whispered, his lips very close to Rebecca Mary's pink ear. "Our hearts are young, aren't they?"

"Yes." Rebecca Mary spoke dreamily, for she felt

as if she must be in a dream world. She couldn't be wide awake and be in Richard's arms. "As long as we have love in our hearts they can't grow old."

"I'm going to live forever!" Joan danced out to tell them her news. "Granny said I should. Are you, dear Miss Wyman? Do you like the golden wedding? I'm disappointed in it," she confessed loudly. "It's just like any grown-up party. I don't see exactly why Granny wanted it so much."

"Oh, don't you, miss?" And there was Granny. "It wasn't like any grown-up party to me, not a bit! You just have one wedding, Joan, and then you'll understand why I've wanted fifty. You understand, don't you, Rebecca Mary?" She put her arm around Rebecca Mary and hugged her after her keen eyes had searched Rebecca Mary's tell-tale rosy face.

"But Miss Wyman hasn't had one wedding." Joan didn't see why Rebecca Mary should understand so much more than she could.

"No, but Miss Wyman is engaged," Granny told her as if it were a great secret.

But every one heard her, and every one was astonished. No one was more astonished than Rebecca Mary unless perhaps it was Richard.

"Rebecca Mary engaged!" Young Peter couldn't

believe it. "That wasn't fair, Rebecca Mary, not to tell a fellow."

"What is she engaged to?" asked Joan jealously, although she didn't understand what being engaged meant.

Granny told them that, too, before Rebecca Mary could open her mouth.

"To a four-leaf clover. Aren't you, Rebecca Mary?" And then she told them what had happened to Rebecca Mary the afternoon when she went to the Waloo for tea, that some one had thrust a four-leaf clover into Rebecca Mary's hand. Consequently by all the laws of romance Rebecca Mary was engaged to that some one.

"But who was it?" Joan expressed the curiosity which was on every face.

"I wish I knew!" Rebecca Mary had quite forgotten the mystery of the four-leaf clover in the greater mystery of Richard's love.

"Don't you know?" Richard asked in a queer sort of a voice. Was he jealous?

She shook her head. No, she didn't know. She never had known where that clover leaf had come from but it had brought her luck. Yes, it had! And she would keep it to her dying day. But she should like to know who had given it to her.

Richard laughed. "Granny," he said, "come and confess."

"Granny!" What had Granny to do with it? A gray-haired old Granny was not according to the laws of romance.

Granny realized that, and she made her explanation apologetically as if she understood that it might not be wholly satisfactory.

"You were such a dear scowling thunder cloud that afternoon that I was sorry for you. It seemed such a wicked waste of a perfectly good girl that I simply had to offer a little first aid. Richard and I talked you over"——

"Richard!" Rebecca Mary remembered very vividly how curiously Richard had regarded her over his sandwich.

"And we decided, I did at least, that you needed a little mystery in your life. You looked as if you had been fed entirely too long on stern reality. It was easy enough to diagnose your case, but we didn't know how to get the prescription to you until we were all jammed together at the door. I had the clover leaves in my corsage bouquet, old Peter Simmons had sent them to me, and I made Richard push one into your hand. He didn't want to do it. He said it was silly and impertinent." Oh, the scorn in

Granny's soft voice. "But I have a very persuasive way with me at times," she added as Rebecca Mary stared at her, her mouth and eyes all wide open. "I told him if he didn't do it I should, and I'd tell you that he did it."

Rebecca Mary swung around to look at Richard. "Then you—you——" but words failed her. It was so altogether as she wanted it to be.

"Yes, I did," admitted Richard with some shame, for there are those who might think it unseemly for a bank vice-president to slip four-leaf clovers into the hands of strange scowling girls. "Granny has, as she said, a very persuasive way with her. I never before did such a thing," he explained unnecessarily. "And I shouldn't have done it then if I hadn't been so sure that she would make her threat good." His voice sounded as if even yet he could not understand how he had let Granny coerce him. "I'll never do it again," he promised with a rare twinkle in his eyes. "But I did do it that afternoon. Are you sorry?"

Rebecca Mary looked from him to Granny and then back at him again. But before she could find breath with which to tell him that she was anything but sorry Granny said slowly, as if she were still visualizing the Waloo tea room:

328

"You were with such a dear looking woman that afternoon."

"Yes," dimpled Rebecca Mary, all flushed and sparkling at the astonishing news she had heard. "My insurance agent. She was trying to persuade me to take out a policy," she giggled.

"And did you?" Joan always wanted to know whether one did or didn't.

"Did I!" Rebecca Mary drew a deep breath as she thought of the policy she had taken out and the long record of payments she had made on it. "I should say I did!"

"That's all very interesting," Richard broke in after she had told them a little more about her memory insurance and they had laughed and trooped away again, "but it interrupted a question that I wish to ask you. What I want to know is, are you going to marry me?" He put the question in his best vice-presidential manner, although there was a twinkle in the far corner of his eyes.

Rebecca Mary laughed and twinkled, too. The old negative phrase never came near her lips. Her cheeks were as pink as pink and her eyes were like stars as Richard's arm slipped around her shoulders and drew her closer.

"Will you marry me, sweetheart?" he asked her

again, very gently this time, not a bit like a bank vice-president.

Rebecca Mary caught her breath. She put up her hand and clutched the edge of his coat with trembling fingers as if to keep him near her until she could answer him. Her eyes crinkled and the corners of her mouth tilted up. My! but she was glad that Cousin Susan had told her what she should say.

"Y-yes," she stuttered, half laughing, half crying. "Y-yes, thank you!"

(8)